To Alice —
Enjoy!
Joy Collini

COMING TOGETHER

By
Joyce Norman
and
Joy Collins

CHALET PUBLISHERS, LLC

Arizona   Alabama

COMING TOGETHER

Copyright © 2009 Joyce Norman and Joy Collins

Cover design: Lynn Smith

This is a work of fiction. Names, characters, places, and incidents are either the product of the author's imagination or are used fictitiously. Any resemblance to actual events or locales or persons, living or dead, is entirely coincidental.

Reviewers may quote passages for use in periodicals, newspapers, or broadcasts provided credit is given to Coming Together by Joyce Norman and Joy Collins and Chalet Publishers, LLC. chaletpublishers@cox.net.

Chalet Publishers, LLC
www.chaletpublishers.com
chaletpublishers@cox.net.

ISBN: 978-0-9840836-2-6

Printed in the United States of America

First Edition

To Clay,
My Greatest Gift.
J.N.

For John,
With all my love,
J.C.

Acknowledgements

To *Joan*, without whose consistent encouragement this book would never have been completed. She surely must know the depth of my gratitude.

To *Patsy and Don*, whose never-ending belief kept me writing. Their prayers lifted me higher.

To *Lynn*, whose talents are remarkable, second only to her spirit. Very special thanks for her beautiful book cover.

To *my BFFs at 26...Harriet, Kate U, Kait S., Aaron, Emily, Matthew, Tommy, Reid, Brandon, and Feizal*. I think of you as family and your support has meant much...the halibut was a motivator, too.

To *PHP Communications, Inc.* for their enormous contribution to this book. Beyond thank you.

J.N.

First and foremost, I want to thank my co-author, *Joyce*, for inviting me to be a part of this project. This book was a product of her heart and soul and I feel honored to be allowed to partake of this journey with her.

To *Lynn Smith*, for the most beautiful cover we could ever have hoped for.

To our readers — *Kathy Harris, Claudia Flowers, Michele Moss, Tracy Voyles, and Deejah Figueroa* - for all their help, unfailing support, and guidance.

To *Nadine Laman and Zanne Kennedy*, fellow authors and kindred souls, for all their support and advice.

Finally, and always, I want to thank my husband and partner, *John*, for always encouraging me, always believing in me, always loving me.

J.C.

ONE

The large wooden double doors fell in with a thunderous noise, like a bomb exploding. Startled, Isabella dropped her fork and stood. When the dust cleared, she saw four Brazilian Federal Police, each holding a machine gun.

"We have orders from the government," one yelled loudly. "Do not move."

The day had started out innocently enough. Isabella Paes and three of the women who regularly helped her had washed and fed all ten of the orphan babies in their care. After the last infant had been put down for a nap, two of the women had turned their attention to preparing the noon meal while Carrie, the American from Alabama who had arrived just two days earlier, sat next to Isabella at the large dining room table.

Isabella was writing a letter to a possible benefactor while Carrie worked on the voluminous paperwork needed to get her new daughter Grace back to the States.

"These forms seem to be never ending. Just when I thought I was at the end, they come up with something else. Isabella, don't you ever tire of filling out all these papers?"

Isabella put down her pen and patted Carrie's hand. "Knowing that another baby is safe and will have a chance for a life without a government like this is what keeps me going. Don't get discouraged. You're in the home stretch now. Soon, you and Grace will be back in the States beginning a new life."

Thirty minutes later, all the women were seated around the large wooden table in the dining room. The room was directly off the hallway and allowed for an unobstructed view of the front door, a fact that, in these troubled times, gave Isabella some sense of peace. The house itself resembled a medieval castle with its stone walls and mullioned windows. It had belonged to her parents and since their death several years ago, Isabella had lived here alone, free to pursue her dream of assisting infant adoptions. Every year she made it possible for at least a dozen infants to find homes outside of Brazil, escaping oppression and poverty.

Isabella looked around the room at the dark wood paneling, the heavy draperies, the tall brass candlesticks, and the high-backed chairs that stood around the huge table like disciplined soldiers. She was a small woman. Her brown eyes sometimes showed both her age and her weariness of the daily struggle with the bureaucracy. A widow, she had raised four children of her own and knew the possibilities that love gave to children. It's what got her through each day. As the food was passed around the table, she once again sent a prayer heavenward, thanking Mama and Papa for leaving her the means to give hope to so many little ones. The house itself was situated halfway up Corcovado Mountain in the shadow of the famous Cristo do Redentor statue. To the south lay beautiful Ipanema Beach but when Isabella looked out her windows at night it was not the sights and sounds of the beach that drew her. Rather, her eyes always strayed to the beautiful statue of Christ the Redeemer with a prayer to get her through another day and help another infant.

Maria passed the bowl of paella to Margarita on her left. Isabella was enjoying the pungent aroma and anticipating a quiet meal when the door was kicked in.

Margarita dropped the bowl. It crashed to the floor, shattering, sending rice and vegetables flying. The combination of noises woke some of the infants and they started crying in the nursery that adjoined the dining room. Maria stood to go to them but one of the Federal Police leaned over the table, placed his hand on her shoulder, and pushed her roughly back into her chair. The chair fell over and she landed hard on the tile floor.

The officer leaned over her and was within inches of her face. "I said do not move."

Maria smelled his hot breath but she made no sound fearing what he might do next.

The officer who had pushed Maria looked at the others at the table and warned, "No one else move or you all will be very sorry."

The women sat speechless.

"Do what you came here to do," barked the Captain to the men standing around the table.

Three soldiers broke from the group and headed for the sound of crying babies. As they did so, somewhere outside a car door slammed.

"Isabella?" called a male voice.

The captain looked at Isabella. "Who is that?"

"My attorney. He was joining us for lunch," said Isabella.

"Grab as many babies as you can and get out," the captain yelled to the men in the nursery. "Hurry!"

The three policemen, two each holding a baby and the other carrying an older child, came running past the dining table. All four men stepped over the debris in the doorway. The last man out stopped and stared at Isabella. "Baby Lady, don't forget my eyes. They will be watching you." The men then ran toward their cars with their tiny cargo. They talked loudly, laughed, and slammed doors. Engines revved and they raced down the hill.

As soon as they left, Maria ran into the nursery.

"What happened?" Alberto asked, as he entered the house of his friend. He gingerly stepped over the remains of what was left of the door.

Isabella turned to face him, tears in her eyes. "What I have always feared. The police have taken some of the babies. I know they took Roberto, our five year old, and two of the infants but I'm not sure which ones." She looked toward Maria as she emerged from the nursery. Tears were streaming down Maria's face as well. She walked up to Isabella and whispered something to her in Portuguese. Isabella nodded and then walked slowly over to Carrie who looked at her with wide eyes.

"Carrie, your Grace was one of the infants."

"Is Maria sure?"

Isabella just nodded. Carrie ran from the dining room into the nursery. Margarita followed her. Seconds later, loud sobs erupted from the next room.

Isabella was unable to speak for a minute. Her heart ached for the babies, praying they would not be aware of what was happening. Her biggest concern was for Roberto, though. He, more than anyone, would be so frightened. She tried not to think about what he was feeling right now. He needed her to remain calm.

Isabella turned to Alberto again. "They would have taken them all if you hadn't come." Then she added, emotion weighing heavily in her voice, "They have taken them to the ..."

"I know, the funabem," broke in Alberto. "Now is when we must trust God, Isabella...and pray," he said as he put his arm around her shoulder. "I will do all I can to get these babies back. You know that, my dear friend."

Isabella smiled at Alberto, then looked toward the nursery where Carrie had gone. "Those two babies were so close to getting out... and they almost made it."

She looked around at the devastation to her home. The remaining babies had settled down and would soon be asleep. The soldiers who had brought the surprising disruption, barking orders, wreaking havoc in this quiet haven on the mountain were now gone, leaving behind the silence that had begun the day.

Two

Several months earlier and thousands of miles away...

Daisy Gardner reached over and silenced the alarm clock's noisy wake-up call. She rolled onto her back and lay there with her eyes closed, not quite ready to get up. Fearing she might fall back asleep, she reached over again and hit the radio button. Maybe some soft music would ease her into the day.

"...days since the hostages were seized in Iran. Here in Washington, President Carter is meeting with ..." Daisy hit the switch and silenced the radio for good. Hearing about the world's continuing turmoil would only serve to heighten her anxiety. Today was going to be tough enough.

She moved her left leg under the covers and, as she did so, she disturbed the peaceful sleep of her bedmate. She and P.D. had been together for a full year now and he was the only male who let her sleep late, even when the alarm clock didn't.

"Sorry, P.D.," Daisy whispered softly as she reached for him in the early morning darkness. A low, harmless, throaty growl sound came from between her feet and P.D., her little brown terrier, made a few small circles before plopping down and going back to sleep once more.

"Hey, little fella, gimme a break. This is an important day for me. I'll probably be growled at enough before it's over, so come on up here and be my friend again."

P.D. slowly raised his head, yawned, and crawled his way up to the pillow next to his best friend. Then, like always, he snuggled up to Daisy's neck and licked her ear until she laughed aloud.

"Cut it out, P.D. I'm sorry I woke you up." She stroked the soft fur on P.D's head. *I'm thirty-two years old and some brown dog has me wrapped around his little paw. Apologizing to a dog for disturbing his sleep…I'm losing it. No, I'm not losing it. I've already lost it.*

Thoughts of Craig immediately flooded her. Craig - her husband of five wonderful, turbulent, unpredictable, never-boring years. Instinctively she moved her left leg to where Craig's had been so many mornings. She remembered the feel of the soft, thick hair on his leg as she would rub her leg across his, the body heat that emanated from him, the sound of his smooth, rhythmic breathing.

God, how she missed him!

Divorce had never entered her mind when she married Craig. Then one day, or so it seemed, it had just happened.

Craig Harris had suddenly stepped into her life years before and she knew she would never be the same. They had met when they were both graduate students in radio and television film at The University of Texas. He was from Houston and she was born and raised in Fort Worth.

They had so much in common even though Craig was five years older. The more Daisy got to know the tall, blond Texan with the reddish moustache, the more she knew without reservation that she was in love with him. Just like in Romeo and Juliet, liking turned to love, and she and Craig were certain that they alone invented fireworks. They were both extremely good with photography. Still cameras and video equipment of all kinds…they knew about them all and how to skillfully use them.

Their documentaries for their Masters theses earned them both high marks. Each seemed to have a special eye and feel how to capture emotions and thoughts and attitudes on film. Daisy, especially, was talented, and after graduation had offers to go almost anywhere she chose. Instead, she chose to go with Craig and be his love and ultimately his wife.

Craig had accepted a job in Washington, D.C. and before their first week was over, Daisy came home to her husband with news that she, too, had a job. She had been hired by a large firm in D.C. to do a video annual report. "Capture our company and all our accomplishments and we'll pay you well," she'd been told.

No one said a word about creativity or uniqueness or great photography, but Daisy gave them these, too. The project yielded her first award.

Soon word got out about her abilities with sights and sounds on film and it wasn't long before she was traveling all over the United States. Then assignments came from Europe and Asia. She missed Craig no matter how busy she was. In the beginning, her return home was filled with love and glorious lovemaking. Lately, though, the homecomings had become tense. Craig stopped meeting her planes, making excuses that he couldn't leave his work or that his car stalled or his watch stopped or...a myriad of excuses, most of them pretty obvious.

One evening, after Daisy had unpacked her gear from her most recent trip to Holland, she decided to bring things out in the open.

"Craig, we need to talk. What's wrong?"

"Wrong? What could be wrong?" he answered sharply. "I mean, here I sit in Washington making films of senators' great humanitarian feats so they can send these marvelous pictorial epics back to their constituency to get more votes." His voice got louder. "No, nothing is wrong. Nothing is boring about my job. My wife, on the other hand, is off filming in the garden spots of America and the glamour capitols of the world. No, everything is just super. I have no complaints that my wife makes more money than I do and is better at whatever it is we both do. I'm very secure. Very secure. Yes, sir, I just love living all by myself in this fancy apartment that you paid for with nothing to keep me company but those damn trophies you seem to be able to collect like baseball cards!" He made a sweeping motion toward the fireplace mantle where most of the trophies stood side by side.

They were both seated in their living room, a room Daisy loved but now, looking at it through Craig's eyes, she saw how it must feel to him. Abruptly Craig quit talking, lowered his head, and stared at his hands.

Daisy spoke softly. "Honey, I'm sorry you feel like you do but I can't help it that people seem to like my work and reward me for it. I love what I do and I want to do it better than anybody."

Craig looked up at her. "That's the whole problem. Better than *anybody*? No, you want to be better than *me* and do you want to know something? You've done it. You obviously are better."

"But, honey, I thought you'd be proud of me, not angry. I *do* want to be the best. We both do."

"No," Craig quickly interrupted. "No, I want *you* to be my wife and I want you to stay home more and I want us to begin thinking about having a baby. But, this can't happen with you going away all the time like some damned gypsy."

Daisy sighed. They had been down this road many times before, each time ending the same. "I do want to have children, Craig. I do. But now is just not the right time. We've talked about this before. I'm getting so much work and I hate to turn it down. Perhaps in a couple of years we could think about having a baby. Just not now."

Daisy knew her husband well enough to know there was more than what he had just said and she wasn't sure she wanted to hear it.

"Daisy," Craig began slowly, "I really want to have children. Growing up as an only child of older parents…well, I know how awful that was. I won't do that to my child. I want the family I never had. This is more important to me than you know. I've tried to stifle the way I feel but I just can't do it anymore. Saying you want to wait to have a child, maybe two years - well, I just believe you'll continue to put it off. You're only getting more involved in your work. With every new award you become more intense. I'm not happy, Daisy."

Daisy sensed a shift in Craig. He had lost his anger – maybe more. She stood and walked over to him. Placing her arms around him she said, "I'm sorry, sweetheart. I'm so sorry. I never meant to hurt you like this."

She touched his hair and stroked his cheek. He raised his head toward her and she kissed him. She felt him respond to her and then slowly they made love where they had argued just moments before. Afterwards, they lay in each others' arms. Neither spoke.

Daisy remembered a time a few weeks after their first date. They had taken Craig's jeep, packed with camera equipment, camping gear, and food supplies and driven out of Austin, passing the University campus on the way out of town. Craig was in high spirits and remarked that it would be good to get away from classes for a full weekend. They were headed for a camping site that Craig knew of near Galveston. He was almost giddy as they drove along, singing, telling jokes and talking.

Daisy had helped Craig unpack the jeep, and although camping was not on her list of favorite things to do, she felt herself get excited and pretty soon was actually having fun. It had nothing to do with camping. It was pure Craig. As she watched him unload the jeep, she realized just how much she loved him and thought how wonderful it was that she had found her true love while she was so young. He wouldn't let her help set up camp and so she watched him build the little campsite, cook the food and make a big deal out of serving her dinner, complete with cloth napkins, real china and champagne.

They had sat together on the beach after dinner and watched the surf play games with the sand crabs. They laughed, ran on the beach and wrestled in the sand and then Craig had gently taken her face in both his hands, looked into her dark brown eyes and had said softy, "It's time, you know, Daze. It's the exact right time. I've made love to you so many times in my mind. Now it's time for both of us to say what we feel, but not with words."

Slowly and so very gently, he removed her t-shirt. Daisy smiled as she remembered the writing that had emblazoned the front of her shirt. As Craig pulled the top over her head and let it drop to the ground she had thought, "I should not have worn this t-shirt. *Slippery Rock U* is not a very romantic addition to foreplay."

It didn't matter. Nothing mattered but that Craig was softly touching and kissing her all over and she gave silent consent with all of herself that he was right. It was the exact time.

P.D.'s snoring brought Daisy back to the present. She stared at Craig's side of the bed, now empty. She could still see him lying there that day, months earlier, when he had shattered her world, their marriage. It had been the morning after their "talk", after they had made love on the living room floor. Craig was lying on his back, staring up at the ceiling. Then, in one quick verbal burst, he had said it.

"I'm seeing someone, Daisy."

"What? What did you say?"

"I'm seeing someone. I've been seeing her for months now. She's not in our business. And she's always there for me."

Daisy sat straight up in bed and stared at Craig. For a few seconds, words just wouldn't come. Then "Do you love her?" flew out of her mouth unbidden. Daisy couldn't believe she was even asking the question. This couldn't be happening. Not her Craig. *Her* Craig.

"Yes. I'll always love you but it's different. I want a family, Daisy, and with her I can. I just want to be happy."

Daisy fell silent. She couldn't even feel angry. She was numb, unable to think – or breathe. Craig's words barely registered. This wasn't happening. Craig had found someone else. In a matter of seconds, he had killed their life together.

Within days, Craig had moved out of their apartment and Daisy knew a divorce was on its way.

Why can't I wake up just one morning without thinking about Craig?

Daisy crawled out of bed and headed for the bathroom. A hot shower was her anecdote for every ill. She did her best planning and thinking under the hot water. But this morning all thoughts were about her eleven o'clock meeting at Georgetown University with Dr. Mikino Tsuru, chairman of the History Department. She had met Dr. Tsuru at a faculty get together six months earlier when she had taught a course in film editing. Somehow they wound up together in the corner of the huge faculty lounge, talking excitedly about cameras and film and the magic they could produce.

"I have a small project," Dr. Tsuru had said to Daisy. "It isn't as exciting as all the film adventures you've been telling me about but I need someone very good to document a small first-time class I'm teaching called *South America — Looking Forward*. I need a video that will aid me in obtaining a grant to set up teacher exchange programs. Will you do it for me? I feel you're just the one to capture what's needed from me and my students."

Daisy listened as Dr. Tsuru, a slightly built man with thick silver hair, told her of his unusual background. Although born in Japan, he had been raised all over South America. He spoke Japanese, Portuguese, English and, of course, Spanish. His father had worked for an engineering company and Dr. Tsuru had studied at the finest universities before going to Harvard to receive a second doctorate. Although he was chairman of the entire History Department at Georgetown, Dr. Tsuru's first love was South America.

"Yes," Daisy answered, "I'll film your class and give you a product that I guarantee will yield you exactly what you need!" Later, she realized she'd sounded awfully cocky. She just hoped she could please him. She had turned in the edited film two weeks before and had heard nothing until yesterday when he had left a message on her answering machine asking her to come to his office at eleven o'clock this morning.

"I bet he didn't like my work. I probably missed the whole point of his teaching. I bet…" Daisy made herself stop this shower psychology third degree. He wanted to see her and for whatever reason she would be there on time.

Out of the shower and wrapped in a thick dark green towel, Daisy picked up the toothpaste tube and squeezed the gel onto her toothbrush. It was green also. I guess this is my green period, she thought. Anyway, she would keep this toothbrush until the bristles fell out. Craig had bought it for her and had said, "This is the third toothbrush you've had in a month. Leave this one behind in one more hotel and I'll buy you another one, drill a hole in the end, insert a string, and tie it around your neck."

Daisy looked lovingly at the tiny brush. *Damn, now he's in the bathroom, too. Oh, Craig, I'm so sorry.* Trying to shake the heavy nostalgia she was experiencing this morning, she hummed as she vigorously brushed her teeth. As she dried off the toothbrush she looked at it once more. *Who knows? Maybe I'll have the darn thing bronzed!*

Thoughts of toothbrushes were interrupted by warm fur against her bare legs. P.D. was up and letting Daisy know he wasn't mad, just wanted some petting. She bent down and picked up the little dog that had helped her keep her sanity in the last few months. She cuddled him to her cheek and faced the mirror. Her brown hair mingled with his fur. "We make a good looking pair. I love you, P.D."

With the towel still wrapped around her, Daisy stepped out of the bathroom and into her bedroom. She walked to her window and threw open the wooden shutters. It was almost winter and, although the days had been extremely cold, there had been no rain or snow. She hoped today would be no exception. Cold temperatures allowed Daisy all the mobility she needed. Add moisture and it slowed her life down considerably. She peered out the window and saw dry sidewalks and streets and sighed, relieved that she wouldn't have to deal with the elements. She knew it was extremely cold though as she watched pedestrians walk by, huddled into their heavy coats and parkas.

Daisy turned on a small television she kept on a wicker table at the foot of her bed. TV was an absolute necessity to her. She had a large set in the living room and another small one mounted under a cabinet in the kitchen. She even carried a tiny two-inch Watchman in her oversized leather purse. A TV was a lifeline to her. She loved the thought of being able to have whatever she needed to know at the flick of a switch. News. Weather. Movies. Documentaries. Whatever. It was all there. She loved television.

She sat on the edge of her bed and turned the television to the news station. More bulletins about the hostages in Iran and meetings at the United Nations. She flipped the stations, stopped for second when she heard President Carter's name, then moved on to the weather channel. The outside temperature would dictate what she wore today. She saw the low and the high predicted and then came flashing on the screen the current temperature. It was twenty-nine degrees and due to warm up a little by noon. That meant her heavy coat. Still, what to wear to look smashing? Even if Dr. Tsuru canned her film, she wanted to look good when he did it.

Daisy's "look" could best be described as pure Banana Republic, the new clothing outlet with the eccentric catalog. She loved khaki, boots, turtle neck sweaters, loose blouses and jackets and pants with pockets everywhere. Her five-foot-eight frame looked good in just about anything and she had a way of looking classy and even elegant in her work clothes. Her long chestnut brown hair was usually worn down or piled high on her head with a leather fastener. Today, however, she wanted to look feminine.

She pulled a cobalt blue wool dress, ankle length, from her closet. She found matching blue knee-high boots, reached inside each one and felt warmly comforted that her heavy wool socks were nestled there. She dressed, brushed her long hair, and headed for the living room to get her coat and pick up her purse. She stopped in the kitchen to pour herself a small glass of orange juice. As she drank, she stood in the kitchen doorway and looked into the living room, thinking just how much she loved her apartment.

Her place was a wonderfully meshed composite of every place she had ever traveled. Thick cream-colored carpeting set off the bright colors in paintings from Italy, temple rubbings from Thailand, twenty or so different kinds of woods carved into as many different shapes. Books lined floor-to-ceiling shelves on two walls; a fireplace occupied the majority of the space on another. Her furniture was contemporary, although the colors in the two sofas were a Polynesian print. Some pieces she'd brought home from Hong Kong, some from France and yet the room was like a page from Architecture Magazine. Not cluttered. Just right with everything looking like it felt comfortable with everything else.

Daisy noticed her watch lying on the kitchen counter and that's when she realized she was running late. She had thought she would walk to Georgetown but she now knew she would have to drive. She opened the closet next to the front door and retrieved her long cobalt blue coat that set off her dress and boots. She would barely have enough time to walk P.D. before she left. She snapped his leash on and carried him outside. P.D. sensed her impatience and quickly did his business, foregoing his usual sniffing. She raced back to her apartment, plopped him down on the sofa, and kissed him on the head.

"Wish me luck," she said in her soft voice. A once easily identifiable Texas accent had been mellowed by time away from home and being surrounded by other languages.

As Daisy stepped out into the brisk morning air for the second time, she caught her breath at the blast of cold air. Adjusting her purse on her shoulder, she walked the long block to her parking garage. She lived in Foggy Bottom because it was a great section of Washington that was so accessible to everything. Usually she would walk almost everywhere she went. But not today. She walked faster. She'd have to take the Honda and press the metal at that!

Dr. Tsuru was waiting for her in his office and said nothing about the fact that she was fifteen minutes late.

"Sit down, Daisy," he said. "I have another assignment for you. This time it will be an adventure to equal any you've had before."

"Oh, then you liked the documentary I did for you. I was afraid you hadn't. I'm glad - and relieved."

Daisy sat down and settled back in a big overstuffed leather chair, feeling her body begin to relax slowly. She half listened as Dr. Tsuru commented about her recent work for him. She took in the room slowly, like a camera panning a movie's location. Dr. Tsuru was obviously a pipe smoker, as beautifully polished pipes were neatly standing in a rack on a long table behind his desk. Photographs of Dr. Tsuru and other professor-type people hung next to pictures of Indians wearing almost no clothing. Three large leather chairs held pillows that looked like they had been hand woven. One had a llama woven into it, another, a mountain.

Small Dr. Tsuru was dwarfed by his huge desk topped with four or five semi-neat piles of papers, photographs, and journals. On shelves throughout the room were stacks of papers, magazines, letters, and more photographs. Mostly, the stacks of typed pages dominated the room. All this room said was two words – South America.

Dr. Tsuru saw Daisy eyeing all the paper piles and interrupted her thoughts. "Those papers contain the words of my next book. It may seem as though this filing system of mine is a bit haphazard but, believe me, Daisy, I know where every chapter is. This room is one of my favorite retreats in the entire world. Everything here has a definite order to it."

Daisy nodded. "My hus- a friend of mine was the same way. It amazed me how he knew where to find anything. But he always did."

Dr. Tsuru walked around his desk and sat on its front edge, facing Daisy. He smiled and said, "How beautiful you look today. The blue of your dress makes your blue eyes even lovelier. I've been enjoying watching you absorb my little world. You are such a curious woman. I believe that is why you are so good with film. You leave nothing out. You see everything.

"Daisy, my very talented new friend, to a certain degree I have tricked you." Dr. Tsuru watched Daisy's face as this last remark of his sunk in and his smile widened. "You did a wonderful job with your last assignment," he continued. "Because of that, I have another job for you. I have written a book I'd like you to make come alive for me. It's a new history book and this time I want it to move and talk and cry and laugh and be alive with all you can do with your wonderful film. It will most likely take you about six months to complete this job. You will be paid well and you may take any assistants you need."

He reached behind him and picked up what looked like a huge dictionary. He held it face down on his lap and said, "Daisy, this book has taken me much time to research, compile, live out, and finally, write. It is everything I know about Brazil. Only you can bring it to life. Here, take it. It is your script."

Daisy took the heavy green book from the professor and turned it over. When she saw the title, she felt her heart skip a beat or two. In large, bright yellow letters were the words *Brazil – The Country and Its People.*

"Take the book home. Look it over and get back to me within the week, Daisy. We'll discuss then what you'll need and who will be going with you to help with this enormous project. By the way, I certainly hope you won't change your mind."

Perhaps she had said goodbye to Dr. Tsuru. Daisy wasn't exactly sure. She made her way out of the history building and across the campus. The wind had picked up and it seemed much colder than predicted. She spotted a bench where she could sit a minute to catch her breath and button her coat. She sat, shivering from the cold and shivering inside from something else, too.

She felt things shift within her. There was unrest there but something else. For the first time in years, Daisy felt sad and alone. Lost. Craig was gone from her life; a new assignment was just around the corner, in another strange city. The unforgiving wind whipped her hair around her face. As Daisy pulled her coat collar up close, she wondered what lay ahead for her and she realized she would begin this new journey solo. She lifted her head high and straightened her shoulders. She was going to be just fine.

THREE

A light snow began to fall as Daisy made the short drive back to her apartment. She decided against listening to the radio. Instead, her thoughts were preoccupied with what she was going to need to carry out the assignment Dr. Tsuru had just given her. For sure, she would need two experienced cameramen. She hoped her two favorites would be free to accompany her to Brazil. They were good, fast, and fun to be with and right now Daisy needed fun. She needed to laugh, to joke and unwind. Of course, it went without saying that she wanted to turn in a fine piece of work to Dr. Tsuru. But there was no harm in enjoying herself while she did that.

The first name that came to mind was Charlie Crawford, an exceptional cameraman and someone she had known all her life. He had lived with his mother in a tiny, white frame house just a block away from her childhood home back in Fort Worth. When the neighborhood kids walked to school together, Charlie was always one of the group. He was a year older than Daisy but they had always been the best of friends, right from the start. There had always been a natural closeness between them.

Daisy had never known who or where Charlie's father was.

They had never talked about that. Once, when he was about twelve years old, Charlie had told Daisy, "Mama's worked hard to raise me without a man around. She gets money from somewhere every month but she never talks about my father. Maybe one day I'll ask her." As an adult, he had never brought the subject up again.

Every Saturday, Charlie was one of the two or three young boys her father, a commercial contractor, always took to his building sites to help with the finishing-up work, as he called it. They screwed the handles on all the kitchen cabinets and drawers, sanded strips of molding, picked up trash, wood and other building material remnants from around the houses. Daisy's father even allowed her to come along on these Saturday work days. When they got older, her father let the boys lay hardwood floors. Daisy thought this was one of the most fun things to do but her father didn't believe a girl could do a good enough job. However, if she persisted in wearing him down long enough, her father would either get extremely angry, yell at her, and make her go sit in the car or sometimes he'd give her a hammer and let her work next to the boys laying floors.

It seemed that Charlie was always around and her father really seemed to like him. He always made a point of praising Charlie when he did a good job. They would pick up Charlie on Saturday mornings and stop at Elsie's Doughnut Shop and buy several boxes of hot, glazed doughnuts for the men waiting at the job site. Daisy enjoyed these times. Her father was relaxed and he smiled a lot. She had heard him tell her mother that the reason he tried to encourage Charlie was because he had no father. Maybe so, Daisy thought. But it simply appeared to her that he just genuinely liked the boy who wore a different kind of crazy hat almost every Saturday. And he always wore cowboy boots and prided himself on being a "real" Texan.

Daisy and Charlie attended the same high school and when Charlie graduated, he went on to the University of Texas on a scholarship. He planned to major in video journalism and when he came home on visits he'd tell Daisy all about what he was studying. His tales of school and classes sparked Daisy's interest in cameras and film-making.

"Next year, when I come to the University I'm going to study all that stuff, too," she told him. "I think I'd be good at it."

Charlie and Daisy worked on many projects together both at the University and, after they graduated. They had been partners on many assignments and Charlie had even been somewhat instrumental in Daisy meeting Craig. Charlie was an excellent cameraman and they worked well as a team. There was a comfort level between them that Daisy enjoyed. They had seen each other through many life crises, including Charlie's bout with alcoholism. That had been a tough time but Daisy was especially proud Charlie had won that battle.

Yet despite their closeness, they had never been more than friends. Romantic love was just something that never happened and they both were grateful for their special bond. For years they had been there for each other and theirs was a comfortable, easy, accepting relationship. When Charlie's mother had died several years before, they had been working together on assignment in Athens and Daisy was glad she had been with him. Charlie had needed her.

The other cameraman she wanted was Jon Tanner. He had traveled with her and Charlie on the last two big jobs in Europe. She knew having the two of them along would make everything easier.

Once inside her apartment Daisy changed into jeans, a warm sweater, and thick socks. She took the phone from a table behind a sofa, retrieved her address book from her briefcase, and plopped down on one of the sofa's overstuffed pillows to call Charlie first. After his mother's death, Charlie had moved back to the old home in Fort Worth near her parents and had set up his home base there.

To her surprise, he answered on the second ring. They chatted about trivial things for a few minutes but Daisy quickly brought up the Brazil assignment.

"That sounds great," Charlie quickly answered, to Daisy's delight. "Do you really think it will take six months? That's a long time to be out of the States. We'll have to get six-month working visas. I hear the Brazilians are pretty tough about Americans working in their country even under the best of circumstances.

I'll contact the Brazilian Consulate in New Orleans tomorrow. Don't procrastinate, Daisy. You get on this visa thing at your end, too. Promise?" As always Charlie was organized. "What other cameraman are you going to ask?"

"I thought I'd ask Jon. You two work so well together..." but Charlie quickly interrupted.

"Sorry, Daisy, no Jon this time. He's in Alaska shooting some kind of documentary for a military guy named Rayburne. That's about all I know other than he just went north, so looks like Jon's not in on this job. Wait, I have an idea. I've heard lots of good things about a guy who actually lives right there in Rio. I met him briefly once at a film seminar in Rome. I've even seen some of his work and Daisy, that guy has the touch. He would be tailor-made for this job. He could be a great help. Hold on, let me get my address book."

Daisy could hear pages turning and Charlie whistling, then, "Okay, I've got it. His name is Luis Campos and he lives near Ipanema Beach. Call him and see if he's available. I'd love to have a chance to work with this guy."

"I'll do that right after I hang up. I'd like to leave in less than a month, Charlie, right after Thanksgiving, actually. Will that work for you?"

"Do you really want to leave so close to Christmas? I don't mind for myself, now that Mom is gone but you —" Charlie stopped, fearing he had opened a wound. "Sorry, I guess with Craig gone..." he let the rest hang.

"It's okay. I'm fine. Craig isn't even a factor. I want to do this job. My parents will understand. They have my brothers. All I need to do is get my visa and arrange for P.D. and I'm ready to leave. Then, I'll fly to Fort Worth to visit my parents and you and I can fly out together from there to Brazil. It will give you a chance to look the script over before we land."

Next, Daisy called Luis Campos. After three rings, the answering machine picked up.

Expecting to hear a message in English, Daisy was momentarily caught off guard by the polite Portuguese words, "Bom dia. Meu nome Luis Campos." He sounded younger than she had expected.

Daisy couldn't help but feel intrigued by the smooth Latin accent.

Hoping Luis also spoke English, Daisy took a deep breath, waited for the tell-tale beep, and said, "Hi, Mr. Campos, you don't know me but I was referred to you by a mutual acquaintance. I would like to speak with you about working on a film project in Brazil. Please call me as soon as you get this message." She left the numbers for her D.C. home as well as her parents in Fort Worth.

After that, things started falling into place very fast and very smoothly. A friend knew a friend who had a sister who would stay in Daisy's apartment while she was away. And, added good news was that the sister loved animals and asked Daisy to leave P.D. in her care. It was a big relief to be able to leave her little friend in his own surroundings.

Daisy was an expert at packing, so getting ready was no big chore for her, just time consuming. Not one used to wasting time, she hooked her tiny Watchman to her belt, put on her headphones and listened to the television while she walked around her apartment getting her things together.

Two weeks later Daisy was in Fort Worth, being pampered by her mother, whom she thought was the best cook in the world. Her pies and breads were legendary. Daisy decided she was going to eat without worrying about extra inches. Brazil was far from Texas and it would be a long time before she would be enjoying such special treats again.

On her second day home, Daisy borrowed her mother's car and rode aimlessly around town. She drove to her high school, parked in front, and just stared at it. Thoughts of parties and rallies and football games flooded her memory. Daisy shook her head, remembering the snob she had been back then. So much had changed.

Daisy left her alma mater and headed for home. She drove down West Berry Street toward home. Her father had said he was going to be home a little early that day and she wanted to spend some time with him. She couldn't remember a time when just the two of them had ever really communicated. Perhaps this was the time.

As she approached her parents' home, she was struck by how small everything looked. The chinaberry tree in the backyard she'd remembered as "taller than a skyscraper" when she and Charlie climbed it as kids wasn't as tall as the rooftop. She turned the car into her parents' driveway and parked behind her Dad's old black Buick. She fought the urge to back up and just drive away. Her stomach tensed, a sure sign that she had not outgrown that feeling of intimidation that her father always caused. All it ever took was a word or a glance and Daisy would find herself scrambling to fix whatever imaginary thing had caused his disapproval. Her father never admitted it was anything he might have done.

Daisy parked the car and went in. Her father was seated at the kitchen table reading the paper. She sat across from him but he didn't look up. A few seconds later, her mother walked into the room.

"Daisy, a man from Brazil telephoned. Said he was returning your call about working on a film. He left his number. Oh, and he said to tell you he would do the camera work. Just call this number," she handed Daisy a slip of paper, "when you get to Rio. His name was Louis something or other. I couldn't understand him too well. His accent was pretty thick."

Daisy stared at the number her mother had handed her. Well, she thought, he's pretty cocky. No exchange of questions. No doubts that I might not want to use him. Just a message that he'll work on the film. I wonder if all Brazilian men are that confident. Then for a brief, flickering moment she wondered what Luis looked like.

Daisy folded the paper and slipped it into her pocket. She turned to her father. "Dad, how's work?"

"It's fine, Daisy, just fine. Just like it was the last time I saw you. Nothing changes when you work on houses. Not the wood. Not the nails. Not the people. Why do you ask?"

Daisy sighed. Why did he have to make this so hard? Why was even the slightest interest in him viewed as a challenge?

She tried again.

"Dad, I think about you a lot. I think about how much alike we are. You know, people pay me pretty well for being creative. I learned techniques and mechanics of directing and editing film at school, but it's the creative part that gets me the jobs and gives me such joy. You're creative, too. I get my creativity from you and I couldn't do what I do without it. Thanks, Dad."

Will Gardner looked up over his paper, his eyes magnified by the thick lenses in his glasses. He stared at his daughter as though he'd heard nothing she'd said. Then he said quietly, "You're welcome."

Daisy got up and went to the sink. Her father's dismissal of her attempts at conversation always hurt her to her core. She poured herself a glass of water and felt her mother's hand on her shoulder.

"Hon, your Dad loves you very much and he's proud of you," she whispered. "I know he is. The other day I heard him tell the fellow who rides to work with him all about your trip to Brazil." Sybil Gardner, always the mediator, always trying to make peace.

Daisy patted her mother's hand. "Mama, it's okay. Really it is." She turned and held her mother close; no one else in the world had that wonderful soft, warm, special smell that her mother had. It was a clean, starched smell and she loved it.

"I think I'll go outside for a bit."

"All right, hon, but don't go too far. Dinner will be ready in less than an hour."

Daisy walked out the back door and looked up at the tall chinaberry tree and on impulse grabbed the lowest branch. Soon, she was sitting on one of the bottom branches of a tree that brought back mental flashbacks of scampering from the bottom to the top of one very much like this one. She looked down and shook her head. What was once so easy now seemed like an insurmountable obstacle. She considered herself good just to be a few feet off the ground now.

Daisy sat for a long time and just looked up through the leaves. Memories flooded her. Of school, childhood, friends…but mostly Craig. *I've hurt you so much. I never meant to. But why couldn't you wait for me, for us? Why did you have to turn to someone else?*

Daisy leaned up against the rough trunk of the tree and sighed. A tear slowly trailed its way down her cheek and she made no attempt to wipe it away. It was going to be a long time before the hurt went away. If it ever would.

The sound of the back door slamming abruptly brought her back to the present.

"Daisy, hon, come on in now or everything will get cold." Sybil walked over to the base of the tree and looked up at her daughter. "Well, now, I see you didn't make it to the top of the tree this time. You know, I can close my eyes and still see you, way high up in those branches. Sometimes you'd get so lost in all those leaves I couldn't even see you. You'd play in that tree for hours, remember? You've always been my special little girl."

Daisy hopped down and hugged her mother.

"You'll always be my little girl, hon. No matter where you go or what you do."

"Dad's right, Mama. Some things never change."

FOUR

" **M**ake sure your seat belts are securely fastened and all tray tables are in their upright positions…"

Daisy had heard this little memorized speech hundreds of times. While the stewardess droned on, she settled back in her seat on the big Pan Am jet at the D/FW airport and waited for takeoff. Next stop, Rio. It was 11:45 p.m. and arrival time was 7:30 a.m. the next morning.

Her parents had insisted on driving her and Charlie to the airport even though her father had cataracts and didn't see well at night. Daisy had gripped her purse in her lap, praying they would make it to the airport in one piece. Charlie patted her hand occasionally whenever they made a turn that particularly unnerved her. This trip to Rio was unsettling enough. She wasn't sure how long she'd be gone, how it would go, what she would find. She didn't need it to start out with this hair-raising ride but she hadn't the heart to tell her father he couldn't take them to the airport. He so often ignored the important things in her life.

Or was it the fact that Charlie was going too that piqued his interest this time?

Too soon after they checked in at the Pan American ticket

counter, it was time to say their farewells. Daisy turned and hugged her mother who had stood off to the side, clutching a wadded tissue and trying to hold back tears. From the corner of her eye, Daisy saw her father and Charlie, deep in conversation. Her father actually had his hand on Charlie's shoulder and she could hear him saying, "Be careful, Charlie. You never know about these foreign countries. Drop me a postcard sometime."

Daisy felt a twinge of jealousy. She yearned for only a fraction of the affection that her father so easily bestowed on Charlie.

"Be careful, sweetheart," her mother said as she hugged Daisy close. "Eat well. Write. Phone when you can. Don't do anything dangerous and for heaven's sake, don't drink the water."

Daisy held her and said over and over, "It's okay, Mama. Please, don't worry. I promise and you have to promise me, too. Promise me you'll take care of yourself. I'll call this week and give you my phone number and address. I love you."

"I love you, too."

From her father she received a stiff hug and a "Do like your mother says. She worries about you."

Daisy played that scene over in her head as the plane's engines revved up for takeoff. A warm embrace, a kiss even – anything but that stiff-armed hug from her father would have been welcome. Was it because she was a girl? Did her father just not know how to relate to his daughter? Daisy tried to remember how her father acted toward her brothers but they were so much older than she was and had been out of the house and on their own for most of her memories. Now, they made it home infrequently but Daisy could swear they got more from their father than she did even sporadically. What was it about Charlie that made it so easy for her father to show his feelings to a neighborhood kid and not his own daughter?

"Can I get you something to drink?" The question from the smiling stewardess broke into her thoughts.

"What? Oh, no, I'm fine. Thanks." The stewardess nodded and moved on to the person seated behind Daisy. Daisy and Charlie had separated as soon as they were on the plane. Charlie was a smoker and wouldn't sit in non-smoking for cold, hard cash. Daisy was glad, actually, that she'd be sitting alone, up front right behind the bulkhead. She wanted the think time.

The December weather had been extremely cold in Texas, too, so Daisy was still wearing a bulky sweater. She had stowed her hooded, insulated jacket in the overhead storage bin. As the plane ascended, she settled back, closed her eyes, and woke up an hour later when the flight attendant brought a tray of nuts, cookies, and juices.

The first of December and I'm on my way to Brazil. Thanksgiving had been good, spending time with her parents and loving all the wonderful food her mother had prepared. She had wished her brothers and their families could have come but they both lived too far away for a short trip to Texas. Both Will and Eric called during dinner and Sybil passed the phone around the table. It had been good to be home but Daisy was also glad to be heading off to a new assignment.

With a start, she suddenly realized she had done nothing about Christmas gifts for her parents but decided she would take the time in Rio to shop and send a package off within the week. It didn't feel like Christmas or at least she didn't feel like it was the season. Daisy knew she wasn't the only person who got depressed during the holidays but this didn't make the month any easier on her. She didn't really know what it was that made Christmas such a downer. She used to love it when she was little. Now, it seemed more drudgery than joy. *Maybe because I'm not a kid anymore. And, it's about Craig, too, and the divorce.*

The cabin temperature was comfortable and after her snack, Daisy dozed for the remainder of the flight. She was awakened when an attendant accidentally bumped her seat with a serving cart.

"I'm sorry," he said. "We'll be on the ground very soon and we have to batten down everything."

Daisy moved over to the empty seat by the window and pressed her nose against the glass. She could see beautiful cloud formations and, as the plane began its descent into Rio, she saw craggy mountains rising from the dark green jungle below. She marveled at their proximity. They were right outside the window. Daisy felt like the plane was a tiny thread being guided ever so gently into the very small opening in the eye of a giant needle. She could see nothing but mountains covered in fog and actually worried if they would make it. She felt reassured when the attendant announced that the plane would set down at Galeao, Rio's international airport, in approximately ten minutes.

As the plane made its final descent into the airport, the clouds suddenly disappeared. The view from Daisy's window was breathtaking. The landscape was lush and green and it made the color back in the States seem like it had been through the wash a few too many times. This was a green to make one forever disappointed in New York's Central Park.

Daisy felt the plane's wheels touch down on the runway and silently marveled at how the pilot had guided the great metal bird to this thriving city nestled between rugged mountains and a sparkling blue-green sea. Everyone stood and the cabin got decidedly smaller as people jostled for room to maneuver as they grabbed belongings from overhead bins and from underneath seats.

As soon as she deplaned, Daisy felt engulfed in a great humid wave of subtropical heat. Welcome to Rio in December.

Charlie and Daisy caught up with each other in one of the customs lines. "Did you catch that view as we landed?" Charlie asked. "Man, this is a beautiful country." Charlie was clearly excited.

Daisy nodded. "Definitely breathtaking. We're going to get some great footage." She stifled a yawn. "I can't believe how much I slept on that flight and I still feel tired."

"I think it's the weather," said Charlie. "I talked to a flight attendant for awhile and she said from now until March, Rio is very warm. I guess even Santa Claus wears a Speedo down here."

"Thank you for that mental image that I will never get out of my head now." Daisy pulled her sweater away from her neck in a vain attempt to feel cooler. "I wish I had thought ahead a little better. I'm roasting in this sweater." She adjusted her heavy jacket that she had looped over her left arm. "I'd gladly trade this jacket for a glass of cold anything with ice in it right now." They cleared customs, Charlie doing all the paperwork on the large suitcases and film equipment.

As they exited the airport, Charlie said, "Okay, Daisy, now where? Want me to get a cab? Where are we staying anyway?"

Daisy took a small address book from her oversized purse and flipped through it. "There's a small hotel near Corcovado. The woman who made my plane reservations reserved two rooms for an unlimited stay. I thought we'd move in there, meet with Luis, and work out a filming schedule for Rio. It's called Tijuco and is on Rua Cosma Velho. She said it was very convenient."

Daisy did not see the figure coming toward her from a parked black Mercedes.

"Seja bemvindo – welcome to Brazil," said a cheerful, familiar voice. Dr. Tsuru stood before them, both hands in his khaki shorts, and sporting a wide smile. He wore a bright yellow sports shirt and white tennis shoes with no socks. Daisy was as surprised to see her professor friend dressed in such a manner as she was to see him in Rio.

"Dr. Tsuru, what a surprise! What are you doing here?"

"I'm here to meet you and give you an education on how to dress for Rio in December. You are dressed for Finland!" They all laughed and Charlie, leaning in to Daisy, whispered, "I think I'm going to like this guy."

After introductions, they loaded the car and took off. Dr. Tsuru maneuvered the big Mercedes in morning Rio traffic like a seasoned taxi driver.

"By the way, if you have reservations anywhere, we'll cancel them. I'm staying in a friend's home on Copacabana Beach. He and his wife teach at the University in Recife half a year and when they are not in Rio they let me have use of their spacious, beautiful home. I have a conference starting here on Friday so that gives me lots of time to help get you organized and to see you settled in. The house is yours while you are in Rio."

"Dr. Tsuru, I am truly touched that you flew all the way down here just to get us set up like this."

"I realized after we talked the last time," he said, "that I could be of much use getting you situated in a nice place to use as a base while in Brazil. As it turned out, this conference presented itself so it gave me the opportunity to be here to welcome you." Dr. Tsuru deftly skirted a car that had driven into his lane and Daisy gripped the door handle to keep from calling out. Dr. Tsuru patted her free hand. "Don't worry, I have been driving on Rio's streets for years. This is nothing. By the way, where is your other cameraman?"

"I'm hiring a local named Luis Campos. He lives here in Rio. I was planning on calling him when we got to Copacabana."

They stopped at a traffic light and Dr. Tsuru pointed straight ahead and up.

"Look there, Daisy. That is the heart of Rio."

Daisy looked to where Dr. Tsuru had pointed. There, on top of the high mountain, arms outstretched to the world, was a statue of Christ. Soft wispy clouds swirled behind Him almost within arm's reach.

"That is one of the most beautiful sights in the world," he continued, "Cristo do Redentor – Christ the Redeemer statue. He stands atop Corcovado Mountain and has a breathtaking view of Rio Bay. You'll never forget your visit to the Christ statue."

Daisy noticed when Dr. Tsuru talked about Brazil there was a reverence in his voice. It was clear he loved this country and it was contagious. Daisy was getting excited.

Dr. Tsuru deftly turned the sleek black car into a side street. "We're almost there. Just a few more blocks. You'll be right on the beach so I trust you brought your swim attire. You must take time to enjoy this country, to have fun, to fall in love with it."

The car turned off Avenida Atlantica into a short drive. Large iron gates automatically opened and then closed behind them. Up ahead, Daisy saw a stark white building with a red tiled roof. With a flourish of his right arm, Dr. Tsuru announced, "Your new home for a while."

They piled out of the car. Each grabbed a suitcase and went in. Dr. Tsuru led the way into the main room and smiled as he watched the faces of Daisy and Charlie register their amazement. Daisy dropped her heavy suitcase on the floor at her feet and turned in a circle, taking the whole room in. All the furniture was contemporary: the fabrics and accessories in whites, yellows, greens, and blues.

Dr. Tsuru smiled, thoroughly pleased that he had impressed his American friends. He walked over to one long wall and pushed a button. The floor length white drapes slowly opened, revealing an indescribably beautiful sight – mountains rising from the deep blue-green water. No one said a word until Charlie broke the silence with, "Eat your heart out, Texas. This is some view."

Daisy turned to their kind friend and said softly in the only Portuguese she knew, "Obrigado. Muito obrigado. This has been quite a welcome. We'll do an award-winning job for you. I promise, Dr. Tsuru."

"Oh, and there's another thing I want to settle. My name. We're friends now. Well, friends are not formal so I do not wish you to call me Dr. Tsuru anymore. My full name is Mikino but most of my friends call me Miki. Like the mouse. Okay?"

"Okay, I'll try," said Daisy, "but it may take some time. Somehow Miki doesn't fit you yet."

Miki laughed again and picked up the suitcase he had carried in. "Let me show you to your rooms. This house has four bedrooms and three levels and even three live-in servants to care for us. Just follow me."

After an hour or so, everything was out of the car and put away. Daisy had chosen a large bedroom on the top floor facing the ocean. It had an area for a small study on one end and the view was unbelievable. After putting her clothes away in the ornate dresser, she changed into a cotton, loose-fitting dress.

She was staring out her window at the ocean once again when someone called out, "Lunch is ready."

Following a small lunch of fresh fruit, cheeses, toasted small breads of all kinds and chilled mango soup, Charlie excused himself and retired to his room for a nap. Dr. Tsuru changed into a suit for an afternoon meeting in town. Alone, Daisy got out her address book to finally speak with the illusive Luis Campos.

She dialed his number and drew circles on a nearby pad while she waited for him to pick up the phone. Five rings and Daisy was about to hang up when a voice on the other end said, "Boa tarde. Luis Campos here."

"Hi, this is Daisy Gardner from Washington D.C. I just arrived this morning and it's wonderful to be in Rio. Sorry I missed you in Texas, but..."

"Excuse me, please. May I call you back in an hour or so? I am busy at the moment," Luis Campos said and promptly hung up.

FIVE

aisy stared at the dead receiver in her hand. How rude! Did she really want someone like that on her team? It was probably too late to find someone new but she was not about to let this arrogant man ruin her project. She'd put him in his place as soon as he called back. He would know who was boss from the start or he could go packing. And if he did, so be it. She'd manage somehow.

It was an hour before the phone rang again. Daisy answered it before the second ring.

"Hello. Daisy Gardner here," she said, mocking Luis's phone greeting.

"Now I can talk to you." Daisy recognized the soft accent. "I will meet you at the Café Garota de Ipanema in one hour. Do you think you can find it?"

Once again, Daisy had thoughts of firing Luis Campos. "Well, I made it to Rio from Texas. I believe I can find you a few blocks away."

Luis either didn't understand her sarcasm or chose to ignore it. "Fine, I will see you soon." And once again, Daisy held a dead receiver.

That was it. The man was toast.

Daisy decided to meet Luis dressed exactly as she was. Even the loose-fitting dress gave no real relief from the humid, hot weather that had replaced the bone cold temperatures of Texas. And, frankly, she wasn't interested in how she looked anyway. This meeting with Luis was going to be short and sweet.

She slipped on a pair of bright yellow sandals, grabbed her purse, and headed for the front door.

Before she left, she propped a note for Charlie on the large, low hand-hewn table between the two sofas in the living room. It simply said where she would be and that she was meeting Luis.

She walked the half block toward the beach and then turned down Avenida Atlantica, the wide street that ran next to the beach. She hoped she wouldn't have too much trouble finding a cab. A breeze from the ocean felt good blowing through her hair. Daisy couldn't resist. She removed her sandals, put them in her large shoulder bag, and crossed the street to the sandy beach.

She marveled at how wonderful the sand felt on her bare feet. She walked slowly toward the water, then stopped and took in the view. In the hazy distance was Pao de Acucar, Sugar Loaf Mountain, proudly pushing itself up from the sea. Behind and above her, high on its mountain, was the striking giant, white figure of Christ with arms outstretched as though in blessing for the entire city that sprawled out below.

Daisy had been to San Francisco and Hong Kong but as she stood there and visually inhaled Rio de Janeiro, she believed this was the most beautiful city in the world. Long stretches of sandy beaches as far as she could see lay before her. Lines of tall, straight palm trees stood stately like royalty's honor guard. She could see mountains up beyond the Christ statue that were covered with deep green jungle and flowers popping colors in profusion. She tilted her head up and followed a large fleecy cloud floating lazily out over the ocean.

Looking south, Daisy saw charming little cottages nestled into the sides of all the mountains surrounding the city. They were painted in a variety of pastel colors and had magnificent views of the ocean. She couldn't help but feel that there was something special about those cottages and made a mental note to look into them further.

She glanced at her watch and realized that Rio had so captured her attention that she was about to be late for her meeting with Luis.

Back on the street, sandals on, Daisy was fortunate enough to get a taxi very quickly. She told the driver the café's name and before she had settled back in the seat to enjoy new views, the driver stopped, turned to her and with a beautiful smile, pointed straight ahead and said, "Garota de Ipanema."

She had not had the opportunity to get any money exchanged so she simply gave the driver a five dollar bill. He was still smiling as she got out of the taxi. It was either too much money or he was admiring his passenger.

Daisy saw no one standing outside the unpretentious little café and decided to go in and find a table by the window if she could.

Lucky again. She sat down, looked out the window, and could see a glimpse of ocean about a block away. So far, Daisy liked everything she'd seen about Rio and was getting excited about capturing so much of it on film.

"Excuse me. You are Daisy Gardner, I believe. I am Luis." Daisy looked up and caught her breath. Luis was taller than Daisy had imagined. Maybe over six feet tall. His hair was dark and curly and his thick moustache had smatterings of gray in it. No one could miss the deep cleft in his chin. He was offering his hand to her and smiling broadly. For a few seconds, Daisy was unable to find her voice.

For the sake of the project, she decided not to fire him.

"I'm pleased to meet you, Luis." *Great, Daisy. That definitely put him in his place.*

"I feel I owe you an apology. I have been extremely busy completing a job in Sao Paulo and I'm afraid my thoughts have not been on the work we will do together. I am, as you may learn, a somewhat single-minded man. But," he added as he sat down opposite Daisy and put his two large hands over hers on the table,

"I am finished with my other project and I am all yours."

Daisy felt a heat from his hands that unnerved her. Were all Brazilian men this forward? She returned his smile but slowly slid her hands back into her lap. "No apology needed, I guess. I know how it is to be involved in something that consumes you like that." She felt she was watching herself from afar and couldn't help but think that she was quickly losing control of this meeting.

"So," Luis said, "would you like something cold to drink? I'm going to have a beer."

"That's fine. Make it two."

Luis called out to the bartender whom he obviously knew and then returned to Daisy.

"This is one of my favorite places," he said. "Actually I guess it's rather famous. You know the song, *The Girl From Ipanema*? The two men who wrote the song, Antonio Jobim and Vinicius de Moraes, were sitting right here in this café when they composed it. There actually was a girl from Ipanema, Heloisa Pinto, and she used to walk past this cafe on her way to Ipanema Beach."

He leaned closer to her and continued softly, "They were sitting there," and he pointed to a small table in the corner by a large window. "They saw this beautiful girl walking to Ipanema Beach and they couldn't forget this tall and tan beauty. They came every day and she walked by that window to the beach. They smiled. She didn't ever look at them." Then Luis sang the last line, tapping out the beat on the table with his fingers.

"You're making this up." Daisy was embarrassed, pleased and totally at a loss for words. She had never met anyone like Luis before. She was captivated.

"Believe me, it is all true, and Jobim and Vinicius made this café famous. They even changed the name to The Girl From Ipanema. When people come to Rio, they always come here. All because of sentimental Brazilian poets and a song. Maybe you should put this place in your film." And he leaned back in his chair and smiled again.

The waiter arrived with their drinks. Daisy looked out the window at the beach. Instead of the girl from Ipanema, she could swear she saw Craig walking into the ocean, disappearing into the surf.

Six

The sounds of Rio traffic awakened Daisy the following morning – horns honking, the husky voices of hundreds of car engines impatiently competing for more space on the road. Daisy turned over in bed and thrust her feet out from under the covers. But instead of jumping out of bed, she just stretched and smiled. So much had happened in just one day.

The arrival in Rio. The gift of this beautiful house in Copacabana. The wonderful treat of seeing Dr. Tsuru at the airport.

And meeting Luis Campos.

Oh, yes, Luis. Daisy's mental run-through of events stopped when she thought of the handsome Brazilian who had caught her by surprise and turned out to be utterly charming and warm. She had not been prepared for this. *And to think I was going to fire him!*

They had sat in the café in Ipanema the entire afternoon and Luis had given her the most wonderful time she had enjoyed in years.

He was so knowledgeable and energetic. Not just about Brazil but everything he talked about. It was easy to see that he truly embraced life. Daisy had marveled at his quick laughter. He smiled often and she found herself enjoying his gaze. There was something both intriguing and yet very comfortable about the man.

After a few hours in the café, Luis had called a cab for Daisy. When Daisy was settled in the back seat of the taxi, Luis had leaned in the passenger window of the cab and said, "I am going to like this job very much, Daisy Gardner. I have enjoyed this afternoon. I have needed the unwinding and you, too, I believe, need much more of it. I will see you tomorrow. Welcome to Brazil. We are both happy you are here."

He motioned for the driver to go and Daisy turned and watched Luis standing by the curb with his arms folded. She watched him until the driver turned the corner at the beach road.

Plans had been made for Luis to come to the house today and meet Dr. Tsuru and Charlie. She knew she had to get up, shower and dress but she was enjoying the luxury of being alone with her new thoughts about this man who had suddenly jumped into her life.

Stirrings she hadn't felt for quite some time welled up inside her. Daisy turned on her side and looked out her window at the majesty of Brazil. The next few months were indeed going to be very interesting. After an on-purpose cold shower, Daisy joined Charlie and Miki in the dining room. It was nine o'clock and the two of them were just having juice and coffee.

"Breakfast is on the way, Daisy," said Miki. "In the meantime, help yourself to the marvelous fruit." He passed a large bowl of guava, bananas, and a mixture of other exotic fruits her way.

"So," Miki remarked as he cut into a juicy mango, "Luis will be here at one you said. We'll let this late breakfast last us until dinner tonight so we can work uninterrupted all afternoon. I've made a work sheet by cities that I think will simplify filming considerably."

"How'd you like Luis?" Charlie asked Daisy. "He seemed like a really nice guy to me when I met him. Of course, I didn't really get to know him that well but he's some kind of master with a camera. He's got the touch."

"Really?" Daisy hoped she sounded more casual than she felt. It would do no good if she let her feelings get in the way of this project. She also didn't want to put up with any teasing from Charlie. "He definitely seemed very knowledgeable about Brazil. I'm sure that will come in handy as we get further along. I just hope his camera skills are as good as you say. We don't have time for any mistakes."

Charlie shot Daisy a look that told her he was either hurt or puzzled. Daisy felt bad. She certainly didn't want to wound her friend but neither did she want to sacrifice her project's success if Luis didn't meet up to expectations. Her feelings about the man were not going to get in the way of doing her best work for Miki.

"Let's see what we can get done before Luis gets here, shall we?" Daisy reached for a piece of fruit and all talk of Luis was dropped.

Charlie continued to talk about all the new video and film equipment with Miki and Daisy was grateful for the distraction.

Yet, every so often, despite all her good intentions, Daisy found her thoughts drifting back to her time with Luis and wondering what it was going to be like to work with him. She knew herself well enough to know that she was definitely attracted to him – and that it could spell disaster for the project if she didn't get her feelings in check. Besides, it was pointless to get so enamored with a man about whom she knew so little. Daisy scolded herself for allowing her feelings to get away from her. Luis was probably involved with someone. Daisy suddenly realized he could even be married. She clearly needed to know more about the man.

Something Charlie said about traveling interrupted her daydreaming and Daisy felt she had her opening.

"I'm sorry, Charlie, you bring up a good point. The hours needed for this project are obviously going to be demanding. I hope Luis' family obligations won't get in the way."

Charlie shot Daisy that puzzled look again. "I've never heard anything said about Luis that led me to believe he wasn't the consummate professional. He often goes to great lengths to get his story. Besides, he's not married. The fellow who introduced us in Rome told me Luis had been married a long time ago and had a young child. I'm not really sure exactly what happened, but he lost both his wife and the child. They said he sort of pulled out of the human race for a long, long time. Pretty sad, actually."

Daisy felt joy at hearing that Luis was unattached and then

immediately felt guilty thinking about the death of Luis' wif
baby. She found it hard to believe that Luis could have known such
sadness. He seemed so happy. So upbeat. So vibrant and full of life.
Another piece of the strange Luis Campos puzzle.

The door to the kitchen sprang open.

Marcelina, the cook, brought in a huge serving tray filled with
delicacies – eggs, ham, all kinds of varied colored sauces, sliced
melons, cheeses, rolls, and jams.

"Yes," said Daisy, coming back to the present, "I believe I can
wait until dinner to eat again. This looks marvelous."

At 1:00 p.m. the buzzer sounded at the gate outside. Charlie
peered through the window. "It's Luis. I'll go meet him." Daisy got
up from the sofa and watched her good friend waving to Luis who
stood on the other side of the gates that were opening slowly.

Once in the house and introductions out of the way, Miki
suggested the four of them sit at the large dining table. "We can
spread out and look at all the maps and books." He gave each one of
them a large yellow pad and sat at the head of the table.

"If you have any questions, just ask me," he began as he held up
his textbook. "Daisy will do most of the editing and be responsible
for the finished film. She has assured me that you, Charlie and Luis,
will provide us with unequaled film work. I believe that, too. Brazil
is a photographer's dream for anyone with an eye and heart for
beauty and extreme contrasts in its geography and people. Brazil
has come a long way but it is still a land of the very rich and the very
poor. It is a place of extremes.

"Perhaps you noticed the little huts and shacks built into and
onto the sides of the mountains," he said, looking primarily at
Daisy and Charlie. "We passed many of them on our way from the
airport. They are called favelas and the very poor live there. We'll
talk more about the favelas later.

"Let's move on. If each of you could just visually skim the
text, read a portion of each chapter, you'll begin to get a feel of the
rhythm of Brazil. And there is a definite rhythm here. Not only in
the music without which the people, rich and poor, could not live

but there is a rhythm of nature and the constant way of things."

The dining room chairs were very straight and formal in design, not conducive for relaxing or getting comfortable. Daisy looked at Luis sitting across from her. He was wearing white jeans and a bright red summer shirt with a design of lime green and yellow parrots on it. With his olive complexion, this stark brightness was quite flattering. He seemed so at ease, so at home. He had been the same way at the café the day before but she had chalked it up to the fact that he was in familiar surroundings. However, he had the same air of confidence and easy manner today. Daisy wondered if Luis was always like this – never seeming to feel out of place no matter where he was. He was listening to Miki and making lots of notes.

Daisy watched Charlie, too, as Miki spoke. He was certainly one of a kind when it came to clothes. World traveler that he was, he always picked up the men's mode of dress from every country he visited. This afternoon he was wearing blue-jean cutoffs and a white t-shirt that read, NEPAL HAS IT ALL. His sandals were from Bangkok. He and Luis were like night and day and yet already she could see the beginnings of teamwork forming between them as they nodded and chatted with each other. Daisy scolded herself for not being more in the moment. She felt restless and if she wasn't careful, this project was going to get away from her. She forced herself to pay more attention.

"I think we should begin filming here in Rio," Miki was saying. He reached into his very full briefcase and pulled out a typed agenda of places in that city. He then turned to Daisy and said, "I'd like for you to talk now and explain how the filming will progress beyond Rio."

As though in planned unison, Charlie and Luis moved their heads at the exact moment and looked directly at Daisy.

Daisy cleared her throat and looked from Miki to Charlie and then to Luis. He was looking attentively at her and she wished very much she knew what he was thinking. But Luis's was not a face that read like a book like Charlie's. Her longtime friend watched her enthusiastically, his wide smile showing the small space between his top two front teeth. Luis, on the other hand, gave no hint of his thoughts as he looked at her with big, warm brown eyes. He watched Daisy expectantly as though she had some startling announcement to make. He seemed poised on the edge of his chair, watching her, yet he was relaxed.

"Daisy," Miki urged when Daisy took a few seconds too long to respond, "you were going to talk about the filming after you finish here in Rio. Where do you think you and the boys will head from here?"

"Sao Paulo," Daisy said softly. She felt her composure return as she spoke. "I believe that will be a logical place to go from Rio. Then from there, we'll break up and Charlie and Luis can work some small villages separately. I see no need for all of us to remain together when sometimes the shoot will only call for one camera. This way, the other camera can be filming in another area of the country. I believe we can conserve time this way."

"And you, Daisy," spoke up Charlie. "Will you stay here in Rio and begin to edit the footage we send back?"

"No, not all the time. I'll need to be with the cameras on the critical jobs, especially in the Northeast and the Amazon region."

Oh, but which camera? And how to decide, Daisy wondered as she looked up and saw Luis staring intently at her.

SEVEN

The informal briefing broke up around 4:30 that afternoon. Luis said he had plans for the evening and Daisy immediately sensed that those plans involved a woman. Again, she was caught off guard by the intensity of the feelings that thought generated.

After Luis left, Daisy retreated to her room and freshened up. For what, she had no idea. All of a sudden, she felt out of sorts, adrift. She wandered downstairs again in hopes of spending some time with Charlie. Miki was reading a book by the window but Charlie was nowhere in sight. Then, bounding footsteps made her look to the stairs. Charlie had changed clothes and was heading out the door.

"I'll be gone all evening. Don't wait up for me," he said as he winked over his shoulder at Daisy.

Miki watched Charlie go. "Well, it seems we have been deserted. Or at least you have. The young and handsome have departed, leaving you with the old and distinguished. Do you want to see some of Rio? Maybe go out for dinner?"

"I do have to get Christmas gifts for my parents and get them mailed or they won't receive them in time. I have no idea where to look or for what. Got any ideas, Miki?"

"Well, as a matter of fact, I do have an idea for gifts. A dentist friend of mine, Dr. Beto Mendes, makes delicate wood carvings. It's his hobby but the sculptures are far better than anything you would buy in a store. Let me make a quick call and perhaps we can go to his studio this evening. He usually works late."

Dr. Tsuru reached for the phone near him and dialed Beto's number. This was the first time Daisy had heard Miki speak Portuguese and although she was fairly fluent in Spanish, she could not decipher what he was saying.

"Okay," Miki said as he put down the phone. "Beto said he can see us now, so let's go. You will like him very much and I know you will be very impressed with his work."

Once outside the gate Daisy was keenly aware of late afternoon traffic in Rio. The streets were crowded with cars and motorcycles and everyone seemed to love using their horns and yelling out the windows to fellow travelers with much enthusiasm, and not always positive.

Despite this, Miki was able to carry on a conversation as if they were taking a leisurely drive through the country.

"I met Beto a few years ago at an art show in Washington, D.C.," he said. "We have remained friends ever since. Wait until you see his home. I know you will be impressed."

Soon they were away from Avenida Atlantica and began to climb steadily, turning right, going three or four blocks and turning left, weaving in and out of narrow cobblestone streets. The twists and turns around hills and mountains and unexpected drives through tunnels left Daisy with no sense of direction at all.

A sharp right turn up an unpaved alley and Daisy asked, "How much longer, Miki? I may not look green but I certainly feel queasy. This is like being on a rollercoaster. Doesn't it bother you?"

"No, not anymore. Besides I have two advantages. One, I can hold on to the steering wheel and the other, I know exactly where we are going."

He stopped the car in front of a beautiful estate with neatly manicured lawns, begonias with yellow blossoms and tall bamboos and huge tree ferns. "Besides, we're here."

Miki gave a short beep on the horn and out of the wooden double doors and down the stone walk hurried a short, balding, smiling man.

"I'm Beto and you must be Daisy, Miki's new friend," he said, opening the door and extending his hand for Daisy. "You're right, Miki, she is beautiful. Welcome to my home." He gave Daisy a hug that engulfed her. "Let's go out to my studio and see if I have something you can choose for your parents." He took Daisy by the arm as they walked through the spacious home. He spoke perfect English with just the slightest hint of an accent.

"My wife and two children are in Germany at the moment but I would like you to meet them when they return at Christmas. Perhaps you can come back and visit."

"I'd love to," Daisy said. She was turning her head to and fro trying to take in the house as they walked through the rooms. Everywhere she looked she saw furniture, paintings, and sculptures of sheer elegance and beauty.

"Beto, I believe this has to be one of the most beautiful homes I have ever seen. The furnishings, the glass walls across the back of the house - everything is so open and simple and yet so unusual."

"Well, thank you very much, but I take little credit for what you see. My wife, Luci, is a decorator and a designer of furniture. Right now, she's remodeling a large home near Munich. She's extremely talented, and has the ability to give each home she decorates that comfortable, you-can-live-in-me feeling. Her philosophy is simple: a museum is for viewing, a home is for living."

Out behind the home was a small workshop. When Beto opened its door and motioned for Daisy to enter ahead of him, she was wonderfully surprised.

"I had expected to see some nice things, Beto, but your work is exquisite."

Beto smiled, happy that he had pleased his visitor. The walls were covered with his artwork – tiny wooden miniatures of everything imaginable. Beto carefully removed one piece from the wall and handed it to Daisy.

"Perhaps your mother would like this one. It is a very tiny window, complete with wooden framework and very small panes of glass set in the frame just like its larger counterpart." Beto held his little masterpiece up to the light. It was no more than six inches long and about three inches wide.

"Look carefully here in the lower right corner of the window. See? There is the same effect as in a larger window when someone throws a rock or other object and breaks the glass. You can see the tiny hole where supposedly a small rock broke this little window. And, just like in a larger pane of glass, there is the spider webbing that occurs around the hole. It is simply that on a very small scale like this, the veining and webbing in the little pane of glass is so intricate it is an artwork within an artwork. What do you think?"

Daisy was enthralled with Beto's creativity and his sensitivity. She bought one of the windows for her mother and one for herself and chose a wood carving of Sugar Loaf, complete with little cable cars, for her father.

The drive back home wasn't nearly as hair-raising. The traffic was lighter and Miki's conversation made the time fly.

The phone was ringing when they reached the front door. Daisy ran to answer it wondering if it was Charlie telling her he was in trouble somewhere and needed to be bailed out.

"Hello?"

"Good," Luis said happily. "I am glad you are home. I had a very good idea during our meeting earlier this afternoon but had to hurry off to deliver some film before I could tell you about it."

Daisy felt relief to know there had not been a woman involved in Luis's plans and then immediately tried to banish the feeling. "So, what is your idea?"

"You have not seen my beautiful city of Rio and before we begin filming I would love to be your personal guide. So, tomorrow I will pick you up early, even before the sun comes up, and we will spend the day introducing you to the most spectacular city in the world. Dress casually and wear comfortable shoes."

"Oh," he added, "I must apologize. Please forgive me. I have just assumed you would be interested in coming with me but I have not even asked. Would you like....."

"Yes," Daisy interrupted him. "Yes, I would like."

Daisy hung up and went to find Miki to tell him of her plans for the upcoming day. She found him in the kitchen scooping white rice onto plates and then gently pouring black beans and tiny pieces of meat over the rice mountain. He looked up as she came through the swinging door.

"It's a bit late, I know, but I thought you might enjoy a very typical Brazilian meal – feijoada completa – rice, beans, and sausage. Marcelina prepared it before she left and kept it warming on the stove. Let's eat and you can tell me why you are wearing the most glorious, unearthly look on your face," he teased.

Daisy smiled and took the plate Miki offered her. "It's nothing really. I'm just glad to be here."

Miki shot her a look that told her he didn't believe her for a minute but he let it pass. He motioned for them to sit at the small table by a window that overlooked a garden in the back. The conversation drifted to talk of art and Beto's family. Daisy found herself enjoying Miki's company more and more. She couldn't help but compare him to her father and the many stilted conversations she had shared with him.

Daisy finished her plate of rice and beans. After she drained the last of her fruit drink she placed the glass on the table and stared out the window. A neon yellow bird sat on a low lying branch and poked at a seed pod.

Miki broke the quiet. "Do you want to tell me about this new flush that has come over you? This new preoccupation? This 'I'm here in body but don't ask me where my mind is.' Don't misunderstand, Daisy. I'm not prying. I'm paying you to make a documentary for me, not to keep me informed about your personal life. However, I consider myself your friend and I thought you might like to talk. If that is not the case, then forgive me for being nosy."

"There's nothing to forgive and I'm pleased that you care what happens to me. The new gift of your friendship is very important and I treasure it."

"You know, Daisy, I have a daughter about your age. Her name is Hisako and she, too, is very beautiful. There are many things about you that remind me of her. Your energy. Your bright mind. Your endless curiosity. You appear to desire to be the best at whatever you do. And something else. Your face is like Hisako's – not in appearance of course, but –." Miki seemed to struggle to find the right words. "How can I put this? Your face is so open. Like Hisako, you cannot hide whatever it is that your heart is feeling."

Daisy was taken by surprise for this was the first time Miki had ever said a word about family. She wondered how much more she didn't know.

"Where does your daughter live?" she asked, genuinely interested and glad to be getting the focus off her.

"At the moment she is studying law at Harvard." The pride clearly showed on Miki's face as he talked about his daughter. "She plans to go into international law and will most likely live abroad. She and I have lived in many countries. She will be excellent on the international scene. She speaks several languages but at the moment doesn't know just where she would like to settle. Frankly, I cannot see Hisako settled in any one place. I'm afraid I raised her rather like a gypsy," he laughed.

"Where is Hisako's mother?"

Miki poured himself another glass of juice. He motioned toward Daisy's glass and she handed it to him to fill. Daisy wondered if he even intended to answer her question at all. She regretted bringing it up; Miki was obviously stalling.

He placed the full glass in front of Daisy and sat back at the table. "My wife Mihoko is a different sort of woman. She was a concert pianist when we met and quite famous in Japan. I was in Tokyo for a year working on a historical research project when we met and fell in love."

He looked away from Daisy and stared at something she couldn't see.

"She was the most beautiful woman I had ever seen. It seemed to me that it was unbelievable she could fall in love with a professor of history, but she did and I was thrilled. We married in her hometown of Osaka and spent our brief honeymoon in a tiny inn in the mountains outside the city."

"Then did you come back to South America?" Daisy asked, completely caught up in his story.

"No. Mihoko had a concert booking for the next year and a half and it would carry her around the world. This seemed to be no problem before we married. I had planned to finish my work in Tokyo, return to South America and she would join me there after her tour.

"Before she was to leave Japan, she discovered she was pregnant. I was happy beyond reason. But Mihoko was not pleased with this news at all. In fact, she was terribly upset and angry. I had never seen her this way. There was no talking to her at all. She just sat and said over and over, 'I never wanted a baby. I never wanted a baby. Now my career is ruined. My life is ruined.' And she would cry for hours until she fell asleep, exhausted.

"I knew in the beginning she would not want children soon and we took precautions. But, Daisy, sometimes babies just happen. I thank God this one did. Hisako is my life and I find so much joy in her."

"What happened to Mihoko?"

"I discovered she had tried to abort her pregnancy two times. She was desperate and wanted a career, not a baby."

Daisy felt a twinge as Miki talked. Painful fragments of her fights with Craig came back to her.

"What happened then, Miki?"

"I talked very seriously to her. I told her that I wanted that baby and I would raise the child. I told her 'Just carry it, have the baby and I will never ask for another thing from you.' I didn't know how she would respond to my proposal, but I shall never forget the way she looked at me nor what she said.

"She told me she would stay on tour as long as she could. Then she would have the baby. But she would return to her music right afterwards. The baby would mean nothing to her.

"And that is what she did. Hisako was born in Australia and I flew down and brought her back with me when she was only two weeks old. Mihoko never saw her again. She never wanted to. So," he sighed, "Hisako and I have been together ever since. I am all the family she has ever known."

"Have you seen Mihoko since Australia?

"No. We never divorced but she lives in Tokyo and teaches in a large university. She trains young pianists for the concert stage. I don't know if Hisako will ever choose to see her mother. We seldom talk of her. I, on the other hand, think of Mihoko every day. She gave away her child and I believe that is a terrible thing to do, but I still love that beautiful woman. Time will write the ending to this story." Tears filled his eyes and one ran slowly down his cheek. Miki didn't seem to notice.

A few seconds later, he took a deep breath and said in a now stronger voice, "I have rattled on and on and haven't as yet discovered the secret you are carrying, Daisy. Why the glow, the subtle smile, the satisfied look? Did you meet someone before you left the States?"

"No," Daisy answered coyly.

"Well, you certainly haven't had time to meet anyone since you've been in Rio. What is it?"

Daisy slowly got up from her chair and put her hand on Miki's arm.

"Let's just say it's the ocean air. I must get some sleep now for I have a full day before me. Thank you for sharing your heart."

Miki watched her walk away and after the swinging door closed behind her, he could barely hear Daisy's soft singing as she made her way up the stairs.

Miki smiled.

EIGHT

It was 5:30 a.m. when Luis's old white BMW pulled into the drive. The lights from his car made giant shadows on the walls of Daisy's bedroom. She had been up for quite some time, mostly thinking about Miki and the evening before. She had seen a side of him last night that she was sure he showed to only a few people and she was moved that he had let her inside his heart like that.

When she heard Luis pull up, Daisy grabbed her oversized purse and tip-toed quietly down the stairs. She opened and closed the heavy front door ever so gently. Luis was standing by the open passenger's door, his arms folded. She could only see his silhouette in the mid-dawn light but she could swear he was smiling, immensely pleased with himself. When she reached the car, he bowed with a flourish and took her hand to help her in.

"I can't see you too well in this light but I'm sure you look beautiful," he said. "You smell wonderful, that I know."

He hurried around to the driver's side, slipped behind the wheel, closed the door, and turned on the inside light.

"I was right. You do look beautiful but what is that marvelous aroma?"

"Jean Naté cologne. Nothing at all expensive. In fact, you can buy it in supermarkets. I've worn it for years. However, I have never gotten this reaction before."

He leaned toward her. "That's because it has never been mixed with the romantic, exotic air of Rio. Let me tell you, the combination is a few centigrades above lethal."

"Luis, I have heard some pretty good lines before but never this early or on such an empty stomach. Sorry to break the mood but I'm starving."

He laughed and started the engine. "Well, perhaps my Latin charms will improve with the day. I trust this is the case. Breakfast awaits us. We are dining on the most beautiful spot in the world."

"On?"

"On! Now buckle up. We have a challenging drive before us." He looked at her and winked. "If we make it, you'll be eating breakfast in half an hour."

Daisy wasn't sure she liked the "if" part but decided it was just more of Luis' teasing. She was amazed at the lack of traffic once they were out onto Atlantica. Usually there was a steady stream of cars on this much-traveled street, but pre-dawn drivers seemed to move in slow motion and were not as intent on plowing one another off the road with horns blaring loudly. They drove in silence for awhile before Luis spoke again.

"Where shall I start? Do you care that Brazil was discovered by Admiral Pedro Cabral in 1500 and claimed it for Portugal?"

"Yes, I care and I'm impressed you know so much." The sound of his voice made it easy to listen to him.

"Any Brazilian school boy would know this fact but there is so much more and it is fascinating. Shall I continue? I think the more you know about Brazil the more useful in the overall filming and editing of this documentary. Besides," he smiled, "I love to tell the story of my country. We have just enough time before we reach our breakfast spot to talk a little about Brazil. My father, too, loved the history of our country and he passed all he knew on to me."

Daisy turned and leaned against the passenger door and watched Luis closely. She loved to watch his expressions. He never just talked.

Every word, it seemed, had accompanying gestures with it.

"Okay, I used the word 'discovered' in relation to Cabral and Brazil. Actually, this sea captain was not so smart and he actually discovered our country accidentally. He did not set out to discover Brazil at all. When he landed here, he thought he had arrived in India but when he looked around and saw no elephants or maharajahs, he realized he had discovered someplace new.

"At first he thought he had found an island and told a search party to walk around the 'island' one time and come back. I think this was very naïve of Cabral for, of course, he hadn't discovered an island at all but the biggest piece of land ever to be claimed in the New World.

"Not really knowing what he had found," Luis continued, "Cabral then sailed back to Portugal, leaving a few men behind to guard his new 'island'. Soon merchant ships came from Portugal and began to carry back loads of a very hardwood, called brazil wood. It wasn't long before the Portuguese people began to call this country the Land of Brazil and soon, simply Brazil."

Traffic was picking up and Daisy was aware that the volume of Rio was slowly being turned up. It was coming alive. Luis continued to talk, his hands intermittently on and off the steering wheel. Still, he was able to maneuver the car up through some very narrow streets, turning sharply, stopping quickly.

Daisy found herself relaxing, lulled by his voice. She sat back. "Go on, continue. I'm enjoying the history lesson. Besides, you're a wonderful story teller."

"Thank you. It's because I like the story. As you know, Brazil is a huge country, the largest in South America. In fact, it's nearly as large as all of Europe. But, sad to say, Brazil has a high rate of illiteracy, a rigid class system based on wealth and a pretty unfair sharing of the country's income. The majority of the Brazilian people today are poorly housed, poorly fed, poorly clothed and most have no education at all.

"The Northeast is the area of Brazil plagued with the most serious problems, I think. The peasants live in little clay huts with dirt floors. There is no electricity, no sanitary facilities, and these poor people live mainly on manioc flour and black beans. They live in chronic hunger and most of the Northeast suffers from intestinal worms, even the tiny babies. They say a child dies up there every thirty or thirty-five seconds. That's a lot of children every day, Daisy."

Luis was no longer smiling. "I do not believe anyone can make life better for these people and there are millions of others just like them all over Brazil, even right here in Rio."

Daisy interrupted, "This is a very different picture from the one I had come to expect. I've always heard that Brazil was a beautiful country with fun-loving, carefree people. You've painted a very bleak picture."

"We'll talk about the fun-loving, carefree people later, for they do exist. But in these backward areas, these peasants accept life the way they have it, very fatalistically. With little energy, education or reason to be motivated, they can do little to make changes. At one time, this area was very wealthy. This is where the first Portuguese discoverers anchored their boats and built Brazil's first capital, Salvador. They became rich from the great sugar mills. All that is changed now and all over Brazil it is the same – a great place to be rich and a terrible place to be poor."

Luis turned to Daisy and smiled, "But that's enough about Brazil for the moment. Perhaps you and I will take an adventure trip and you can see for yourself. Now there is breakfast and Rio. We're almost there."

Daisy had been listening to Luis and not paying much attention to her surroundings. The car stopped and on a gate in front of her was a sign – Serra da Tijuca.

"Where are we?"

"We are about to begin our steep drive to the granite peak of Corcovado and we will drive through the rain forests that are behind the mountain. When we reach the top we will catch our breaths for this is quite a stretch ahead of us. Are you ready?"

Looking into the black, smiling eyes of Luis Campos, Daisy felt ready for anything. "Yes, let's go. I'm ready," she answered.

Luis popped the BMW into first gear and off they went, up,

straight up the mountain road to the top of Corcovado. One thing for sure, Luis knew how to handle the car and the road. The hairpin turns were challenging, to say the least, and there was not much straight road. Once she relaxed and knew she could trust Luis' driving, Daisy experienced a feeling of exhilaration as Luis maneuvered the quick turns and they climbed higher and higher. She couldn't see anything but the sides of the mountain, covered with an abundance of lush, green foliage, rushing by outside her window.

Then suddenly everything fell away. Before her was nothing but sea and sky and for several moments she couldn't say a word.

"I feel like I'm floating or suspended in space," Daisy finally said. "This is truly the most spectacular view I have ever seen! It's unbelievable! Luis, even you are speechless." She watched him stare out to sea, a faraway look in his eyes.

He didn't turn his head for a few minutes, just looked straight ahead and said, "I've lived here all my life but this sight never becomes commonplace to me. I love it."

Luis abruptly turned off the ignition. "Now, for our feast." He got a large wicker chest from the trunk and steered Daisy to a small clearing near the base of the famous statue of Christ, standing high above them, the head almost covered in clouds.

"We'll have our breakfast here, okay?"

But Daisy wasn't ready to eat just yet. She kept staring out onto the view below. "I can almost see the entire city from here."

Luis set the chest down, walked over to Daisy, and put one hand gently on her shoulder.

"Nearest to us and right below, at the very entrance to Guanabara Bay is Sugar Loaf Mountain – Pao de Acucar." He tapped her cheek and pointed, "Now, look to the right of Sugar Loaf, outside the bay and to the west. See that long stretch of white? That is Copacabana Beach and beyond that is Ipanema."

His voice was soft and his breath warm against her ear. He could have been saying the alphabet and Daisy wouldn't have moved.

"To our left you can see all of Guanabara Bay, deep blue and smooth this morning, just for you. Directly below, the skyscrapers and streets look like miniature replicas of a large city."

"I'm curious. How did Rio de Janiero get its name?"

"Rio was discovered by Captain Andre Goncalves in January in 1502. When he sailed into Guanabara Bay, he thought he had discovered a great river and from this mistake the city got its name – Rio de Janiero, the River of January."

"How do you know so much or are you making all this up?" Daisy laughed.

"I minored in history at the University of Rio de Janeiro but I think I would have remembered all this and more from my father. He loved Rio very much and, as I mentioned to you earlier, told me all he knew. I'll tell you about my father later. Surely you are hungry by now. Let's have breakfast."

They sat down and Luis removed parcels of food from the chest, a thermos, and a colorful cloth that he spread out before them.

"So, I have brought much fresh fruit, several kinds of bread, jam, some wonderful cheeses, and this thermos of coffee, the best in the world." He poured the dark, strong liquid into two cups he had tucked away in the chest. "Taste it. This is one thing the rich and the poor can both enjoy. This is Brazil." Luis took a long sip from his cup and smiled at Daisy.

Daisy took sips of the hot coffee, looked out once more at the view, and said, "If this isn't paradise, it can't be far away." She turned to Luis. "I think I'm in love."

Luis' eyes widened a bit.

"With Rio, silly," Daisy said quickly.

"Oh, you have fallen in love with Rio, have you?" Luis said. "Be very careful with this city. Don't fall in love with Rio too quickly. She is the Mistress of Romance. You can think you're in love, but protect your heart. Let Rio make the first move."

Daisy sipped her coffee again and watched Luis from the corner of her eyes. She wondered if he was talking only about Rio or if there was another meaning behind his words.

NINE

On the drive down the mountain, Daisy pretended to watch the scenery so that she could think in peace. Her thoughts were as jumbled as Rio's rush hour traffic. She knew if she wasn't careful, she could very easily have feelings for this intriguing Brazilian and right now that was the last thing she or her project needed.

When they reached the bottom of the mountain and were about to enter Atlantica traffic, it was clear by now that all of Rio had awakened. The decibels were high and getting stronger. Traffic was congested and drivers were making lanes that did not exist. At last, Luis found an opening and hurried into the flow of traffic. He sang absently as he drummed his thumbs on the steering wheel. His voice was low and, husky and Daisy found herself tapping her foot in time to the Brazilian song she'd learned about the day she had met Luis in the café.

Luis gave her a sideways glance and smiled. "I see you like my singing." Daisy stopped tapping. "Don't be shy. Brazilian music is habit forming."

"Well, you definitely are a man of many talents, I'm discovering. You're also an exceptionally knowledgeable guide. What's next?"

"Well, I thought I would take you to Video Brazil and introduce you to Paulo Sancho, my friend who can help us with our editing. He has a very sophisticated studio with the most up-to-date equipment. Perhaps within a few days we can begin filming here in Rio. I think it is important for you to see some of Paulo's work and decide for sure if you want to work with him. His price is reasonable and he speaks fluent English, a big plus."

"Perfect. I'm anxious to get started. We have a lot to do in a short period of time. If Paulo is as good as you say, then I'll be very relieved." Daisy waved her arm in the direction of traffic. "Lead on."

It was almost noon when Luis and Daisy left Video Brazil and walked down the wide sidewalk to their car.

"You were right, Luis, I do like Paulo and I love his work. His editing is tight and dramatic. It's more than I had hoped for and I feel very good about letting him work on this project. I also like his idea to get an original, typically Brazilian musical score done for the film. Let's talk with Charlie about all this soon, okay?"

"Good. Now let's have something to eat. I know just the place."

"Why am I not surprised?"

They walked past the car and stopped at a very small, open-front space in the wall. It could hardly be called a restaurant or even a snack bar, but the aroma of something delicious filled the air. Luis ordered for them and when he was handed two little fried pies filled with pork and shrimp, he said, "Now, let's get something to drink." He gestured for Daisy to walk down the street.

At a tiny store down the sidewalk they stopped at a little cubicle that had tall stalks of green limbs stacked against the back wall. Seeing Daisy's quizzical look, Luis quickly told her, "That's sugarcane and this place has the best drink in town. It's pressed sugar cane juice."

When the shopkeeper handed them their drinks that were in tall hard plastic cups, Daisy was surprised to find the cups ice cold. The frothy liquid went down refreshingly as Luis explained, "They keep ice behind the counter and they prepare it like a martini, mixing ice with the liquid and shaking it vigorously until it is cold."

"What's in the pies?"

"Our lunch. Let's walk about a block and have lunch in a park that overlooks the bay."

They soon reached the grassy spot and Daisy said, "You surely have an eye for beauty. This little green oasis squeezed among the concrete is just beautiful and I've never seen such a variety of colorful and unusual flowers."

They sat on the grass and Luis handed her the warm lunch packet.

"This smells so good," said Daisy.

"You will like them. They're filled with all kinds of delicacies. These have pork and shrimp but they use all kinds of different meats and vegetables. They take all the ingredients, blend them well, and roll the mixture in a pie crust and then they cook the pies in hot coconut oil. It is very good, especially with a tall, cold sugar cane drink."

"This little park, how did you know it was here? I'm afraid I would have blinked and missed it completely."

"Oh, this was once a much larger park," said Luis. "I am surprised it is still here at all."

"Why?"

Luis took a bite and swallowed quickly. "Rio is growing too fast. For example, look at Copacabana," he gestured with his pie. "Skyscrapers, overcrowding, pollution, ear-splitting noise, traffic, and miles of concrete."

"And that's bad? Most big cities look like this."

Luis had finished his lunch and was looking across the bay in the direction of Copacabana. Daisy could see that he was sincerely concerned.

"You know, Daisy, they tear down skyscrapers not even ten years old to build newer, taller ones. And they are cutting down more of Rio's beautiful trees every day. They are destroying the natural beauty, our gardens, and parks, to build more tunnels, wider highways. One of our philosophers once said that life should be a balance between man and nature. I believe Rio is today an unbalanced city."

Daisy, finished with her lunch now, too, said, "But, Luis, there has to be progress and change."

"Yes, I realize that, but the city of Rio is in a constant state of construction. They are covering everything with concrete and with progress so much of Rio's history and heritage is gone forever. Rio seems to be obsessed with forever modernizing itself."

Luis was standing now, leaning against an old, gnarled tree. He turned toward her and looked into her eyes.

"Daisy, to me, it is as though Rio has raped herself. We are like no other city in the world. For example, Rome's historians can dig down and uncover layer after layer – each layer representing several centuries. In Rio, you would only see a few layers, representing only a few decades."

He walked over to Daisy and kneeled down and spoke in a softer voice, but the intensity was still there.

"Rio has no peer. It is not an historical city like Rome or Florence. It is not a great commercial city like New York, or a political city like your Washington, D.C., or even a spiritual city like Jerusalem."

"Then, Luis, how would you describe Rio?" Daisy was getting caught up in Luis' emotions.

"Rio's name conjures up romance, excitement, and exotic living. This is definitely a sensual city."

"Is that bad?"

"Daisy, until 1960, Rio used to be the capitol of Brazil. Now Brasilia is the new capitol. Rio used to be the commercial center of Brazil, now Sao Paulo holds this title. So, Rio has become Brazil's biggest holiday attraction – a beach resort, open all year round. It stands for fun, carnival, soccer, the beach. I suppose we are the biggest sandbox for adults in the world."

He was quiet for a moment, then, "And we could have been so much more. I'm not sure I can live here for the rest of my life."

Daisy was caught off guard by Luis' admission. She wondered what it was about this country that made people admit so much about themselves to almost-strangers. First Miki, and now Luis. Her discomfort made her want to change the subject but to what?

"Where were you born in this city, Luis?

Luis' eyes clouded over. "I'm afraid that is not very interesting. I will tell you sometime."

Trying again, Daisy said. "Luis, those little colorful huts up there scattered over the mountains. What are they? Do you know?"

Luis lay back on the grass and looked up and slowly turned his gaze to the little houses nestled into the mountains across Rio.

He sighed. "Those are called favelas, Daisy. Dr. Tsuru spoke about them briefly yesterday. They are the slums of Rio and only the very poor live there. Actually, I don't think I should have used the word 'live' for that hardly fits the conditions in a favela.

"Perhaps the better word is 'exist'. There are over three hundred favelas in Rio, more than any other city in Brazil. In fact, over one-fourth of Rio's population lives in the favelas. They are no more than brightly painted hillside shacks."

"I had no idea, Luis. In America, the slum section of a town is usually outside the perimeter of the city proper. These little huts are mixed in everywhere."

"Yes, Daisy, the poor are very lucky," Luis said with a smile that was totally devoid of humor. "They can look over into the backyards of the very rich. As poor as they are, they have the most beautiful views in the world – gorgeous, expensive mansions and this breathtaking view of Guanabara Bay. However, the lifestyle they have never seems to change for the better. Most of the young girls and women are maids for the wealthy and the men work in factories if they can find work at all."

"How did these favelas get there, up on the mountainsides? There's something so sad about that."

Quickly Luis said, "Oh, don't feel sorry for the favelados, the hill-dwellers. They manage. They are born to fight and to try to survive. Some actually manage to graduate from the favela and live in the city of Rio and do important jobs. A few. And they are very lucky and very grateful."

Luis had gotten up again and had his back to Daisy.

"Luis, are you alright? Do you want to talk about something else?"

"No, let's finish about the favelas. They will need to be in the film, and besides, you need to know about them." He turned to face her but his expression told her his mind was somewhere else.

"Around 1900, young Brazilian soldiers returned to Rio from a battle in Bahia. They had no real purpose, no money, and no place to live. Near Bahia, they had been camping on a hill they named *favela*, after a wildflower that grew wildly all over that hill. So, when they came to Rio they called their first settlement of shacks 'favela', too. Soon all the other shanty towns were called favelas. These soldiers married Indian girls, slave girls and the racial mixture of the favela was the coming together of many different kinds of blood – Portuguese, Indian, French, African and who knows what else."

Daisy noticed that Luis's voice was lower now and he spoke of the favelas with a reverence and compassion.

"As you can see, many of the shacks are painted bright colors and that is why they look almost beautiful when seen from a distance. Up close there is nothing beautiful in a favela, except the little children who play with colorful, homemade kites and anything else they can find. Daisy, conditions are so bad that one out of every five children dies before he is five years old."

Daisy noticed tears in Luis's eyes. She stood and walked over to him. She longed to wipe the sadness from his face. She wanted the smiling, singing Luis to return but wasn't quite sure what to do. Instead, she just reached out and put both her hands over his.

Luis turned to her and seemed to see her for the first time. "I was born in a favela, Daisy. And sometimes I feel guilty to be one of those children who survived. So many don't."

TEN

Luis extended his hand to Daisy.

"Walk with me," he said and they walked along the streets hand in hand as he pointed out one thing or another.

His touch was electric. When he first reached for her hand it seemed like the most natural thing in the world and Daisy knew they had crossed an invisible barrier and wondered what it meant for the film -- and for her.

After an hour of walking, they found themselves back at the car.

"Ready to go back home, Daisy?" Luis asked.

"Honestly? No. I'm having a wonderful time and I don't want this day to end. I'm learning so much and enjoying the company."

"Me, too." Luis said softly. He motioned to a nearby wooden bench set within the park they had left over an hour ago. "Let's sit for a while?"

Daisy nodded and walked ahead of him to the little area he had pointed out. She sat on the bench and inhaled the sweet fragrant flowers. "Luis, is all of Brazil like this?"

Luis sat beside her. Daisy noticed he kept a safe distance, careful not to touch her and wondered if he regretted their earlier closeness.

"No, Daisy, sadly all of Brazil is not like this. There are many parts that are quite ugly. Maybe not in looks but certainly in spirit. But we'll see them soon enough. Right now, I want to know more about the woman I am going to spend the next few months with. Tell me about Daisy. I have done most of the talking today. I would like to know more about this American who will be in charge of my life in the coming months."

A soft breeze caressed her face, moving her hair ever so gently. Daisy tucked some stray strands behind her right ear. She was stalling and hoped Luis hadn't noticed. "What do you want to know? I'm pretty simple, really."

"I find that very hard to believe." He smiled that smile again, the one that warmed her heart and caused it to beat faster. "Is there someone back in the States? Are your parents in Washington, too? What do you do for fun? Tell me what makes you, you."

"Oh, so nothing really personal, right?" Daisy teased. It was so easy to be herself with this man. She felt her reserve slipping again and knew she had to be careful. "Where to start? Well, let's see. No, there is no one back in the States. My work pretty much prevents that right now. There was a husband a while ago. Craig."

"And this Craig - he was stupid enough to let you go?"

"No, not stupid. I think I have to take the blame for that."

"Why do I think you are just being kind?"

"No, it's true. Oh, we had a wonderful relationship — in the beginning. But, as it turned out, we really had nothing in common. We wanted very different things. Looking back with brilliant hindsight I see that now. And, a very important part was that Craig wanted to start a family very soon and I didn't feel ready to have babies. I put him off many times. Too many, as it turned out. I realize now I was selfish and I set the stage for the breakup. With me, there seemed to be no compromise." Daisy looked down at her shoes, unable to look at Luis while she talked of another man. "I honestly hope he finds happiness and a family. That's what he wants."

"Your film work. What about that? Couldn't you share your common love for that?"

"No, Luis, because now I realize there was competition between us. I did want to be the best. When he confronted me with my awards and job offers and travels abroad, I viewed him as immature and totally lacking in understanding. I simply saw him as jealous. Now, I see myself as being the jealous one. I think this feeling was subconscious but present just the same. I wanted to be the best, just as he said. He was right about a lot of things.

"I think my relationship with my father had a lot to do with my marriage to Craig, too. Just as I always knocked myself out to please my father, I realize now I was doing the same thing with Craig. And, of course, that was the worst possible thing to do. Eventually, it broke us apart."

"And having a baby?" Luis asked quietly. "Have you changed your mind about that, too?"

"I'm not clear on that one," she answered quickly, wondering if Luis was thinking about his baby, the one he'd lost. "I've given it a lot of thought over the past months and I think the timing was just off. That, and Craig's unbending insistence that I have a child right then, in that moment, just because he wanted one. I believe I want children," and she looked into those deep, black eyes of Luis's and said, "Yes, I'm sure I want children."

The sun was now lower in the sky. Luis turned to Daisy and said, "Let's have dinner before I take you home. I want to tell you about my life in the favela and especially about my Papa. I would not be here today if it were not for Vitor Campos. I know a wonderful place in Niteroi and you will love the drive. A bridge links Rio to Niteroi and it's quite a sight. Five miles of the journey on the bridge over Guanabara Bay is over water and the shimmering lights of Rio are beautiful from the bridge. The restaurant is called Beijo and I will tell you later what that means in English. Okay?"

Luis and Daisy sat outside on a large patio that had a magnificent view – the sparkling lights of Rio, like fireflies, danced in the distance and the water of Guanabara Bay sent back reflected images of millions of lights.

"This is breathtaking, Luis. I know I've over used that word too much today but I honestly don't believe I've ever seen anything so beautiful. I'm glad you brought me here."

"This just happens to be my favorite view of the Bay."

"Well, then," said Daisy, "I'm happy you consented to bring me along. I do love this view and I may have to agree with you, although I've not seen nearly enough of Rio yet. I've just seen enough to know I want to see all of Rio. It's so different from what I've ever been told."

"What do you mean? How different?"

"Oh, I think my conception was that Rio was a very large city with one huge beach. I guess that's about it. And even though you say there is no lengthy history here, I believe I feel a pride from the few people I've met. A pride in this city that is a part of a huge country that definitely has a history. From what I've learned today, Brazil has a fascinating past. Don't you believe there will come a time when Rio will settle down and, as it were, begin to build memories, keep things of importance and stop destroying so much beauty to make way for 'progress'?"

"No, Daisy, and I realize I sound very pessimistic. We are running out of land. Rio can only grow vertically because we have used up our horizontal. In addition, I explained to you the attitude of the builders and politicians. Make Rio modern whatever the cost to the past. That, I'm afraid, will never change."

A waiter appeared and spoke to Luis in Portuguese. Luis laughed and then, in English, introduced Daisy.

"You know many people here, Luis. This man, however, seems exceptionally friendly. How do you know him?"

"He's my cousin. Carlos said a very nice thing about you. He is a true Carioca and you would appreciate his sentiments much more if you understood our language. But, I shall try to translate as closely as possible. He said, 'The lady makes the lights of Rio lose their glow, for her beauty far outshines them tonight.'"

"My, he must be a poet."

"No," Luis said and smiled. "He is a typical Brazilian who thinks with his heart and does not forbid his mouth to speak what his heart thinks. He is most charmed by you. And so am I."

Daisy thought Luis was going to say something else but he

didn't. He changed the subject quickly with, "How about some wine? We'll have a glass and decide later about dinner."

He held up two fingers and very soon Carlos returned with two large goblets of dark, red wine.

"To a beautiful day with a lovely lady," said Luis as their goblets touched.

"A true Carioca speaking?" she asked.

"No, an honest man," he answered. "And a man who would like to share with you about his father. I credit him for everything I have ever accomplished in my life. Oh, but I have told you so much today. Perhaps I should wait."

"No, I am in no hurry and I'm enjoying this setting. Please, tell me about your father. I really want to know."

Luis took a long drink from his wine and began.

"As you know, I was born in a favela, in a tiny hut with a dirt floor. The little, fragile hut hung precipitously from a mountainside. Every time we had a heavy tropical rainstorm we just knew our little house would be swept away.

"My mother died in childbirth and I was frighteningly small — three-and-a-half pounds at birth. My grandmother lived with my mother and father and took care of me. There was no electricity, no running water, no drainage system for water and garbage and as I told you this morning the infant mortality is extremely high. Meningitis kills so many little ones. My father was so proud to have a son that he came down off that mountainside determined to get a job — one that paid enough money to take care of us."

"Had your father not worked before you were born?"

"Not much," answered Luis. "He and my mother were so young when they married. She ironed to make money and he got jobs wherever he could find them. Both were born in favelas so they knew nothing of a trade or any skilled work. After I was born, my father went to the house where my mother had ironed and asked to speak to the man of the house. He told him, Andre Pinto, about my mother's death and that he had a baby son to care for. He told the man he didn't want his son to be like him. He told him he wanted me to be able to go to school and learn a trade that would get me out of the favelas. 'I will work hard, Senhor Pinto, if you will help me find a job.'

"My father used to tell me that story about going to Senhor Pinto's house many times. It was a turning point for him so I understand why that moment was so important. Senhor Pinto was a very wealthy architect and designer of the mosaics that edge the avenues and beaches in Rio. He gave my father a job crushing the large, very hard black and white stones into the tiny pieces the mosaic workers used. My father smashed those stones with a heavy hammer for years. He worked very hard but Senhor Pinto didn't forget my father's desire to provide for me. One day he asked my father two questions: one, if he would like to put that hammer down and never pick it up again. Papa thought he was going to be fired but Senhor Pinto told him he was being promoted to a new job – actually putting the tiles in place and helping make the large designs that had become famous all over the world." Luis stopped and took a sip of wine, clearly enjoying his tale and watching Daisy's interest.

"And the second question, what was it, Luis?"

"He asked my father if I, who by that time, was twelve and making money any way I could, would come and work for him in his office. He asked Papa if I knew the city of Rio well and Papa assured him I did. Anyway, he told my father he would pay me to be an errand boy for his office staff. I was so excited when Papa told me about Senhor Pinto's offer. Also, Daisy, when I was born, my father did not know how to read at all. He told Senhor Pinto and that man arranged for Papa to go to school at night where he learned to read and when he learned, he read everything and then passed it onto me."

"Your father sounds like such a wonderful man. I would love to meet him."

Luis looked out toward the Bay and slowly turned back to Daisy. "Papa died last year when I was in Italy filming. Senhor Pinto called me in Naples and told me. Somehow it was not such a big surprise for me. Papa had a bad heart and I had asked him not to work so hard. He always laughed and said, 'Luis, good, honest work is like medicine. It will make me strong. You will see.' And so, he continued to work but his heart just couldn't take it.

"But I have great memories of my Papa. It was as if his only real job in life was to teach me everything he learned. And he gave me the greatest gift you can ever give anyone – he loved me and he was man enough to show me. You know, there are times when I can still feel his strong hands on either side of my arms, lifting me high to sit on his shoulders. He told me he loved me many times."

Luis looked out at the water, a soft smile on his face. "I remember one special time when Papa took me to the beach – Leblon, I think. We built sand buildings, not castles, and Papa took some little pieces of tile out of his pockets and worked so patiently for a long time making miniature mosaic sidewalks around my sand city. I remember I wished I could have taken a picture of that. Those little mosaic sidewalks and pavements were more beautifully designed than any in all of Rio. I believe my father was a very creative man.

"After the sun set, we continued to sit in the sand. Papa leaned against a big rock and I sat between his widespread legs and leaned back on his chest. He told me the story about where the idea for mosaic pavements came from – Lisbon, Portugal, where mosaics were laid in an ocean wave-design to commemorate a great earthquake and flood that had hit Lisbon in the 1700's. He told me he would like to visit Lisbon some day and see those mosaics. All the while he softly talked to me, he touched my hair with his fingers. His hands, so strong and rough from the kind of work he did, but so soft when he touched my curly hair. I never doubted Papa loved me. I will never forget him.

"Then when I was seventeen, Senhor Pinto called me to his office and talked to me about my work. He said I was like my father, hard-working and honest. He told me he and his wife, Lily, had never had any children and that they both had grown quite fond of me over the years I had worked for him. He said he had talked to my father and he wanted to do something special for me – it would be a gift to my father and to me. And then he told me he would like to send me to the University of Rio."

"Oh, how wonderful, Luis," Daisy broke in. "I know you were excited."

"Yes, very much. I went to school and worked for Senhor Pinto when I had time off. Every new course I took, Papa asked to see my books and made me promise to tell him everything I learned. He was proud of me but not as proud as I was of him. I believe Papa would have worked twenty-four hours a day to see that I went to college.

"At my graduation, Senhor Pinto and his wife and Papa sat on the front row of the auditorium. Papa had bought himself a new suit and he looked so handsome. I will never forget when I walked across the stage to receive my diploma, I heard Papa say in a not-so-soft voice, 'Luis, you have done it. Your mama would be proud. No favela for you...'"

Carlos brought a third glass of wine to Luis and that seemed to bring him back to the moment. "I believe I have again talked too much. It has been such a long time since I have thought of Papa and Senhor Pinto."

Daisy reached over and placed her hands over Luis'. "I'm so glad you shared that beautiful story with me. I think you must be a lot like your father and I know he was very proud of you."

"Yes, I believe he was. We were father and son but we were best friends, too. The night of my graduation, Senhor Pinto had invited us to his home for refreshments. My Papa surprised me when he said, 'I appreciate your invitation but I have a party already planned for Luis. May we come again, another time?' Of course, they said we could and we left the school and headed for Leblon, our old beach spot. Papa went behind some rocks and pulled out a plastic chest filled with ice he had placed there earlier that afternoon. He opened the lid and pulled out a bottle of champagne, the first of far too many we emptied that night.

"'For us, Luis,' my father said proudly. 'You are a man and a college graduate so let us celebrate your future.' We cheered and drank and cheered and drank and for the first time *and* the last time I saw my father subdued by the spirits of drink. Around midnight we walked up the beach and Papa put his strong arm around my shoulder. In that moment I knew I would love my father forever."

Eleven

It had been three weeks since Daisy and Luis had sat and talked at Beijo in Niteroi. Much had happened in the meantime.

Soon after Daisy and Luis went on their day long tour of Rio, Miki had been called back to Washington and within hours, he was on his way back to the States. The university had called asking him to come back for an important meeting with the president of a large international plastics firm. Jonathon Erick Petras, the president and an alumnus of Georgetown, had expressed interest in giving a sizeable sum of money to the history department, especially earmarked for South American studies. Miki was badly needed in D.C..

Daisy had returned home that night to find a note from Miki on her bed:

> *"Daisy,*
> *If you are still in the mental state you were in the other evening, perhaps you have floated off into thin air.*
> *I have been called away to urgent business in Washington. If you return to earth and find this note, give me a collect call at my office in D.C the day after tomorrow.*
> *Love, M."*

The day after Miki returned to Georgetown, Charlie and Luis started filming in and around Rio in earnest. Daisy began some initial work with Paulo at Video Brazil on the musical score for the finished product and between them, they decided on a voice to narrate the documentary. Sergio Neto was known as the voice in Brazil, so deep and resonant and so clear with just the slightest hint of an accent. When the script writers at Georgetown finished, Daisy would send Paulo and Sergio a copy of the film and they would lay down the voice-over to fit the film perfectly. Paulo would also do the musical editing for the film when it was finished.

Now, three weeks later, Daisy and her team sat around the dining room table, discussing the rough footage from their work in Copacabana.

"This looks great, guys. Even better than I had hoped for," Daisy said.

The evening before they had watched the film over and over, each making comments. Now over a midday meal, they were all taking turns talking excitedly about the project so far.

"It's all better than I ever thought possible!" gushed Daisy. "The color is so sharp and brilliant. You two have done a marvelous job."

"See," spoke up Charlie, an army fatigue hat with tiny sergeant's stripes on it plopped on the back of his head, "I told you Luis was the best photographer."

"Well, my friend," said Luis, "you have much talent yourself. Your ideas about how to shoot Sugar Loaf were outstanding. Daisy, he filmed the mountain from a cable car as it made its approach to the summit. The viewers will get the feeling they have made the trip themselves. Then, Charlie suggested I begin shooting the exterior of the approaching cable car to show the height and panoramic view from the top. This way you get a much better idea of the starkness and beauty of Sugar Loaf in comparison to all that is around it."

Charlie and Luis talked animatedly to each other about the shoot. Daisy interrupted with, "Okay, you two. You're good. No, you're great but let's finalize the next step. Luis, we talked quite a bit about the favelas and I know there is a terrible infant mortality rate in Brazil. But, what happens to the babies who *do* live and the mother gives them away? Let's address this in the film. Do they go to an orphanage, a state institution, are they adopted, do..."

"Hold it," said Luis. "Some of your answers require a yes, some a no. But, there is no beautiful state-supported institution with little freshly painted baby beds, nutritious food or swing sets on grassy lawns in the country of Brazil. We'll go to one of these places later and we'll film it if we are allowed and you can see for yourself. They are called funabem. Adoptions? If any, they are done privately without much knowledge of the Brazilian Federal Police. The government does not encourage adoptions outside of our country. It is a matter of pride."

"But, Luis," Daisy broke in, "why would the government object to a little child being placed in a home that wants a baby? That just doesn't make sense to me at all."

"Nor to many, many other people, Daisy. These officials do not want to admit that we cannot care for all these abandoned children ourselves. So, they put these little ones away in the funabem where they usually don't survive for long, I'm afraid. But, we were talking about the possible adoptions and I know of one small home, called A Candeia that helps in getting infants out of Brazil legally.

"Adoption in Brazil is a lengthy process and very difficult but these wonderful people at A Candeia have been fighting government officials for years. They have managed, with no help from the Brazilian government, to get a few babies out now and then. When I say 'out'", continued Luis, "I mean to England, America and a couple of babies have gone to waiting parents in Australia, I believe. A Candeia is located in the Cosme Velho area so we'll go by there tomorrow when we finish our shoot at Corcovado."

"Yes, I would like that," said Daisy, deeply touched by what Luis had just told her about the babies. "I really believe it's an important issue that needs to be included in this documentary of Brazil. We need to give the whole picture of this country, don't we? I've read that many die of unsanitary birth situations, diseases, even by their mother's own hands when they know they cannot care for them.

I'd like to highlight the problem of what happens to those few who are born and do survive and nobody wants them. I've heard some babies are just wrapped in newspaper and put in garbage cans or left on doorsteps and a hundred other ways of 'passing them on' for someone else to care for."

Soon after, Charlie and Luis left to shoot some footage of the sun setting on the beach. Daisy decided to take this time alone to call her parents.

As she waited for someone to pick up in Texas, she placed her hand in her pocket and caressed the note that Luis had scribbled and handed to her as he walked out the door.

"I'll come back tonight after we finish. I never did tell you the definition of 'beijo'. It has a beautiful meaning."

"Hello," her mother's soft voice said on the other end of the line.

"Mama, it's Daisy. How are you? Did you get the Christmas gifts I sent?"

"Daisy! So good to hear you, sweetheart. Yes, your friend, Dr. Tsuru sent them from Washington and put a lovely note in with them. He seems to think a lot of you."

"He's a very nice man. I know you would like him, too. Did you like the gift? It's really one of a kind."

"I love it," her mother answered. "I have it hanging on the wall in front of our bed. That way, every single morning when I wake up I can look at that little window. Your dad likes his wood carving, too. It was thoughtful of you to get these gifts for us, you being so busy. I wish I could have sent you something."

"Just get ready to make me some of your fried apricot pies when I come for a visit. I could eat twenty right now and some of your cornbread and fresh green beans…and oh, that fried okra!"

"Hon, it sounds like you need me to send you a care package. Are you getting enough to eat?"

Just like her mother. Concerned. Caring. Daisy suddenly felt homesick and hearing her mother's voice made her eyes misty.

"I love you, Mama. I think of you a lot. You'd love it here. I wish I could fly you and Dad down especially since Christmas is right around the corner. It feels strange not to be bundled up for Christmas. But we're not going to be in one place long enough for you to come. I'm learning so much."

"How is your Brazilian cameraman working out? Are you pleased?"

"Yes, ma'm," she answered, trying to give nothing away in her voice. "I'm very pleased." Daisy wished she could tell her mother just how happy she was since she had met Luis. But her mother had loved Craig so much and the divorce had been difficult for her. No, this was not the time to talk about Luis. "He is an excellent cameraman, Mama, and he and Charlie work very well together. If one of them has a good idea, the other is quick to try it. So far we've only filmed in Rio but we'll be finished here tomorrow afternoon. Then we'll split up and go elsewhere so we can get the work completed sooner."

"Is he married?"

"Is who married, Mama?"

"That Brazilian cameraman," she answered.

"No, not anymore," said Daisy. "He lost his wife and child a while ago in an accident, I believe, but I don't know any more than that. He doesn't talk about it. Anyway, we've been working pretty hard and haven't really had time to get to know each other very well yet."

"Here, hon, your Dad just walked in. I know he'll want to talk to you." Daisy heard her mother's muffled voice telling her father who was on the phone and to "be nice."

"How's the weather? It's fifteen degrees here," her father abruptly said. "Just hope it doesn't rain. Then there'll be a sheet of ice."

Daisy was surprised that her father's voice could immediately put her into a state of unease, despite the miles between them.

"I'm fine, Dad. It's about ninety-five degrees here today. You ought to see the girls out on the beaches in their swim suits. That would take your mind off the cold weather," she laughed.

"Maybe," he said. "How's Charlie doing? Working hard?"

"Yes, sir, we're all working hard."

"Tell him I was asking about him, will you?"

"Yes."

"Okay, well, your mother wants to say something else. Here, Sybil." and Daisy could hear the exchange of the phone to her mother's hand.

"Bye, Dad," Daisy said softly to the open line.

"What's that, hon? Did you say something?" her mother asked.

"No, Mama, I didn't say anything. Just cleared my throat. I guess I better go. I'll call again next week. You've got Dr. Tsuru's number in case you need to reach me, right? I love you, Mama."

Daisy hung up the phone and called Miki. They talked mostly about filming, Daisy telling him how smoothly it was going. He mentioned that his daughter, Hisako, was coming to Washington in a few days to spend Christmas and he was very excited. Daisy then told him Charlie would soon be headed to Sao Paulo to film and that she and Luis were either going to Brasilia or up to the Northeast. She promised to call him again in the next few days.

After Daisy hung up with Miki, she looked at her watch and saw that she had a little time before Luis came back, so she decided to head for the beach to walk off the frustration of the call to Texas.

She walked vigorously for over an hour before she turned back in the direction of the house. Luis would be coming soon and she wanted to shower and change before he arrived. Charlie had mentioned he was having dinner with Paulo to talk about some new fast-speed film.

Daisy went to her bedroom and stepped out of her shorts and panties. A tan line, she noticed, very pleased. She removed her blouse and bra and walked over to the full-length mirror that hung on her closet door.

Not bad, she thought, as she eyed herself carefully. Then, immediately her thoughts drifted to Luis.

What does he see when he looks at me?

She walked over to her bed and lay across it on her stomach. It felt good to be unencumbered by clothes and to be alone to think.

Her thoughts were interrupted by the sound of the front door slamming shut.

Daisy suddenly sat up. "Who's there?"

There was no answer.

She quickly grabbed a robe and hastened out to the landing. "Who's here?" she called out again.

"Daisy, is that you? I'm back," said Luis. "Where are you?"

Daisy leaned out over the railing.

"I thought I heard a door open. I'll be ready before too long. Just make yourself comfortable." Daisy called down to him.

"What do you say, Daisy? I could use a shower. Okay if I use the downstairs bathroom? I've got some fresh clothes in my car. See you in a bit." And he hurried off before Daisy could say another word.

By the time Daisy showered, changed into a lightweight pale pink dress and came downstairs, Luis looked like a different man.

"Luis, you could make the cover of GQ. I am impressed."

"Obrigado," Luis said. "Let's go have dinner. There's a place not far called Carioca and they have wonderful steaks. That sounds good to me. How about you? You're awfully quiet, Daisy."

"It's just that I've never seen you wearing a tie before or a jacket. My, how handsome. What's the occasion?"

"To be honest, this was the only clean outfit I had with me. I usually keep a jacket and tie in the car in case of a sudden business meeting, important interview, or dinner with a beautiful woman at Carioca," he smiled.

Luis took Daisy by the arm and led her out the door. She thought that he should wear light blue more often. He looked wonderful.

The restaurant was unique. Luis asked if they could sit out back on the terrace. They were led to a table near a large wild fig tree and the view overlooked forested hills and bright, sparkling stars overhead. The table was covered in a multi-colored cloth and they sat in chairs that Luis told her had been carved out of huge chunks of brazil wood.

"What does Carioca mean?" Daisy asked after Luis ordered them a couple of rum drinks.

"It's simple. A Carioca believes there is no one else in the whole world like him. He is wondrously outgoing, talks rapidly, and uses his hands wildly as he talks. Sometimes his conversation and actions make no sense at all. He is definitely an individual, easy-going and above all else, loves, no, adores having fun. This is symbolic of how most people in Rio see themselves."

"I see. Does the rest of Brazil see the Cariocas that way?"

"No, some see him as lazy, funny, not very ambitious, and many think he is totally insane."

"Why insane?" asked Daisy, knowing Luis had an answer.

"Because he has to be in order to eat black beans and drink rum in this heat. Cheers," Luis laughed and they clinked glasses.

After dinner they drove back to Copacabana in silence. Luis popped a cassette in the car's tape player. A soft samba filled the little space. Daisy closed her eyes and let the music sweep over her. It had been a good evening.

They pulled into the drive. Luis hopped out of the car and came around to help Daisy exit the passenger side.

They walked silently up the walkway and stopped at the front door. Daisy turned to Luis. "You know, you never did tell me what Beijo means."

"Why don't I show you instead?" Luis took her in his arms and kissed her deeply. His arms encircled her and she melted into his embrace. He kissed her neck, her throat and then, softly at first, found her mouth again and she believed heaven was indeed on earth. At last, he pulled back from her and whispered, "Goodnight, Daisy. This has been a wonderful evening. I will see you in the morning for our final day's shoot in Rio." Then, he simply turned and hurried to his car, backed out onto Atlantica, and drove away.

Daisy stood there, rooted to the spot. She put her fingers to her mouth where Luis' lips had been just moments before.

What just happened?

And she abruptly went inside and headed up the stairs to a cold shower.

TWELVE

The phone's sharp chirp awakened Daisy but she rolled over and ignored it. Whoever it was could wait. Daisy wanted to go back to her dream – to Luis' arms, his mouth…

"Daisy, the phone's for you. It's Luis," Charlie yelled up from downstairs.

Daisy couldn't get to the phone fast enough.

"Good morning, Luis."

"Charlie told me you were still asleep. I apologize for waking you. I am going to make a little visit this morning before we start filming and I thought you might like to go with me. Remember, I told you my grandmother took care of me when I was a baby? Well, Vovo Maria is ninety-eight years old and is still wise and charming and I visit her as often as I can. I think it will be a treat for you to meet her. I wasn't sure if I would get to see her on Christmas Day so I wanted to drive over there now. I must warn you though. She still sees me as a young boy and she speaks to me like one."

"Where does she live? I think I just assumed she wasn't still living. Is that rare here in Brazil, for someone to live to be so old?"

"Yes, it is rare," answered Luis. "Few people live to be in their eighties or nineties. Vovo Maria has worked hard all her life and even now, I believe, has a very strong heart. She lives in the north zone of the city where the majority of the lower working class lives. My cousin, Josefina, cares for her. I told Charlie we'd meet him at the top of Corcovado at 11:00 this morning. That will give us time for a short visit with Vovo Maria. Also, do you still want to go to the little orphanage, A Candeia? It's near Corcovado so we can go there after our filming. Can you be ready in half an hour?"

"Yes, I'll be ready. See you soon."

Daisy stood in the kitchen drinking her coffee and looking out the window at the gorgeous view. She wore a loose-fitting white cotton dress that she'd bought over a year ago. She never dreamed her first time to wear it would be in Rio de Janeiro.

Right on time, Luis came through the gates, beeping his horn and waving. Daisy hurried down the front walkway and plopped into the passenger seat of the BMW.

"You look especially beautiful this morning. That color makes your hair shine and your eyes sparkle." Luis flashed that smile again and Daisy wondered if he knew the effect he was having on her.

"You sound like a commercial for shampoo and eye makeup," she said. Without thinking, she reached over and gently touched his face with her index finger. "Thank you, Senhor Campos."

Luis didn't respond. Instead, he just turned quickly and started the car. Twenty minutes later, they pulled up in front of a rather dismal little house squeezed in between other dismal little houses. Daisy marveled how the area seemed to change block by block. Just a half block before they arrived, Luis had pointed out to Daisy the Brazilian Observatore Nationale. Now, the street was crammed with small little houses. The entire street was situated on a steep hill and Daisy counted twenty-five narrow steps from the curb to the front door of Cousin Josefina's house.

Luis opened the door and called out, "Josefina? Vovo Maria?" He motioned for Daisy to follow him into the house. "Come on in. They are probably in the back room. It has many windows and Vovo likes to sit and look out at the ocean." He took Daisy's hand and they walked toward the back of the house.

Daisy wasn't sure what she expected Luis's grandmother to

look like but she certainly wasn't prepared for the bright-eyed, distinguished looking woman with eyes like coal who faced her from her wheelchair near a large window. When this woman saw Luis, she smiled broadly showing beautiful, straight, white teeth. She had a cleft in her chin, too, and there was a remarkable resemblance between grandmother and grandson. It was plain to see the white-haired woman was thrilled to see the man who dropped Daisy's hand, moved to her chair, and knelt beside her.

"Vovo, que seudade," Luis said softly and kissed his grandmother warmly.

"Eu tambem, Luis," she answered, stroking Luis' hair gently. They talked quietly for a few minutes. Luis turned and motioned for Daisy to come closer. In Portuguese, he introduced her. Vovo took Daisy's hand and smiled. She turned to Luis and said something in Portuguese that was totally lost on Daisy. Daisy looked questioningly at Luis.

"You two have me at a disadvantage. What did she say?"

"Vovo said she thinks you are very pretty and that we would make beautiful children together. Does this embarrass you? Vovo has always spoken freely what is on her mind."

"No," answered Daisy, "tell her thank you."

Luis said something to Vovo that sounded like it was something far longer than the simple thank you Daisy had requested. Vovo Maria laughed out loud and grabbed both of Luis' hands and kissed them.

Josefina came out of the kitchen, carrying a tray of iced suco fruita. She, too, spoke no English, so while Luis and Vovo talked energetically, Daisy and Josefina sipped their drinks and looked uneasily at each other, both wanting to ask questions but having no words.

Luis reached over and hugged and kissed his grandmother again and said, "Daisy, we must hurry or we'll keep Charlie waiting. Just shake Vovo's hand. She understands you speak no Portuguese."

Daisy bent toward the smiling older woman and took the hand that was extended. Without warning, Vovo pulled Daisy down to her and kissed her gently on the cheek. In a whispered voice she said, "Luis? Amor?"

Daisy stooped near Vovo's ear and said, "Luis? Amor? Si."

Vovo squeezed Daisy's hand and her smiling black eyes looked directly into Daisy's. She held Daisy's hand, caressing it softly. After saying goodbye to Josefina, Luis and Daisy hurried down the many steps back to their car.

On the drive to Corcovado Luis was quiet. Every now and then he would look in Daisy's direction and smile but appeared to be in deep thought. Finally, he turned to her and asked, "What did you think of Vovo? I realize it was difficult, not being able to talk directly with her."

"Oh, I think she is wonderful, Luis. I'm very glad I met her. You know, you have told me a lot about Rio and its history. But today I saw some real Brazilian history and there is more worth in that one person than in all the buildings and historical landmarks in the world. Your Vovo is nearly a century old, Luis! Just think what knowledge is in her head. What impressions. She is very much a part of all you have shown me. I can see she is special to you and I consider meeting her a real honor."

"It was important to me that Vovo meet you. I wanted to know what she thought of you."

"And...?"

"And she liked you very much. I don't need Vovo Maria's approval on anything I do, you understand. It's just that I wanted the two of you to meet. I don't get by to see her often enough but I wanted you with me today. I hope that was all right with you."

"Oh, it was definitely all right." Daisy reached over and patted Luis' thigh. "Definitely all right."

The filming at Corcovado went well. Daisy stressed that they get enough footage of the 700-ton concrete figure of Cristo Redentor that looked down over Rio from the peak of Corcovado.

"I want to make sure we capture how imposing a figure this statue is," she told Charlie. "Almost any hour of the day or night every citizen of Rio can look up and see this Statue of Christ on the mountain."

Charlie and Luis both assured her, as they packed up their equipment, that they had gotten some unusual and striking film of the statue.

Luis and Daisy said goodbye to Charlie who headed for Video Brazil. They walked back to Luis' car.

"All right now, let's go to A Candeia," Luis said. "It's just below us on the side of Corcovado Mountain. We can run by and I'll broach the subject about us doing some filming there."

"What does A Candeia mean?"

"In Portuguese it is the candle or the light and I think it is a perfect name for this place. You'll see."

"I have no idea how it could fit into the video at this point but if the owners will let us, let's set up a time to come back and get some footage. Maybe we can use it later and edit it in somehow. What I really want to do is get up to the Northeast and see the conditions there."

"Yes, Fortaleza will give us many vivid pictures of abandoned babies and children, and in general, the overcrowding and poverty that is so prevalent in that area. But, for now," he said, "let's go to A Candeia."

"Do you know the owners?"

"I met the woman who owns the large house where the babies are kept but I've never been to her home. She was being interviewed about adoptions on television about three months ago. I was impressed with her courage to get on television and defend what she and her little staff are doing. She's received some negative press lately but it doesn't seem to have stopped her. Her name is Isabella Maria Paes. She is a widow, about sixty, I think. But her energy makes you believe she is much younger. Her father was German and her mother English. For some reason they moved to Rio when Isabella was small. Oh, one more thing. Make sure Isabella knows this film is a documentary and not for commercial or general public viewing."

"Why?"

"Because if she gets the opportunity she will use any form of media to push her cause," warned Luis. "And if she thinks this film is for the general public she will make a strong, not-too-subtle plea for funds. Right now, Isabella is not too popular with government officials on both the Brazilian and the American side. She's doing nothing illegal but her manner with most officials is – well, she comes across very pushy and demanding. If things are done a certain way and this way doesn't exactly suit Isabella's time frame, then she gives people a hard time. She is a very good person and, I believe, has what is best for each baby uppermost in her heart and mind. But sometimes her tactics lose her valuable ground. One week a minor's court judge will sing the praises and unselfish work of Isabella and things will be smooth for awhile. Then, the next week there will be an article in the newspaper about her causing a scene somewhere or demanding her rights and that sets her work back."

"She sounds like a real character," said Daisy.

"Yes, that she is. Don't misunderstand me. The babies she finds are her life. She works all day going from one legal office to another and she is up all night caring for the babies and trying to keep up with all the legalities of each case."

"Doesn't she have any help?"

"Some, but Isabella wants to be involved in everything when it comes to the babies. It is hard for her to turn loose, to delegate. And I have heard that she has a special bond with each child in her care. People have told me she knows as much as most pediatricians about how to care for well and sick babies. They say she can tell by the baby's cry if it is sick or hungry. She has saved many babies' lives, I believe, and she has been responsible for getting many adopted out of the country."

Luis made a sharp, quick turn off Cosme Velho onto an extremely small cobblestone path that was as steep as it was narrow. The car jostled and bumped higher and higher on the little rough road until at last Daisy saw the top of a house ahead. Luis pulled into the drive next to a motorcycle and a dune buggy.

"They must have visitors," Daisy said.

Luis took her by the arm. "No, the motorcycle and dune buggy are their only means of transportation."

He led her to the front door which was actually a back entrance that led directly into a large airy kitchen. A large bell with a gold chain attached hung over the door.

"You do the honors, Daisy," Luis said, pointing to the chain.

She pulled the chain and, at its ringing, she was sure at least half of Rio must have heard its voice.

"I'm afraid I've awakened the babies. Maybe I should have knocked," she said to Luis in a whisper.

Luis laughed. "Why are you talking so low? The bell has certainly announced our arrival."

Daisy heard footsteps on the tile floors and dogs barking, and the door opened and a woman in a white apron motioned them to come in.

In Portuguese, Luis asked her if Dona Isabella was at home.

"Si." She motioned for them to follow her into a large dining room. An imposing dining table commanded the center of the room. Beautiful leaded glass windows looked out onto the gardens on three sides. The furniture was old but classic and looked to Daisy as if it would have been at home in a castle on a mountainside somewhere in Europe.

The woman left them and Luis turned to Daisy. "It will be just a moment. She said Dona Isabella would be in to see us as soon as she finishes feeding a baby. See what I mean? Always the babies."

Daisy walked over to one of the windows and pushed it open. There before her was a stunning sight – right in front of her and just a little above, was the Christ statue with arms outstretched. Clouds floated slowly in front of the face, hiding it momentarily, and then passed, revealing once again the beautiful Christ, high in the sky.

The silence was broken. Isabella had entered the room.

"Welcome to A Candeia and to my house," said a husky voice behind Daisy. Daisy turned and was surprised to see the person who stood in the room. The woman with the short, graying hair was no more than five feet tall.

"I am Isabella Maria Paes," she said extending her hand first to Luis and then to Daisy. "Have you come about adopting a baby? Do you have all the necessary paperwork completed? Are you aware of..."

"Hold it," Luis broke in quickly. He explained why they had come to A Candeia. By now they had followed Isabella into the living room and were all three sitting on a large, sectional sofa. Isabella was listening carefully.

Finally, she spoke. "I have no problem with you doing some filming here. We are not very large and for many reasons we are unable to get more babies out of Brazil into homes with adoptive parents. I would ask, however, that you show our struggle, our fight, and the hardships that we face every single day."

Daisy looked at Luis and their eyes met. He had been so right about Isabella. "We will do our best to show your work," she said to Isabella. "But I am more interested in getting shots of the house, how the children are cared for, the system for getting the babies from here to their new homes, and of course, show the babies. Little ones always warm the hearts of the viewer. I definitely want to get close ups of the babies."

Isabella was not easily deterred. "I want the American people to see the injustice done to these children by the Brazilian government's selfishness."

Daisy took a short breath and tried again. It would not do to get on Isabella's bad side.

"I think we can make a film that will help us both."

Isabella kept on as if Daisy hadn't even spoken. "If I could tell you the stories of the many babies we have found in garbage cans, in open fields in the Northeast, in filthy stables and God knows where else, then you would understand why I work day and night to get these babies out of Brazil. These babies are little fighters."

Daisy softened as she listened to this dedicated woman talk from her heart. She saw the deep, dark lines under Isabella's eyes and the bone tired look from her gaze.

"All I want is for someone to see the vision I see of getting these babies into homes where they will be loved," Isabella continued. "It would be nice to be supported and encouraged and assisted by some of these officials who persist in fighting me. Do you know that I've been accused of selling babies to pharmaceutical companies for use in experiments? Of selling babies to rich Americans so they can turn them into slaves. Of smuggling them out of the country and making millions of dollars.

"Look around you. Do you believe any of that? Listen to me." Isabella's voice raised an octave and she clasped her hands tightly together. "We celebrate and rejoice every time just one little child is issued a Brazilian passport and flies out of here with his new parents. I would give my very life to give life to any one of these children."

Daisy believed her. She immediately liked this small woman and felt tears welling up in her eyes to know that someone could care so much.

"May we see the babies now?" Daisy asked, regaining her composure.

Isabella was on her feet. "Follow me. We now have eight infants, five girls, and three boys. It seems there are always more girls than boys, especially when most of the adoptive parents right now want boys."

Daisy couldn't believe it was so quiet with eight babies in the house.

Isabella started talking to the infants before she even got into the room.

"I'm coming. Isabella is coming. Do you know who loves you? Well, I am going to tell you."

Isabella opened the door to the room that had been turned into the nursery. Daisy and Luis saw eight tiny woven straw baskets with handles on them. They had been placed on tops of tables, chests of drawers, night stands, and even large empty boxes. On the end of each baby's basket hung a clipboard. Here were recorded times and amounts of feedings and all bodily functions. The room was clean but not spotless. A gentle breeze wafted in through the unscreened window. One table held stacks of clean, folded diapers, blankets, sheets, and tiny terry cloth jump suits.

Isabella picked up one baby and loudly kissed him under the neck, from ear to ear, saying over and over, "I love you. I love you. How are you today?" She put this baby down, picked up another who had begun to fret and said, "Why the fuss? Do you want some good conversation? Okay, then you stay with Isabella awhile while we talk." She nestled the tiny baby in the crook of her left arm and reached for another one with her right hand. "And you with the big eyes, what do you see with those big eyes? Will you tell me all about it? For now, this is your home and you are loved," and the kissing began again.

God, Daisy thought, the Pied Piper of Rio! These babies are mesmerized by this woman and they certainly must feel the love she pours out on them. While Isabella changed two babies' diapers, Daisy bent down and looked into the remaining bassinets. The last little straw basket sat on a large cardboard diaper box. Daisy looked quietly in, expecting to see a sleeping baby. What she saw was a baby with more hair than she had ever seen on an infant before, two big, bright eyes that were wide open, and a small fist stuck in a tiny mouth.

"Isabella, is this a boy or a girl?" Daisy asked.

"That is Senhor Laid-Back. He rarely cries, just eats, sleeps, poops on schedule, and lies in his little bed and looks around. He is a very good baby and nothing seems to bother him. He's only four days old but seems to like this world so far.

"Don't just stand there," ordered Isabella. "I need all the help I can get. Pick him up and feed him. He's very hungry. That's why his fist is in his mouth. His bottle is in the refrigerator in the kitchen down that hall. Warm it in the pan of water on the stove and feed him."

Daisy looked at Isabella and then back at the baby sucking his fist and his fingers, making all kinds of sounds. Pick him up? All right, there's always a first time. She gingerly scooped the baby into her arms.

"Isabella, are all these babies waiting to go to the States? Do they all have families waiting for them?"

"All but the one you are holding," she answered. "I had notified a couple in Wisconsin and they were to be here this week. However, the woman phoned me last night and said she just found out she is pregnant and they don't want to have two babies so close in age. So, we begin again with that one. He'll probably be with us for a while."

Daisy held the tiny baby on her shoulder and, as she headed for the kitchen, asked, "How do I know which bottle is his?" She brushed her cheek against the thick, silky hair and wondered how anyone could give up something so wondrous – no matter what the cost.

"He uses the blue plastic bottles with the little yellow bears on them. Oh, and make sure the milk isn't too hot. You've done this before, haven't you?"

"Not that I can remember," Daisy answered.

"You'll do fine and you will soon learn that babies don't break easily. Anyway, he will tell you if you don't prepare his lunch to his liking."

Daisy tested the milk on her arm as she had seen others do. It felt fine so she carried the baby, who now was trying to get both fists in his mouth, to the living room. She sat in a large chair by an open window. Earlier she had seen the beautiful statue through this window. Clouds now covered the statue's face and her attention was drawn back to the baby who had taken the nipple quickly and had begun sucking in the warm milk. Daisy looked up and there stood Luis, looking down at her and smiling.

"You look natural feeding that baby, Daisy. I wish I had my camera." He turned quickly and left the room.

The nursing infant grabbed hold of Daisy's little finger and squeezed it.

"You're strong," she said softly to him, "and very beautiful. I'm sorry about that family in Wisconsin. You probably wouldn't have liked it anyway. It's too cold up there. Besides, I bet there's a special home just waiting for you."

She looked up at the open window and in that moment the clouds moved from in front of the statue and Daisy Gardner found herself looking straight into the face of Christ.

THIRTEEN

After Luis and Daisy left A Candeia, they drove to Copacabana. Luis had telephoned Charlie at Paulo's studio but was told he had left for home. They hoped they could reach him there and explain about A Candeia. Their plan was to pick up some equipment and then return to get some footage of the facilities and the babies before Isabella changed her mind.

"Luis," Daisy said as they drove through heavy traffic and headed for Copacabana, "I'm curious about something. The babies I saw this morning - each one is a different shade of brown. Two of the children are very dark with straight, black hair while another is a little lighter in skin coloring with still lighter straight hair and the one I held and fed is very light with brown hair. In fact, he's just slightly darker than I am – maybe as if he has a little tan. They're not all from the same place, are they? I mean, even their features are different."

"No, they all come mainly from the Northeast and there is much Indian influence there. However, the baby you held was born in the little village of Fuegas, just outside Rio, so he has an entirely different look. He will resemble more the Mediterranean or European people. As I've told you, Brazil is a melting pot, a coming together of many nationalities. It will be good to show this in our film."

A driver cut Luis off and he beeped his horn as he deftly drove around him. Daisy put her hand on the dashboard to brace herself.

"Don't worry, I'll get us there in one piece. This is nothing. Just everyday traffic."

"If you say so."

"Tell me your thoughts about Isabella. How are you planning to handle her in the film?"

"Very carefully," laughed Daisy. "I see what you meant about her intensity. I thought that with the voice-over, we could show some of the problems she faces but not get into a preaching, pleading kind of thing."

Luis nodded. "You're absolutely right. I think we need to be very careful. Just the facts, no allegations directed to the government. Not only would we not have a film, we could get a first-hand view of the inside of a federal prison. I think it would be good, too, if we can interview some minor court officials, maybe some judges, and some attorneys here in Rio and Fortaleza. Just let them have their say. What do you think?"

"I think that would add a lot to the film but would these officials even speak to us? I mean so many of them are against Isabella's work and slow her down at every turn. Do you think they would actually give us any information? Of course, the judges who are against Isabella's efforts, they wouldn't talk or want to be shown on a video."

"You may be right there. No," answered Luis, "Isabella's legal enemies would definitely not give their opinions but surely there are some, and they are even a few who would give us some facts on the film. I'll check into this. Hopefully, we can find some who are willing."

"We should get right on that. I had wanted us to fly out to the Northeast very soon, right after Christmas. It would be great if we could square away some of those officials as soon as possible."

"I'll see what I can do. We can film people who are willing to talk when we return from Fortaleza and then edit in those parts."

"Fine, and Luis, I think Charlie should fly down to Sao Paulo and then head for Brasilia. Afterwards, we can all meet in Belem and do the Amazon portion together. I'll plan to do all the editing at one time, so let's just stay up in the Northeast until we've completed our filming. What do you think?"

"You are the boss, Daisy, but I have a problem with part of your plan. Only Charlie and I will go to the Amazon region for the filming. We can do it in one day. We will take a helicopter and fly in, get our footage and then, zip, we're back safe and sound with you. I see no need for you to go on this trip."

"Is it that unsafe? Maybe you and Charlie shouldn't even go. We can always get some stock footage and edit it in," said Daisy.

"Hold it. Luis Campos has never used stock footage when he can film a scene himself. We will be in and out without a hitch. Don't you worry. You'll hardly have time to miss us."

"All right but I don't like it, Luis. Not even a little." Daisy felt an uneasy twinge in the pit of her stomach.

Luis turned the car into the drive at her condo and shut off the car's engine. "It's such a beautiful day, let's take an hour to walk on the beach."

"You're on."

Luis locked Daisy's purse, along with his camera, in the trunk. Daisy walked slowly up Atlantica to wait for Luis to join her. The cars were zipping by so fast it was impossible to even count them. There was no traffic light at this corner and it was difficult to find an opening in the mass of automobiles in order to get across to the beach.

Luis had joined her now on the curb. "Oba, wow, the traffic is heavy today. Hold my hand and we'll make a run for it. Let's wait for a clear moment."

But Daisy didn't wait for Luis. She thought she saw a chance to get across Atlantica and jumped off the curb. She was making a dash for the beach when two taxis swerved, barely missing her. Both cabs were up on the sidewalk, yelling profanities in Daisy's direction. She dodged and made it to the other side.

Luis caught up with her and grabbed her arm and pulled it behind her back. With teeth clenched, he said, "Don't ever do that again! Ever! I will not tolerate it. Don't you ever run out in front of traffic like that again. These people will not stop for you. They would smash you like a bug and keep right on going. Do you understand me?" All the while he kept applying more pressure to her arm.

Daisy was frightened. This usually soft-spoken man was both hurting her and scaring her with his strength and harsh words.

"Luis," she finally spoke, "let me go. If you bend my arm any more you'll break it. I'm sorry. My God, I will never again step off the damn curb without holding your hand. But nothing happened. I'm okay. Now let me go!"

Luis released his hold on her and walked slowly ahead onto the sand. In a few minutes, she caught up with him.

"Hey, what's wrong? Won't you talk to me?"

He turned slowly and Daisy saw that his face was wet with perspiration but his eyes were soft once more.

"Daisy, you frightened me so much just now. I lost control. Please forgive me. But you were lucky. You could have been killed."

He took her gently by the arm and led her to a bench nearby. "Daisy, several years ago I was walking back to my apartment from a film shoot. I had my camera on my shoulder, just walking along, singing as usual, not a care in the world. I had brought my baby girl a little doll, my wife some beautiful earrings and I couldn't wait to get home and give my presents to my family. I happened to glance across the busy street and I saw Anita and the baby on the other side. Anita waved at me and pointed to my daughter. They were out for a walk and she smiled and motioned for me to go on home and they would follow. In the brief moments she was focused on me, our baby girl darted out into the traffic and when Anita saw her she thought of nothing but to save her."

Luis could scarcely talk. His voice was filled with emotion and Daisy could hear his grief in every word.

"Daisy, they were gone in an instant. I saw it all and I couldn't do anything but watch. They were crushed beneath those cars and I lost everything. So, today, when you started into the traffic, it all came back. I am very sorry I hurt you."

"It's alright but you upset me so. I'm glad you were here today. I can't begin to tell you how sorry I am about your family. I'm glad you told me."

"Thank you, Daisy. I consider you my friend. You have helped me in the past month more than you could ever know. I have talked, I have laughed, and I have kissed a woman with passion for the first time since..."

"Let's go get Charlie," Daisy said abruptly. "We have to get back to A Candeia and do the filming while the light is good."

Daisy, Luis and Charlie arrived at A Candeia and began their filming as they drove up the steep hill leading to the main house. The large structure was a classic Brazilian residence, probably one of the oldest and better built homes in Rio. It was a mixture of French, Spanish and English décor and had three levels – a large loft for the staff's sleeping quarters, a main level that housed the kitchen, a wood-paneled dining room with a long, formal table and chairs and a living room with a marvelous view, depending on which window you chose, of either downtown Rio, the bay or the Christ statue. The room that had been converted into the nursery, a bathroom, and a small study were also on this level. The bottom level contained a series of small cubicle-like bedrooms and a large bathroom. Charlie zeroed in on the grounds surrounding the house – the tall palm trees, the profusion of colorful flowers, and the green lawns, all neatly mowed and trimmed. Daisy felt the viewers would be pleased to know abandoned babies were being cared for in such pleasant surroundings. This was Isabella's home but she gladly opened her doors to any child.

They also took footage in the nursery of Isabella, and Isabella's sister, Lito, as well as Carrie, an American who had arrived the day before to begin her paperwork for one of the baby girls.

As luck would have it, all the babies were in varying stages of waking up, being fed or being changed. Daisy walked over to the baby boy she had fed earlier that day lying in the last bassinette. She leaned down and looked into those big, round, dark eyes once more.

"My, you have the longest eyelashes for such a little guy. I missed you, yes I did. It felt nice to hold you and feed you." Daisy extended her pinkie finger to the baby and he grabbed it and held it tightly.

"Isabella, does this baby need feeding again?" Daisy asked. "I'll be happy to lend a hand. By the way, it seems so cold to continue referring to him as 'this baby'. What can I call him?"

"The couple in Wisconsin had sent the name Clay and we were calling him Clayzinho, or little Clay," said Isabella. "But we cannot continue to call him that, I suppose, as new parents will give him another name. But, no one else has completed the necessary documents in order to come for him. I spent most of last night going through my files and although many just lack their visas or the U.S. immigration work, or their passports, they are not ready to come to Rio until all is in order. Foreign adoption is an involved, complicated process so I'll just have to wait. In the meantime, I guess we will think of a substitute name for him. Do you have any ideas?"

Daisy looked at Isabella and then at the baby and then back to Isabella. "I like the name Clay. It's simple and short and seems to fit him. Can I call him Clay when I come to visit?"

"Why do you wish to 'visit' this baby?" Isabella asked. "You will only become attached to him and then you will have to say goodbye. And you must know that a baby, even this tiny, begins to bond with the one person who shows love to him. He, too, would have to experience a loss when I find parents for him. I am curious. Why do you want to come back and see this one?"

"I'm afraid I don't know," answered Daisy. "I just know that ever since I held him I've thought about him. And I have this crazy, senseless opinion that he needs me. If a baby needed anything, it certainly wouldn't be me."

"Don't be so hard on yourself. You are already giving something to Clayzinho. Every time you look at him, touch his face or hands, talk softly to him or just stand by his little bed, that is giving and this baby already knows you care," Isabella went on, holding an already-asleep baby across her lap and moving her legs from side to side while she held another and fed him.

Daisy was still standing by the bassinette, the baby now asleep, her finger wedged snugly in the crook of his tiny finger.

Isabella looked straight at Daisy. "Why worry about this baby? I have the perfect solution. You adopt him! Why not? I can begin some of the paperwork from this end. I'll go ahead and put your name on his first documents. Now, why didn't I think of this before? I will just..."

"Whoa! Enough! Isabella, I'm in no position to become a mother. Look, my marriage broke up partly because I wouldn't have a baby with my husband. Then to come to Brazil and try to adopt a baby? Everyone I know would think I had lost my mind!"

"What do you think, Daisy?" Isabella asked.

"I think you'd better keep looking for parents for Clay because I'm not your woman." Daisy looked up and saw Luis leaning against the door jam, putting the lens cap back on one of his cameras. "Are you finished with the babies?" she asked.

He stared at her with the strangest, most quizzical look on his face and answered, "Yes, I am. But are you?"

Fourteen

That evening, Charlie, Daisy, and Luis sat in the large living room. Polaroid photos from the day's shooting were strewn across the heavy coffee table. To keep things in sequence, Charlie always used a Polaroid camera to give everyone an idea of what they had filmed earlier.

Daisy held one photo especially long. "The shots of the Christ statue are outstanding," she said enthusiastically. "I really believe we've got some never-before seen footage, and I can't wait to see the film." Daisy continued. "I'm anxious to begin editing the film, too. Who shot these Polaroids? Even these tracking shots are breathtaking."

Charlie raised his right hand over his head, bent his wrist, and let his index finger point to Luis. "There's your genius with the touch. What did I tell you, Daisy? It's like watching magic."

Daisy loved her old friend Charlie and this last gesture was one of the many reasons why. He was always so eager to give credit where it was honestly deserved. He was as proud of Luis's work as anyone.

"I am flattered, my friend," said Luis. "But don't give me so much praise, Charlie. Understand that I have lived in Rio all of my life. From as far back as I can remember, all I had to do was go outside and look up and there stood Christ on the mountain peak. I have seen that statue from every possible angle and so I try and put myself in the place of someone who has never seen it and show them with my camera what I want them to see."

"And that's why you film such great stuff, Luis," said Charlie, patting Luis on the shoulder.

A few minutes later, Charlie excused himself, saying he was tired.

"I think I need to go soon myself. It's been a long day," Luis said. "I just want to finish my coffee."

Charlie waved over his head as he headed up the stairs. "See you guys mañana."

Daisy and Luis sat in silence for a few minutes. Daisy started to speak several times and then each time decided not to.

Luis sipped his coffee and finally broke the silence.

"This has been a very productive day for us, Daisy. Charlie and I filmed everything on Dr. Tsuru's agenda for Rio plus a few things more. I'm anxious to get to the Northeast. Wait until you see it. It is worlds apart from Rio, like another country."

Daisy didn't hear anything Luis said. She just started out the window, her mind miles away, looking at a baby in a bassinet.

Luis gently touched her shoulder. "Daisy, where are you? You are not with me tonight. Are you all right?"

"I'm sorry. Yes, I'm fine. I was just thinking about Isabella and A Candeia and…"

"And the little one you seem to like so much? What did you call him?"

Daisy turned and faced Luis. "I called him Clay. I can't explain it, Luis. It makes no sense but I actually missed him when I left there today. I liked how he made me feel when I held him. Does that sound crazy?"

"No, it's not crazy. We can't predict what our heart will do." Luis looked away and stared into his coffee cup.

Daisy didn't notice and kept on talking. "Luis, Isabella asked me today if I would like to adopt Clay. Can you imagine? I told her I was the last person in the world who needed a baby!"

Luis took her gesturing hand and gently held it. "And now?"

"What now? There is no now. I've had enough troubles with almost every relationship in my life. I can't add another human being. I screwed up my marriage, cannot carry on a single conversation with my own father…"

"That's nonsense, Daisy. You are more upset than I could ever imagine you being. That little baby is not upset or worried. Little Clay is in his bed right now without a care in the world. Look, I'm not making light of your feelings for Clayzinho. I simply want you to stop being so hard on yourself."

"Funny, that's the same thing Isabella scolded me for today," said Daisy.

"Marriages break up all the time, usually the fault of both people, not one. As for your father, I'm sure he bears part of that blame, too."

"I wish I could be as sure as you."

"In your heart, you know I'm right. If he has chosen to ignore you and miss having the love of a daughter, that's his loss. Let it go. Maybe he notices you much more than you realize. Maybe he just doesn't know how to say how he feels as you do."

"That's what Mama says. She's always said that and I've never believed her."

"And Craig? Maybe the baby issue was just a part of the reason you broke up. All I'm saying is that I don't want you feeling so inferior and inadequate at the thought of caring for another person— and having someone care for you."

They were both silent for a moment and then Luis said, "Maybe you should really think seriously about Clayzinho, Daisy. I think you would make a wonderful mother."

"But, it's all happened so quickly. Besides, I'm sure this feeling will pass. It's probably just because it's almost Christmas. It's sort of like seeing a puppy in the window at a pet shop."

Luis smiled. "Well, not exactly, but I know what you mean. I have an idea. Why don't you ask Isabella if she will hold on to Clayzinho until we get back from the Northeast? Then see how you feel about that 'puppy' then. Give yourself a little more time to think about this. How does that sound?"

"I guess so. Thank you, Luis, for not making fun of me. I'm scared at the thought of making such a commitment, but I honestly want to be open to it. Wouldn't that be something? Me, a mother!" She hugged her knees and smiled at the thought.

"This trip has brought you things you never even imagined, hasn't it?" Luis yawned. "Sorry. I think it is time for me to go. Walk with me, Daisy."

Daisy walked him to his car. Luis opened the driver side door but didn't get in. Instead, he leaned against the opened door and took Daisy's face in both his hands. He kissed her gently on the lips.

"Think about what we discussed tonight, okay? Promise me you will think about it."

"I will, Luis. I honestly will. I have a lot to sort out. Tomorrow is Christmas Eve. Please come for a late breakfast. We all need to settle some assignments in Sao Paulo and Brasilia and I'd like you to brief Charlie, especially about Brasilia. And you and I need to make some definite plans about Fortaleza. Goodnight, sweet person. Obrigato. Thank you."

They kissed again, quickly, and then Luis drove out of the driveway.

Daisy stood in the darkness for a while and wondered what else Luis Campos thought. He had talked about the baby, her father, Craig, but he didn't mention their relationship. Daisy knew that something very deep was developing between them, unspoken, but there nevertheless. How that was going to play out – especially if she adopted baby Clay – only time would tell.

The next day, Charlie, Luis, and Daisy ate a huge mid-morning meal that Marcelina had prepared. After the dishes had been cleared away, Charlie turned to Luis.

"About Brasilia, what do you think, Luis? Should I zero in on the buildings, the newness of the city or go for the political aspect of the place? I mean, it's not exactly your typical capital."

"You're right. I think we'll need much of the ultra-modern architecture in the center of the city. Some of these are very pretty, some very unattractive. One of the satellite towns you need to film is Taguadinea. Get the buildings for sure. President Kubitschek built this city in the middle of the wild and empty, flat plains and unbelievably, the job was completed in just three years, with all the materials either brought in by truck or flown in. Quite a task."

"You're kidding," said Charlie. "They built an entire city in the middle of nowhere in three years? That's really impressive. I'm anxious to see it."

The phone rang and Daisy reached over to the little table it sat on. It was Beto Mendes inviting her to visit that evening.

"My wife is back from her work in Germany. We are having a special Christmas Eve dinner tonight. I would love for you to come over and meet her. Bring a friend with you, if you like," he said.

"I'd like to bring two if that's okay. My two cameramen are here and I'd love for them to meet you as well and see your home. What time shall we come?"

"Cocktails and a light snack will be at six. I'm looking forward to seeing you again, Daisy."

"I am, too. Thank you, Beto. Can you give me directions? I'm sure I don't remember how Miki got there." She wrote on a small pad next to the telephone while Beto dictated.

Luis and Charlie stared at her after she hung up.

Charlie spoke first. "Where are we going and do I have to dress up? Keep in mind the answer to question two will affect my response to question one."

"No, you don't have to dress up but can you get rid of that awful purple and orange shirt?"

Charlie looked down at himself. "What's wrong with this shirt?"

"Nothing, if you are going to Carnival," said Luis.

"Okay, I'll change but..." Charlie was interrupted by the phone again. This time it was Isabella telling Daisy she had a five-year-old at A Candeia now. "When you have time I would like you to come see him. His name is Roberto. He's about the size of a three-year old and was born with a crippling lung disease. He cannot live like other children and every breath he takes is extremely difficult for him. But, he is a joyful, happy child and very smart."

Daisy told Isabella they were going out later in the day but would stop by on their way. Just before hanging up, Isabella added, "Have you given any more thought to adopting Clayzinho? The more I think about it, the better it sounds to me."

"Isabella, all of this sounds like a dream. I don't know if I'm ready for a baby and…"

"Who is ever ready?" burst out Isabella. "If every person waited until they were ready I'm afraid there would be fewer babies around. A baby is a part of one's life, my dear child. A baby is even a vital part of our growing up. Whatever you think you know now, you will discover it is not very much when a baby enters your life. They not only help us grow, they help us know and they show us how to love and what sharing really is. My philosophy is that every household should have at least four!" and she laughed loudly, thinking of her own four.

Daisy liked Isabella more and more. She was gruff and sometimes abrupt but she said exactly what she felt. "I'm thinking seriously about it, Isabella. But I need more time. Let's talk some more when we come to see Roberto." She said goodbye to Isabella and hung up the phone. Charlie and Luis were hunched over a pad of paper and talking and paid her no attention. Daisy tried to follow their conversation but her mind kept going back to tiny Clay. She had to admit she knew little about babies. Why the special feeling toward Clay? With all the people wanting babies it certainly wouldn't take Isabella long to find a home for him. The thought of Clay going to someone else jolted Daisy in a way she wasn't prepared for.

Daisy slipped quietly out of the dining room and walked out into a small garden behind the condo. She watched the butterflies flit from flower to flower. Overhead, birds called to one another. Daisy sighed. She knew she had made a decision, even if she hadn't admitted it to herself yet. Tears flowed and Daisy felt a great sense of relief that at last she knew what she was going to do.

Later that day, Daisy and Luis walked on the beach, holding hands and talking about the filming they had done in Rio. Charlie had left, saying he would meet them at Beto's at six. They came to a low wall. Luis brushed the sand from the top and they sat down.

"Daisy, something is going on in your head. You've been preoccupied all day. I feel that I can't get through to you today.

What's going on?"

"Clay…" The words were difficult to utter.

"What about him?"

Daisy took a deep breath. It was time to say it out loud. "I've made up my mind, Luis. I want that baby. I know it's crazy. I know I have to figure out how I'm going to work and travel and raise a child. I can't explain it but I want him to be my son."

Hearing herself say the words out loud for the first time, Daisy felt tears running down her cheeks. Luis gently put his arm around Daisy's shoulders. "I know you love Clayzinho. I saw your need for that baby the first day you held him. I will help you all I can because it will not be easy to for the government to release a baby in this country and then to get them to let you take him legally to the States."

"Oh, Luis, I didn't know what you'd say or if you'd think I was crazy. What do you think about Clay?" Daisy spoke rapid-fire.

"Wait a minute. One thing at a time. I am saying that I believe you are quite sane. I am saying, as I have before, that I think you will be a wonderful and loving mother. I am saying that I am very proud of you because this is not an easy task you have undertaken."

"But, what do you think about Clay?" Daisy insisted.

Luis's eyes were moist and he looked out to sea and said quietly, his voice shaking with emotion, "I think he is the luckiest little boy in the world and a beautiful baby. He will grow up to be a handsome man, I'm sure. But, most of all, I am thanking God that another child will have escaped the favela."

Luis went to his apartment to change clothes, and Daisy took a cool bath, trying to find some relief from the humidity and unwind before the remainder of the day's activities. She was finding it very difficult to relax. Her mind was racing, filled with many thoughts, especially Luis's response to her decision to adopt Clay.

She got out of the tub and dried off. Wrapping a towel around herself, she walked over to the window and pushed the shutters outward. The mountains in the distance looked like humpback whales rising from the ocean.

Soon, she hoped, she would be flying over them, a baby in her arms.

FIFTEEN

The first sound Daisy and Luis heard as they drove up the steep hill to A Candeia a little after four that afternoon was the barking of a dog. As they pulled up in front of the house they saw Isabella's large German Shepherd running in playful circles in the courtyard just outside the kitchen. Then they heard the sound of a child's laughter and as they walked closer they saw him – tiny, and frail. He wheezed loudly and his coughs shook his little body while he awkwardly threw a rubber ball for the dog.

"That must be Roberto," Daisy whispered to Luis. "Isabella was right. He is awfully small for a five year old."

"Yes, but look at his face, Daisy. He has the expression of a much older child. There is pain there but also wisdom, I think."

Luis walked over, bent down, and spoke gently to Roberto. "Que pasa, mi amigo pocito?" Roberto dropped the ball he was holding and ran into the house as fast as his little legs could carry him, the dog following close behind.

Daisy and Luis walked through the open door at the same moment Isabella entered the living room, her right arm around the little boy's shoulders. He looked up at Daisy and Luis with huge, round, black eyes and held tightly to Isabella's skirt.

"Well, I see you all have met. This is my special boy, Roberto," she said caressing his hair. She spoke to him in Portuguese, pointing to Luis and Daisy. He listened carefully and then walked over and extended a hand to Luis.

"May I take him outside in the gardens while you and Daisy talk?" Luis asked Isabella.

"Of course. Just be careful. He is very weak and extremely frail."

Daisy looked out the window at the two, now seated on a bench under a palm tree. Roberto seemed happy sitting on Luis's lap as Luis spoke softly to him and played little finger games.

"What will happen to him, Isabella?" asked Daisy. "Will there be a home for him?"

"Perhaps yes, perhaps no. When he came to us, we could tell he was badly malnourished in addition to his other medical problems. So, before we even think about beginning a search for parents for Roberto, our job is to get some weight on his little body and to let him know he is loved. The only humans with whom he has ever had contact were doctors and nurses in a charity hospital in the Northeast. He has lived in that hospital all his life and although he's been loved by the hospital staff, he has never lived in a home environment.

"As it happened," she went on, "one of the doctors in that hospital went to the university with my oldest son, Eduardo, and when I was in Fortaleza last month, I went to dinner with Eduardo and Jorge, my son's friend. He told me about Roberto and that the medical staff had done all they could and they felt now he should be in a home to try to have a normal life. They had asked many families but no one, it seems, wants a child with such a handicap as Roberto. I told Jorge that I would take him and in time, find a home for him in the States. He was abandoned at the hospital when he was a tiny baby. He is now a ward of the court."

"How did you get him to Rio, Isabella?" Daisy prodded.

"I went to the minor's courts, saw judges, and social workers. I told them what I would do for Roberto. How I would work day and night until I found him a home. I pleaded and begged and after several weeks, I convinced them to sign over all the papers to me -- so here he is. And today, I was rewarded. Playing with the dog this afternoon is the first time I have heard him laugh. What a joy that was! He is so bright, so quick to learn and already knows that when he is stronger he will go to America to live with a real family who will want him very much. At lunch today, he told me he would be the best boy in the world – so good that a mother and father would want him soon."

"Do you really believe you can place him?

Isabella gave Daisy a look that told her she was foolish to ever doubt Isabella's intentions. "Of course, I believe that. I have no business doing what I do if I don't believe every day that I can do this. I don't give up easily. I have kept the doors of A Candeia open through some pretty rough times. I believe there are three stages to every undertaking – impossible, difficult, and done. Yes, I believe there is a couple out there who has the ability and the courage to love this little boy. My job is to look for them."

Daisy watched Roberto sitting with Luis and she thought how beautiful he was. She wondered if someone out there would really adopt Roberto and love him as their own. If they could see him it would make such a difference. A written description of this little boy might frighten some people. But to see him, to watch his tiny fingers hold onto Luis's hand and examine his watch, play with the dog – only the hardest heart would not be moved. Daisy was already captivated by Roberto.

Then she thought of another child.

"Isabella, I've come to a decision about Clay."

"You want to be his mother, don't you?"

"How did you know? I just made up my mind today."

"No, I believe you decided the first day you saw him. There was something special about the way you looked at him and that look has not gone away." Isabella hesitated a moment. She nodded her head toward the open window in the direction of Luis and Roberto. "What about your young man? Is he in agreement about the baby?"

"Actually, I don't know if calling him 'my' anything is accurate.

I thought I knew him pretty well but now I'm not sure and I'm very confused. We get along so well and there is definitely something between us. However, today when I told Luis of my decision to adopt Clay, he merely encouraged me and said nothing to indicate his feelings toward me."

"Did you think you could use Clay and the adoption to force him into speaking his mind?"

"Definitely not, Isabella! I'm not playing games with Luis. I did think my telling him would force some conversation about us. But, he said nothing that gave me the slightest hint about the two of us. Maybe he merely enjoys the pleasure of my company. He really loved his wife and baby and he's probably not over that loss yet. I guess I've been too presumptive about Luis. It appears that way at the moment."

"Daisy," Isabella said softly, "perhaps it is up to you to make the first move. Do you honestly feel you are *in* love with him?"

"Oh, yes, I have no doubts about that," Daisy answered quickly.

"Then, let him know it. All Brazilian men are not aggressive or smooth talkers. Some are shy and quite reserved."

"Do you really think that is the case with Luis?" asked Daisy.

"I do not know Luis, therefore, I cannot say if he is shy or not. He may be and then again, he just may be waiting to be sure. I don't know. But, I believe you are going to have to make the first move in discovering his true feelings."

"Maybe so, Isabella, but not today. Tell me what I have to do to begin the adoption process."

"Pray a lot," Isabella smiled.

"Will it be that difficult?"

"Well, it won't be easy. The young biological mother signed papers giving me custody by way of a power of attorney. Now, we have to transfer all those legal papers to you, making you the legal mother of Clay. All this must be done before a minor's court judge in this state and this is difficult because the judges in these small villages sometimes go for days without coming to court. Once your name has been entered before a judge then everything has to be witnessed, certified, and entered in the city records of his birthplace. This is not going to be easy and I can do nothing to get around the way Brazilians do their work. You better be sure you are ready for all of this because you will lose your patience and your sanity will be tested to its limit.

"Also," added Isabella, "this must take place before you can even apply for Clay's passport. And, you cannot take him out of the country without that Brazilian passport. I must also warn you, Daisy, that there will be many, many delays and ploys to discourage you from taking this baby out of Brazil. You will be questioned from every angle. These people will move very slowly, partly by their nature and partly on purpose. Don't rush them. Don't let them see you getting agitated with them. Play it their way and you'll get results, or otherwise...." and Isabella stopped talking.

"What?" asked Daisy.

"There is no otherwise."

Isabella and Daisy looked at each other in silence. For the first time, Daisy felt fear and she knew Isabella was trying to arm her for what lay ahead.

"All right, let's continue this little orientation. When all the documents have been approved they will go on file at the Brazilian Consulate. Once everything is filed with the Brazilian government, Clay will be your son. Are you ready for all of this?"

"No, but I'm better prepared than I was an hour ago. When do we start?" Daisy asked.

"We can start now. I will need your passport, your birth certificate – you do have a certified copy with you, I hope. Some people don't carry one with them."

"Yes, I have mine. I've run into sticky problems in other countries before so I've learned to bring along a copy. What else?"

"For now that is all. It is Clay's papers that really matter at this point. I'll set up an appointment with the minor's court officials and A Candeia's attorney."

Daisy looked out the window and saw that Luis and Roberto were slowly making their way into the house. The child was smiling up at Luis and speaking rapidly in Portuguese.

"I've been trying to teach him a little English," Luis said as they stepped into the living room. "I told him he will need it when he goes to America to be with his new mother and father. So, he has learned 'mother' and 'father' but it is clear he would rather speak in Portuguese."

"Well," said Isabella clapping her hands and smiling at Roberto, "that is not a bad start. One of these days soon, Roberto will have parents. In the meantime, there is much to be done to get him ready."

"Speaking of ready, Luis, we must hurry. Beto is expecting us very soon and I haven't even seen my soon-to-be-son today. Just a quick hug and we'll be on our way. Besides, I haven't told him the news that I'm going to be his mother! What a Christmas this is turning out to be!"

Beto met Luis and Daisy at their car as they pulled up in front of his home.

"Welcome back, Daisy," Beto said as he lightly kissed her on each cheek. "Introduce me to your friend."

Luis came around to join Daisy and Beto on the stone walkway and Daisy made the introductions.

"Your friend, Charlie, called earlier and said he would be here in about half an hour. My wife's sister, Carla, is visiting from Argentina so we will have a nice little party."

As they entered the foyer, a voice called out, "Beto, darling, is that your friend Daisy?" Luci entered from the other room. She was a small woman with smooth olive skin. Her long black hair flowed down her back and swayed gently as she approached them.

Introductions out of the way, Daisy and Luci went to a side patio where there were several small fountains making soft, subtle, trickling sounds.

"Let's sit for awhile, shall we?" A tray sat on a side table with two glasses of red wine on it. "Won't you have some wine with me? We can talk quietly while Beto shows Luis his workshop. My husband is a marvelously talented dentist but his work with wood is the real love in his life. I sometimes tease him that wood is his mistress. In any case, she is a fair one for she never takes him away from home." Luci laughed heartily, showing extraordinarily straight, white teeth.

"I've seen some of Beto's work. It's so intricate and beautiful. I sent two pieces of his work to my parents when I first got to Rio. Luci," Daisy said, looking around at the exterior of the house and the well-manicured grounds, "your home is beautiful. Beto told me you were responsible for its look."

"I'm glad you like it. I enjoy things that are comfortable as well as beautiful and to me, this house is exactly that."

Daisy watched Luci's long, slender fingers gently pull her jet black hair back behind her ears. A very large diamond sparkled on her left hand.

"How did the renovation project go in Germany?"

"Very well." She tucked her bare feet underneath herself while she talked animatedly of her trip to Germany and the family she worked with. The red wine reflected the light of the many candles placed around the patio.

Daisy felt very comfortable with this woman and found herself opening up to her in a way she rarely did with someone she had just met. *Or maybe it's just this wine.*

"What you and I do is very similar," said Daisy. "I look at a scene, and by filming and editing and adding music and other effects, in a sense I've remodeled that scene."

Daisy looked up and saw Luis standing in the doorway. She had no idea how long he had been there. He smiled at her and she smiled back.

"My," he said, as he walked over and sat down next to Daisy, "you two are getting very deep, so academic. I am very impressed." He took Daisy's hand. Luci excused herself to refill her wine.

"Beto has a beautiful home. So filled with love." He turned to Daisy. "I was going to visit Vovo and Josefina tomorrow. I would love for you to come with me again. Would you like that?"

Daisy looked down at the ground. "Sure. That would be nice."

"Daisy, you seem sad despite your smiles. What's wrong?"

"Nothing, I'm just missing my family, that's all. I thought

coming here would be a good thing but instead I find myself thinking of home even more. Then you mentioned your family and...it's just the Christmas blues, I guess. Ignore me."

"I could never ignore you." Luis placed his hand under Daisy's chin and tipped her face to him. The air between them seemed thick with emotion. He kissed her softly on the lips. Just when she was about to respond in kind, she felt him pull back.

"Luis, what's wrong?"

"Nothing is wrong, sweet one. I, too, am having some blue feelings. It will pass. Perhaps we should rejoin Beto and Luci."

He stood and extended his hand to Daisy but she did not attempt to get up. "Daisy?"

Daisy looked at Luis. "You are a puzzle, you know that? These past weeks have been wonderful. I find I have very strong feelings for you and now I think you feel the same way. In fact, I've stood on the brink, waiting to give you everything but you always seem to close the door like you did just now. Then today I tell you I'm going to try to adopt a baby and you wish me well, just like any friend would do. I don't know what to think." Daisy looked down at her hands in her lap and toyed with a loose string from her blouse. She swallowed hard, afraid she would cry, the last thing she wanted to do in front of this man.

Luis sat down again and looked at Daisy for several long seconds. Finally, he said, "Let me take you home. I'll explain to Beto and Luci you aren't feeling well. Maybe we should talk a little."

Daisy got up and walked directly to the car. Luis emerged from the house a few minutes later. They drove in silence for a while and then Luis spoke.

"Daisy, I cannot expect you to understand me. I don't even know myself most of the time. I know you love me. I've known for quite some time now. I adore being with you. We..."

He continued to talk but Daisy tuned out. All he needed to say was "I love you" but he never did. Through the narrow streets they drove. Luis had stopped talking, and Daisy's mind was racing, thinking about Clay and how she could possibly learn to live without Luis in her life.

They drove through the gates of the condo and as soon as the car was stopped, Daisy jumped out.

"Thanks for the ride home," she snapped as she raced up the walkway.

Luis ran after her and reached the front door at the same time she did. He placed his hand over hers as she unlocked the door.

"Daisy, please, let me..." They both heard the phone ringing.

Once inside, Daisy ran to the phone and picked up the receiver. She looked blank for a moment and said to Luis, "An operator has put me on hold. It's long distance.

"Yes, this is Daisy Gardner. Mama? It's so good to hear your voice. What? What did you say? When? Are you okay? I'll leave tonight. I love you. Hang on, I'm on my way."

As Daisy placed the receiver back on the hook, she said without any emotion in her voice, "My father has died. I have to go home."

SIXTEEN

When Daisy landed at the D/FW airport the following afternoon, she was met by her two older brothers, Eric and Will. They waved as soon as they saw her and she immediately felt the tension leave her when she felt their arms around her. Looking at them closer, a wave of sadness washed over her.

Both her brothers, many years older than she, looked so much like their father. Daisy felt the loss all over again. Ever since the call came from her mother, Daisy had been unable to stop the tears. Luis and Charlie had done what they could to help her get her things together and get to the airport as quickly as possible. Charlie had seemed especially upset about Will Gardner's death. Daisy had expected some reaction since her father had always been so kind to him, but Charlie's grief had surprised her in a way she hadn't expected. She had asked him to return with her but he had refused, saying it was a time for family only and he felt he would be an unwanted intruder. Besides, he could keep the project going with Luis while she was away.

Daisy looked intently at her brothers. Will, eighteen years older than she, had a ranch in Montana and was rugged looking, tanned and lean. He was married to Marlena and had teenage twin boys who were replicas of their Dad. Eric, a year younger than Will, lived in California and was the host of a morning talk show in Los Angeles and looked and dressed like a Hollywood actor. Eric had never married and Daisy was fascinated by him. They seemed to share a creative, artsy quality.

"Where are Marlena and the kids?" she asked Will.

"Back at the house with Mom."

"How is Mama?"

Eric answered her question. "Holding up pretty well, considering the shock of this."

"How did this happen?"

"You know Dad," said Will as they watched the luggage go around on the conveyer belt. "Doctors are for sissies. He had a minor car accident about a week ago and hit his head on the steering wheel. There wasn't anything but a bruise but he had some headaches. Mom couldn't get him to see a doctor, though. He was at work yesterday morning and his brick layer said he sat down in the front seat of his car, grabbed his head, and just fell over. That was it."

"Daisy, will you be able to stay awhile?" asked Eric. "Mom's going to need some support after everything's over."

"Sure, I can stay a week or so. I won't leave until I feel she's really all right."

There were so many cars at the house, Will had to park on the street, about a block away. Despite the holiday, the house was filled with friends and family and through the crowd, Daisy finally saw her mother, sitting on the sofa, holding the hand of an older woman. When she got her mother's attention, Sybil stood and hurried to her daughter's side. They embraced and Daisy felt her mother tremble. For the first time, Daisy realized just how tiny and fragile this strong woman really was.

"It's all going to be alright, Mama. I'm here for you."

Her mother looked at her, more composed now. "I'm fine, hon, really. Thank you for coming so soon. I feel better now that you're here." Sybil grabbed her daughter's hand and squeezed it. "Craig's here, Daisy. He was in town giving a seminar and heard about your

Dad. He's in the kitchen. He's been waiting for you."

"Craig?" Daisy looked toward the closed kitchen door. Did she really want to do this? Her mother nudged her forward.

"Go ahead. I'll be okay in here. Talk to him."

Daisy pushed open the swinging door to the kitchen and saw Craig leaning against the counter top, drinking a cup of coffee. He saw her immediately, put down his cup and hurried to her.

Taking her in his arms, he held her quietly a moment and said, "I'm so very sorry, Daisy. Please let me know if there's anything I can do. I want to help."

Daisy hugged Craig awkwardly, unsure what to do. Here was the man who had caused her so much pain just months before. Craig took her silence as acceptance. Holding her at arm's length, he said, "It's really good to see you."

Daisy eased out of Craig's embrace. For a crazy moment, she thought of Luis and felt as if she were betraying him with Craig. She leaned against the kitchen counter, keeping a safe distance. "I can't believe you left your family on Christmas but I appreciate it very much. You're looking good, Craig. How have you been?"

"I've been good, Daisy, really good. Your Mom told me you were in Brazil filming a documentary. Sounds like things are going well for you."

"Yes, they are. It's a huge opportunity for me and I'm having fun as well. And you? What are you doing these days?" *God, this is so awkward.*

Craig looked down at the floor, sighed, and looked up again. "I guess there's no easy way to say this. My family's here with me in town."

Daisy looked at him, confused.

"I'm married, Daisy, and my wife's pregnant. Can you believe it? I'm going to be a father."

The words hit Daisy like a glass of ice water. She could feel herself catch her breath and for a second felt numb. She wasn't sure what she had expected Craig to say but this certainly wasn't it. No time wasted on making babies, she thought. Maybe they'd started work on this before the wedding. Daisy tried to push such thoughts from her mind and suddenly, the kitchen seemed too small and noisy.

"That's wonderful, Craig," she said after a few silent awkward seconds. "I'm happy for you. I know that's what you always wanted."

"Daisy, are you all right? I wasn't sure if I should tell you but..."

"No, I'm fine. Why wouldn't I be? We're over. We both have lives to live. This is good. Listen, I really need to get back to Mama. Thanks again for coming." Daisy hurried back into the living room, her head buzzing

Thankfully, one of her aunts grabbed her arm just then and with tears streaming down her face, embraced Daisy. She didn't see Craig again after that. Somehow, he slipped away, unnoticed.

The simple funeral service was the following day and the chapel was filled to overflowing. Many of the mourners trickled by the house afterwards. Daisy's mind was tired from making small talk. She was anxious for everyone to leave. She knew her brothers were flying home the next day and she wanted to spend time with them.

Finally, at six that evening, the last of the visitors left. Marlena took the boys back to their hotel. Sybil excused herself and went upstairs to lie down.

Will, Eric, and Daisy sat around the kitchen table. Will had made a pot of coffee and Daisy cut them each a hefty piece of pecan pie that someone had brought the day before.

"Well," said Will, "it's a shame it takes something like this to get us three together but it's really good to see you, Daisy. Eric and I keep in touch but we seem to only know about you through Mom."

"Exactly. You were just a little cotton-headed eight-year old when we left home," added Eric. "Now look at you. Mom said you were filming some movie in Brazil?"

Daisy smiled. "Not a movie. A documentary. And yes, I was in Brazil just a couple of days ago. It's hard to believe so much has happened in such a short time." She took a sip of her coffee. "I still can't believe Dad's gone. I keep expecting him to come through that back door and ask about dinner."

"I know what you mean," said Will. "Dad's always been just a phone call away. So many times, I've had a question about one thing or the other and it was so good to be able to just pick up the phone and ask him. Now…"

"See? That's what bothers me," said Daisy. "You guys always seemed so close to Dad. I never felt as though I ever got to know him. It was like there was a wall between us. And no matter how hard I tried, I could never get through to him."

Will put his hand on Daisy's arm. "Don't be so hard on yourself. Dad was much younger when we came along and his business was doing very well. You grew up when Dad's business wasn't making much money and I know he wasn't happy with his work. He was just an unhappy man. It had nothing to do with you." He turned to his brother. "What do you think, Eric?"

"I think it's more than that. I really think he liked you best, Will. He saw himself in you. He couldn't relate to anyone who was different from him. I think Daisy and I are more alike. I can understand what she's saying. I felt it, too." Eric took a bite of pie before he continued. "When I was in high school, I always felt I could never please him. I was in the speech and debate clubs, in the men's chorus and all that seemed to make him angry. He even nicknamed me 'Sis' because I didn't enjoy working with him building houses. He was certainly right about that part. I hated construction work."

"But, Eric, he was proud of you when you went into the Army and became an officer," Daisy said.

"I know. I think Dad just didn't know how to show his feelings. But, like you, Daisy, I never felt I knew him."

"I'm glad we're talking about this." Daisy placed her hand on Eric's arm. "You guys are making me feel better. I always thought you two were so close to Dad. I guess I wasn't the only one he didn't communicate with. It seems we have a lot more in common that I thought. The odd thing through all of this is Charlie. Dad never seemed to have any trouble showing affection to him."

"There's a reason for that." No one had heard Sybil enter the room. They turned as one and looked at her.

"There's a reason your father had special feelings for Charlie," she said again. "It's easy to understand when you know the truth." Sybil sat in the empty chair at the kitchen table and looked at each of her children. Her eyes were red and swollen and it was obvious she had been crying. "I've been struggling with this all day and I think it's time I was honest with you." She reached across and squeezed Will's arm. "Before I tell you this, I want you to promise me that you will never hold what I have to say against your father. I want you to know that he loved each of you very much and this has nothing to do with any of you."

Daisy looked at her mother, fear clutching at her. "Mama, what's wrong?"

Sybil looked down at the table. A tear streaked down her cheek and plopped onto her hand. She looked up again and sighed, resolute, determined to force the words out. "Charlie is your father's son."

The words hung in the air. No one spoke. Daisy was distinctly aware of the hall clock ticking, the sink faucet dripping. She looked from one face to the other. Will and Eric seemed just as dumbstruck as she was.

Eric found his voice first. "What? What did you just say?"

"Charlie is your brother, your half-brother. Your father had an affair many years ago and Charlie is his son."

Will stood up with such force that his chair almost fell over. He went to the sink, looked out the window, and then slammed his hand on the counter. Daisy jumped at the sound. He turned to face his mother.

"How long have you known?" It was evident that Will was desperately trying to contain his anger.

"Since before Charlie was born. I've wanted you all to know for so long but never felt the time was right. But, tonight," she twisted the tissue she had been holding, "just now, when I heard you from the other room, questioning and groping and wondering about your Daddy, well, I knew I shouldn't keep it a secret any longer." Sybil rubbed her finger tips tenderly across the wood grain of the table. She looked from one of her children to the next.

"Mama, how could he do this to you?" Daisy choked the words out. "You've lived with this for so long with Charlie right under your nose all this time? I can't imagine." She jumped up and hugged her mother. Sybil patted her daughter's arm.

"It hasn't been all that bad. Don't get me wrong. I'm no long-suffering dishrag. Your father and I had many arguments back in those days when this all came out. I thought our life together was

over. But we got past it. We found a better love that we had before."
She patted Daisy's arm again. "You're living proof of that."

Sybil slipped her arm around Daisy's waist and pulled her close.
"It was certainly no mistake that you happened. I've always found
such joy in you, Daisy."

Daisy was touched by her mother's words. "I know, Mama, I
know." She didn't know what else to say.

Will took a long drink from his half-filled cup. "Mom, this
whole thing must have been hell for you. How did you and Dad
manage to stay together? And keep all of us from knowing?"

"Will, I wouldn't call it hell at all. Yes, there were some bad
months when I first found out about the affair. It wasn't easy
knowing she lived so close to us. I never thought a thing about your
father doing that work on her house but then I started getting the
phone calls from so-called friends telling me about your Dad going
by her place. I tried to ignore their remarks but I knew in my heart
something was going on."

"Didn't you confront him with it?" asked Eric.

"Yes, I talked to him. I asked him straight out if there was
any truth to the rumors I'd been hearing. He was defensive, very
defensive. That was my first assurance that there really was something
to all the talk. He told me she was lonely and only wanted someone
to talk with. He felt sorry for her. He insisted there was nothing to
all the gossip and wondered how I could believe he'd get involved
with another woman. He was angry and didn't want to talk about
it."

"I guess not," spoke up Eric. "When you get caught, you get
angry. Yeah, I'm sure he didn't want to talk about it." He made no
attempt to hide his contempt.

"What happened after that, Mama?" asked Daisy.

"He said he would stop going by her house. Told me he guessed
he couldn't be a friend to her anymore. Said it was awful when
two people couldn't just be plain friends. Well, I later found out he
didn't stop seeing her right away. Then, one night he came in the
back door and just stood against that kitchen counter. I knew he had
something on his mind. Tears were in his eyes. I went to him and
put my arms around him. That's when he broke down and told me
Maggie was pregnant and that he'd been lying to me all along and
that he was sorry for hurting me. I asked him if he loved her because

that's all that mattered to me."

"What did he say?"

"Daisy, he told me the truth then. I could always tell when your Daddy was lying, but he looked me straight in the eyes and said, 'Hon, I only love one woman and that's you. I know you can't understand all of this. I'm not sure I can. But it's over.' I don't know what happened that night but I knew in my heart, he meant it that time. He promised me he'd never see her again except as it concerned the baby. He said that he had an obligation to help take care of the baby. It's almost funny, but your Daddy and I were closer from that night on than we had ever been."

Sybil got up and joined Will at the kitchen counter. She turned and faced her children.

"A few months later, Charlie was born. Your father was true to his word. He provided for Charlie but he never saw Maggie alone again. But then as Charlie grew, I knew he wanted to have some relationship with him. After all, Charlie was his, even if no one knew it. So, he took Charlie with him a lot, even brought him to the house. Whatever it was that prompted the affair, he got it out of his system. I know your father loved me and he showed me until the day he died."

"Does Charlie know?" Daisy asked.

"Yes, Maggie and your father told him just before he went away to college. It wasn't easy because Charlie is a very sensitive person. He's handled it with amazing maturity. He's always been respectful of this home."

"Do you think that's why he didn't come to the funeral?" Will asked. "Do you think he's angry with Dad for not claiming him?"

"No, I don't think he's angry. Charlie and I have talked about it since his mother died," Sybil said. "He understands how it had to be. He knew you all didn't know and he respected your father's wishes about that. I know he's hurting at the loss of your father - his father, too - but no, he wouldn't intrude."

Daisy stood up and walked to the sink. Looking out into the Texas night she said, "Well, Charlie, old friend, this explains why you never made a pass at me."

She then turned to face the trio at the table, raised her coffee cup in a toast and said, "To Charlie, our brother."

SEVENTEEN

Will, Marlena and the boys, and Eric left the following afternoon. Daisy and her mother drove them all to the D/FW airport and they promised to stay in touch. Daisy never told them about Luis or the baby. She knew this wasn't the right time. Everyone had had enough surprises for the moment.

Daisy and her mother worked hard the week following Eric and Will's departure. There were legal affairs to settle, decisions to be made about what to do with her father's clothes, his assortment of western novels, and boxes of caps and hats he had collected over the years. A picture of Charlie wearing one of his many hats came vividly to her mind. Yes, the caps would be Charlie's.

Daisy was given the task of cleaning out her father's closet and boxing up his things. She retrieved a short stepladder from the closet and began cleaning off the shelves above the clothes rack. A faded red metal box caught her eye. She stood on tiptoe and inched it off the shelf. She put the metal box on the bed and went over to look out the window to make sure her mother was still in the garage, going through her father's tools and the trunk of the car. She saw her mother sitting on a sawhorse reading something she'd found in the garage. This is probably good therapy for her, Daisy thought.

I doubt she's ever been in the garage by herself. That was always Dad's domain.

She returned to the metal box, satisfied that her mother would be in the garage for a while and lifted the lid of the square container. It appeared to be over half full of paid-out receipts for various things like living room furniture, several used cars and other items, all paid for on time. On top of the pile of all these papers was a plain white envelope with one word written on it in her dad's beautiful script – *Daisy*. She removed the envelope and held it against her heart. It wasn't thick but just knowing her father wrote what was inside, made her heart beat faster and she felt like she could spit cotton.

Daisy placed the metal box next to the clothes and other boxes and wondered what to do about the letter. She decided to save it until she was on the plane headed back to Brazil. Better to be alone when she discovered what he had written.

There have been quite a few surprises in this family lately and if this is another one, I want to be inside a metal bird high above the clouds when I find out. Daisy felt a growing fear rising inside her as she tapped the white envelope against the fingernail on her left thumb.

Two days later, Daisy said a sad farewell to her mother at the airport.

Now she was sitting in a Verig airliner bound for Rio and it was time to open that letter and read her father's last message to her. She removed the folded paper from the envelope and sat staring at it, wondering what he could possibly have to say to her. He'd said so little up to now.

"Would you care for a cocktail or soft drink?" asked the flight attendant.

Daisy thanked her but declined any refreshment. She unfolded the white paper and saw her father's familiar handwriting.

My Dearest Daughter,
This is, as you know, the first letter I have every written to you and one of the very few, in fact, I have ever written in my life. I never thought I had too much of anything to pass along to anybody so I let the writers of this world juggle the words.

I assume, since you are reading this letter, that I am gone so I need to make sure that you know some things. I'd never say them to your face and this is the only way I am brave enough to tell you how I really feel. That sounds sort of weak for a man, I guess, and I never considered myself anything but a strong man but I'm taking the easy way out in writing to you.

I know you'll probably spend the rest of your life running around in some foreign country and that's your business, but please don't neglect your mother. She loves you.

Now, while I'm on that subject, I'm going to say what I've never said to you and I am ashamed to admit it. Daisy, I've loved you since the day you were born and I am proud of you. The boys are fine fellows but you have done a good job with your life. You've got that Texas grit that's a combination of determination and heart. Just keep both these balanced or you'll go off the deep end some day.

I'm sorry I never let you get close to me. Sorry for you and for me. I missed you every time you came home and then left. I always wanted to say something like "I love you." Daisy, I just didn't have the heart but I did love you.

Miss me if you can but forgive me.
Dad

Daisy let the letter drop to her lap and stared out the little airplane window into the blackness. *How about that?*

Tears trickled down her cheeks and she just let them flow. She touched the letter without opening her eyes. *Of course, I forgive you but I will miss you the most. We could have been such good friends.*

And the tears continued to flow until sleep rescued her.

Eighteen

Daisy awoke just as the plane was making its descent into Rio and her thoughts immediately turned to Luis and Charlie. She had been unable to reach Luis the day before. Instead, she had called Charlie who had promised he would have Luis pick her up at the airport. Once through customs she began to look for his familiar face but instead she saw Charlie.

"I know, I'm a sorry substitute for the man of your dreams but Luis insisted I pick you up," said Charlie, as he gave Daisy a hug. "Considering all that's happened, he figured we'd have a lot to talk about. Your mother called me and told me you know everything. Daisy, you don't know how many times I've wanted to just blurt out the truth to you but I promised I wouldn't say anything."

Daisy squeezed his hand. "I know. It's okay. I know now and we have the rest of our lives together to make up for lost time."

They were outside the airport now and Charlie carried Daisy's bags to the car parked by the curb.

"I thought we'd go by the house first," he said after he started the engine, "so you could shower and change. I asked Marcelina to have a meal waiting for you. Afterwards, I'll take you to Luis'. You're not anxious to see him, are you?" and he winked at her.

"As a matter of fact, I can hardly contain myself, Charlie. I tried to call him several times this past week but got no answer. Is everything all right?"

Charlie hesitated for a moment. "Luis can fill you in on everything when you see him, Daisy."

"Something is wrong, I feel it. Is Luis okay?"

"Oh, yeah, Luis is fine. I really haven't seen much of him in the last two weeks. I went down to Sao Paulo and finished the filming there and Luis flew to Brasilia to work.

"We thought we would switch assignments to save time. He knows that area better than I do. He finished up in two days. He said he thought we all three should go to the northeast together, get the Amazon region done and then we'd be finished. See, we've been good, hard-working boys while you've been gone."

Daisy knew Charlie was changing the subject. Something had happened that he didn't want to talk about. But she also knew him well enough not to press it. She would find out soon enough for Luis would tell her what was going on. She stared out the car window at the traffic. It was good to be back in Rio and it would be good to see baby Clay again, too. She just wished she could shake the feeling that something was not right. The car pulled into the drive and while Charlie retrieved her luggage, Daisy walked ahead of him into the house. She put her purse on a sofa and went straight to the kitchen. The aroma of omelets and freshly baked bread filled the room.

Marcelina spoke no English but got Daisy's message when Daisy smiled and held one thumb in the air in the cook's direction. She had missed these sumptuous late breakfasts where hot food and fresh fruits filled the dining table.

"I'll take your luggage to your room." Charlie called from the living room on his way up the stairs.

"The luggage can wait, Charlie."

"No, it's okay. I'm halfway there," he yelled from the staircase.

Daisy was already eating when Charlie returned. They ate in silence for a few moments and then Charlie asked, "How are you, Daisy? I mean, how are you, really? And your mother? Is she all right? I thought you might bring her back with you."

"I'm fine, I think. It probably won't hit me for quite some time that Dad's gone, that he's not with Mama in Texas, that I won't ever see him again."

She stopped briefly then added, "Mama seems to be fine, but I don't think the full impact has hit her yet, either. Friends are still coming by and taking her to lunch and visiting with her. When things settle down, I believe she'll have some rough times." She looked straight at Charlie. "Those two had been together a long time and gone through some pretty heavy duty problems. As far as I know, they weathered them all and from talking to Mama this trip I have no doubts they loved each other very much."

"Daisy," Charlie began, his napkin now folded and placed by his plate. "I'm not going to apologize for having been born and I think I know you well enough to know you feel the same. Our new relationship may be awkward, but I hope we can be okay about it. But I'm concerned about Will and Eric. Are they angry?"

"A little. But not at you. They are their mother's sons. They're naturally protective of her. Their main concern was Mama. She made sure she let us all know that she and Dad had a wonderful relationship right up to the end." Daisy reached over and squeezed Charlie's arm. "This must have been so hard on you after you found out."

Charlie looked down at his food and pushed a piece of egg around his plate before he spoke. "I'll be honest with you, Daisy. I felt a lot of resentment. And anger. Yes, it was hard. If your - my - father had been willing to acknowledge me, it would have been different. I thought maybe after my mother died, he would come clean. But he didn't. I have a lot of unresolved feelings about all that. And now that he's dead, I have to sort it all through. But it doesn't change how I feel about you." He looked into Daisy's eyes. "I love you and I'm so glad now I can openly call you my sister."

"But," said Charlie, changing the subject, "how about you get decked out for Luis while I finish the film schedule for the Northeast. Then, I'll drop you off on my way over to Video Brazil. That Brazilian made me promise I wouldn't keep you too long. He loves you, Daisy, but I guess you knew that."

Daisy got up from the table and headed for the stairs. "I'll be down in a few minutes."

Charlie dropped Daisy off at Luis' and waited until he saw Luis open the door before he drove on.

Inside Luis's living room Daisy held onto him and kept saying over and over, "Hold me tight, hold me tight. I've missed you, Luis."

Luis interrupted her words to kiss her long and passionately. She had forgotten how good he smelled, how good he tasted. And she wondered how long she could live without having all of this man who had captured her heart. Luis led her out to a small balcony off his dining room and they sat in wicker chairs and looked at each other for a long time.

"Daisy, I am afraid I have some very sad news for you. Some soldiers went to Isabella's yesterday afternoon and took a couple of the babies and little Roberto, too." Luis stroked Daisy's cheek, aware that what he was about to say was going to destroy her world. "My love, Clayzinho was one of the babies. They are in the funabem, seventy miles from here. We can visit but I'm afraid there is no chance of getting Clayzinho out of there. Few ever leave that place."

Daisy was silent for a few seconds while the full import of what Luis had just said sunk in. Then she stood and ran to the door. Luis caught up with her and pulled her back into the house. "Daisy, where are you going?"

"I have to get to Isabella's. We have to do something," she cried. "My Clay…"

"Listen to me," Luis said, shaking her by the shoulders. "Listen to me. There is nothing we can do."

"I have to see him. Don't tell me there's nothing we can do. We have to get him out of there. He'll die." Daisy fell against Luis' chest and sobbed uncontrollably in his arms.

Luis hugged her close and stroked her hair. "Shh, shh. Okay, okay. We'll go there this afternoon and see if Isabella has any new ideas about rescuing the babies. But you have to understand. It's like Isabella has told you, you have no legal rights to that baby at all. Not one piece of paper that gives you any authority. All you can do is ask if you can see the baby. They can refuse and you can do nothing."

"After driving all the way up there?"

"Daisy, my love, those people do not care about you or how far you have come. You are an inconvenience to them. Come with official papers from the right people and that's another matter."

"But, Luis, how can I get those papers? What can I do? Can you do anything? Please, help me. I have to get my baby back."

"Tomorrow I will ask two of my judge friends here in Rio and if anybody can come up with the proper papers, one or both of them can. But, Daisy, they have to be so careful with this government, too, and they could be totally ignored or worse. But, tomorrow we will begin. Today, let's talk to Isabella and see about driving to the funabem. Strengthen yourself, Daisy, for you are not prepared for what you will see there."

NINETEEN

That afternoon, while Luis, Daisy, Carrie, and Isabella drove north out of the city, Isabella explained to Daisy why she feared for the children who had been taken. Daisy sat in the front seat and turned to face Carrie and Isabella, who were in the back seat, a big box of clothes, formula, and other things for the babies between them.

"I hope they at least let the babies have this formula and that they give Roberto these vitamins and the sweaters. He gets chilled so easily and then becomes desperately ill quickly. They call themselves a child welfare agency, the funabem, but it is by no means a model of anything but neglect and cruelty. They put on a good front but the children's faces tell the real story. You will see, Daisy."

"Isabella, should I really be concerned about Clay? I mean, can they keep him? Is there a possibility they won't ever let me have him?"

Isabella did not hesitate. "The answer is yes to all your questions. They can do whatever they like and whatever you ask has little to do with anything."

Luis stopped the car just before they reached the orphanage. The steep mountainous roads had taken their toll on his BMW. The car was heating up and he got a can of water out of the trunk and poured it in the radiator. "I'm glad I brought this along. That should do it until we start for home."

They drove through two large stucco columns that held rusty worn gates that had closed at one time. Now the gates just protruded from the columns like some kind of ugly abstract sculpture. They drove up a long winding gravel path to a two-story brick building devoid of any imaginative architectural touches. There were no trees nearby to soften the institutional appearance. There it sat, cold and uninviting, surrounded by millions of pieces of tiny gravel and the new-looking gate that closed everything in. There was no children's playground in evidence.

"This looks like an outdated mental hospital," Carrie said. She grabbed Isabella's arm. "I'm really frightened. I can't imagine our babies inside that place. What kind of people work here? It looks like a prison."

"Yes, it does, Come, help me with these boxes, and let's go in," said Isabella, her voice showing signs of strong emotion.

Luis opened the gate on the fence and pushed hard on the big wooden door of the funabem. They entered a small waiting room where a heavyset woman was seated behind an old dark metal desk that had been placed exactly in the middle of the tile-floored room. The walls had been originally painted a light green, but now they could only be classified as filthy.

"Yes, may I help you?" the woman asked. "Visiting hours are not for another hour. You will have to come back. As you can see, there is no place to wait here."

"But, we just drove up from Rio. We have no place to go. Can we not see the children? At least the babies?" Isabella's voice was shaking.

"That is impossible. The babies are sleeping."

Daisy wondered how every single baby could be asleep and if they were, this strange woman certainly would have no way of knowing it.

Isabella did not back off.

"Then may we see a five-year old named Roberto? I have some sweaters for him and I promised I would come visit. Surely, he is not asleep, too. I am Isabella Maria Paes, the Director of A Candeia in Rio. It is a small adoption agency and we find homes for children who have none. These few children here were taken away from us before they could be placed. I beg you, please let me see Roberto. I have made promises to him."

The woman said nothing but pounded hard several times on a bell next to a metal clipboard on her desk.

Within moments a stocky dark-skinned woman appeared in the doorway behind the desk. She was wearing a dark blue uniform with her name embroidered in gold thread above her left breast pocket. She walked to the woman acting as receptionist and they talked in hushed tones. The uniformed woman used large exaggerated gestures as she talked and she appeared angry. Finally, the matron in the uniform turned and faced the three visitors.

"Follow me up to the nursery," she said coldly in Portuguese. "You can only stay a moment." Isabella relayed the instructions to Daisy and Carrie and the little group made their way down a narrow dark hall.

Daisy noticed the smell first and it made her sick. Apparently, the place had been scrubbed with a strong, undiluted disinfectant and as they walked down the long corridor Daisy's eyes began to burn. The odor was oppressive.

"I can hardly breathe and my eyes are watering. How in the world do the babies tolerate this?"

"They don't," answered Isabella. "But they have no choice."

Carrie put her hand to her mouth and stifled a sob.

The woman stopped in front of a door that was locked. She noisily fiddled with a huge brass key ring that must have held every key to every door in the place.

"Isabella, why would they need to lock the door to a nursery? None of the little inmates can walk out."

"That's just the way things are done here, Daisy. You'll fair better if you do not question everything. Here there simply is no logic to most of what goes on and you must know that they will stop us from coming again if we make any trouble for them. A simple question. A remark they consider unnecessary. A look. It won't take much."

"Isabella is right," whispered Luis as the woman continued to search for the key to the door. "We must be silent, see the children, and then go. These people do not need a reason to make us leave or keep us from ever coming back."

At last the door was opened and they were told to go in. Isabella and the woman talked briefly.

"She says we have five minutes. Our babies are in the last row near the window. Let's hurry. She means five minutes!"

Daisy spotted Clay even before she reached the row of small metal beds. His thick dark hair looked like it hadn't been brushed since he had been there and she saw immediately that he had thrush. His lips, tongue, and the inside of his mouth were covered with a white film. He was crying and Isabella said, "The thrush is very painful. I doubt they are treating it. That is a telltale sign that things are not sterilized here. A dirty bottle, using the same changing table, and with all the other babies, I'm quite sure they do not clean between diaper changes. Oh, this hurts my heart so much. We must get them out of here as soon as we can. Daisy, quickly pick up the bottle in Clay's bed and hand it to me. If I can, without the guard seeing me, I want to see what they are feeding these babies."

Luis was standing near Clay's crib and quietly reached for Clay's bottle. He palmed it and handed it to Isabella. He then went to talk to the guard to try to divert her attention long enough for Isabella to inspect the chalky white liquid.

Isabella squeezed the nipple and the contents dripped onto the palm of her left hand. She licked her palm and looked at Daisy.

"It's watered down formula. None of these babies are getting enough to eat. Clay was always so content but just look at him. He is fussy and crying and he is very hungry. Pick him up, Daisy. He must feel love or he will not last long."

"Isabella, did the guard say it was okay to pick up the babies?" Daisy asked, her hands shaking.

"Well, she didn't say it was *not* okay, so pick him up. You, too, Carrie. Pick up Gracie."

Carrie and Daisy both did as they were told. As soon as Daisy lifted Clay up she could tell he had lost weight. He snuggled close to her neck and began sucking.

"Oh, my little Clay, you are so tiny but you must hold on and fight. I am doing everything I can to get you out of here. God, how can I leave you behind?"

Isabella walked up behind her and handed her a small, four-ounce bottle.

"Be very careful the guard does not see. I smuggled this in. Clay needs it badly. It is not much but it is full strength formula with vitamins. You don't have much time and he shouldn't drink it too fast but get as much down him as you can. At this point, every single drop is a lifesaver. He must have nourishment."

Clay practically inhaled the bottle Daisy had given him. His little jaws worked hard as he strained to get mouthfuls of the formula he remembered. He hardly stopped sucking to take a breath but he got down all four ounces and was now searching for more when Daisy removed the bottle and put him on her shoulder to burp him. He had one fist in his mouth and made loud sounds as he looked for more to eat.

"Hush, hush, little man. That's all there is this time but I'll be back and somehow I'll get more to you." Daisy was afraid to hug him too hard but she kissed him all over his face and neck and never stopped talking to him.

"Five minutes is up," the woman yelled.

Isabella called to Daisy, "Put Clay down now. If we don't obey her this first time, we will never be allowed to return. Now, Daisy."

Daisy held the tiny infant one moment longer then put him back in his crib.

"I love you, little one. I love you. Fight hard for me."

She turned quickly and headed for Luis who was standing at the door. He saw her tears and put his arms around her.

Daisy buried her face in his chest. "Luis, I just can't bear to leave him. He's so little and no one here holds him or tells him they love him. I'm afraid he will die. I don't think I can walk out that door."

"Yes, you can, love," he whispered. "Don't underestimate Isabella. She doesn't lose often and I can assure you the government won't hold these children long. Trust me. And with everything you have, trust Isabella and God. We'll be taking Clay home very soon."

Luis hoped that what he had just said to Daisy would come true.

Isabella and the woman walked ahead and Luis translated for Daisy and Carrie.

"We've been given five minutes with Roberto and the guard just told Isabella that Roberto doesn't want to see her. That's probably not true. You know Roberto adores her."

The guard opened another door and they entered a large room with two long tables where dirty chairs had been stacked on top of dirtier tables. A janitor dipped a filthy mop in a pail of filthy water and slung the mop around accomplishing nothing but getting the floor wet. Roberto stood at the end of one long table. His gaze was at the floor and when Isabella ran to him he backed away slowly.

"Don't touch me," Roberto yelled in Portuguese as Isabella tried to hug him. "You promised to come for me. You promised to get me a home. You promised to get me a family. You lied to me. Nobody wants me and now I am in this place and I will never get out." Tears rolled down his grimy, little face.

"Oh, but you will, and soon, Roberto," Isabella pleaded. "You must hold on to my promises. You must know I will never lie to you. I am trying very hard to free you and the babies. I will never give up." Roberto looked down at the floor, his arms at his sides.

"Look, lady," the guard snarled "I see this kid every day. He has stopped eating and he won't take any exercise at all. His physical condition is not good but I guess you can see that. Who would want to adopt him anyway? "

Daisy had seen Isabella intense about her work at A Candeia but she had never seen her so angry. It came like a lightning bolt from nowhere.

"I have to be nice to you or I will not be allowed to visit again," Isabella said in slow, measured words, "but if you say one more unkind word about this little boy, I will kill you with my bare hands. We are leaving now but we will come back soon. I will not be stopped. These are my babies and soon I will walk out the main gates with them in tow."

She turned to Roberto, stooped down and spoke softly in his

ear.

"Please hold on, my Roberto. I will keep my promises. You must believe me. I will give my life for you if I have to."

She kissed him and walked quickly to the door. As she started out, Roberto called out. "Dona Isabella, I believe you."

Back in the car all four were silent for a long time as they drove back to Rio.

Isabella finally broke the silence, her voice shaking. "Tell me, please, how do you explain to a child about injustice, politics, bureaucracy and total lack of caring? Roberto believed me. I made him have hope that he would have a family and a future. I taught him how to trust and how to dream. Now..." Her voice trailed off.

The women cried openly. Luis swallowed hard, trying to keep his emotions in check.

Before long they rounded a mountain and there before them lay Rio. The Christ statue was very clear. No clouds blocked the view.

As they started down the mountain, Isabella looked at the statue of Christ with arms outstretched and said quietly, "I believe in You, but with all my heart, right now I wish You could come down off that mountain and open the doors to that horrible place and free those little ones."

As Luis looked in his rear view mirror, he saw Isabella looking out the back window at the statue. In that moment, she didn't look strong, authoritative, in control, or confident. She looked like a little child herself, afraid and hurt. Luis glanced out his window at the Christ and knew how much they needed intervention in order to free those children.

He turned toward Daisy and she looked back at him.

"Luis, next time you will have to borrow a bigger car because we are not coming back without the children."

He put his right hand gently on hers and squeezed it lovingly.

"I know," he said. "I know."

TWENTY

Luis, Daisy, Carrie, and Isabella sat around the large kitchen table at A Candeia. Isabella had poured each of them a large glass of freshly squeezed orange juice and set a platter of small meat pastries before them.

"Will this be enough or shall I prepare dinner? I've not been myself since the children were taken, I'm afraid."

"This is fine, Isabella," Carrie said. "Sit, please. You must be as exhausted as we are."

"Yes," said Luis. "Daisy and I haven't had a chance to spend much time together since she's been back so I thought I would take her to a quiet place for dinner later. Right now, let's just put our heads together and see if we can find a way to bring the little ones home."

Daisy had never seen Isabella so quiet. Normally so animated and talkative, she just sat and stared out the window at some unseen object. Finally she spoke.

"I feel like my hands are tied. I have a few contacts in the Minor's Court here in Rio and a trusted attorney friend who has helped A Candeia in the past but I doubt the courts will want to get involved with a state agency. At this point I am not sure whom I can really trust."

"Not even your Minor's Court judge or attorney?" asked Carrie.

"Not even Gustavo. He has been a family friend for years. He has helped us with estate procedures and forming the business of A Candeia but this is a federal matter and he would be risking too much to become involved."

"But, could you at least talk with him?" asked Luis. "Perhaps he would have some suggestions. He has a soft spot for your work."

Carrie's face suddenly brightened. "Isabella, all my paperwork is just about complete for adopting Gracie. Surely, that makes a difference. Maybe they will release her. What do you think?"

"Carrie," said Isabella, her eyes sparkling for the first time. "You have just given me an idea. Let me think out loud a bit. This just may work. And it could work for Clay as well. The biological mother signed a power of attorney, giving me full and irrevocable custody of Clay, so at this point, although he has no permanent parents, I am his legal guardian. The key word here is 'legal.' We've got to play everything by the books, even though they don't.

"If all your paper work was completed, Daisy, I could release my power of attorney to you and you would be free to leave the country with him. However, you haven't even begun, so that's out. But what's preventing me from using this power of attorney to try to get Clay out of the funabem? I would be his parent because it says so in the notarized document. I'm thinking I might just be able to get him out. Gracie should be even easier. It may work – for both babies."

Daisy jumped up and hugged Isabella while Carrie put her hands to her mouth to keep from screaming.

"Then you could keep Clay here while I get all the red tape completed for me to legally adopt him," Daisy said.

"That's no small or easy task, though. You have a lot of work ahead of you, Daisy. First of all, you must have a home study and the only place you can obtain this is back in your city of residence."

"I can't go off to the states and leave Clay. At least, not with a good feeling. How long will it take?"

"Daisy, my little friend, you are going to find that all of this adoption business is, in many ways, more difficult than giving birth to a baby. Carrie can tell you."

Carrie nodded. "The home study work could possibly be speeded up if you knew a social worker in a children's aid department," she said. "Maybe a month if you explain the dire need here. Normally, it takes many months. It did for me. I had the home study done even before I knew I had a baby waiting for me."

"What will that entail?" sighed Daisy, showing obvious signs of disappointment.

"A home study is an in-depth, very thorough report that evaluates parental suitability for adoption and actually will represent the adoptive home to the proper officials here in Brazil. Also, you will need copies of your birth certificate and, in this case, your divorce decree. You will need a letter from your doctor stating that you are in good physical and mental health, a notarized statement showing your assets and liabilities..."

"Surely, this is all, Isabella," interrupted Daisy.

Isabella shook her head. "Oh, no. You will need letters from your employers for the last five years showing the length of employment at each and annual salaries, four original letters of recommendation from people who have known you for over five years, police records of every place you have ever lived in the past five years..."

"Enough," said Daisy. "This is overwhelming! It's a wonder any child ever gets adopted."

Isabella patted Daisy's arm. "There is still more. We will need a psychological evaluation. For the Immigration and Naturalization Service, there is another long list of requirements."

"And there's no way around any of this?" asked Daisy.

"Not one small detour. This way or no way."

Luis leaned back in his chair, folded his arms across his chest, and smiled at Daisy.

"It's surprising, isn't it, how much work is involved just to get one little favela baby out of this country? And he's like most of the babies born up on the sides of Rio's hills. They are certainly not planned and when they are born they are either thrown away, given away, or left to die with some relative or neighbor."

"But why," Daisy asked, "is so much required to adopt these unwanted babies if no one wants them in the first place?"

Isabella spoke up quickly.

"First of all, it is required by the INS, and that's that. And never forget, the Brazilian government. And, you will need a professional, government approved translator. I did know of a wonderful translator here, an older woman who had a passion for being a part of getting children placed in loving homes." Isabella's eyes softened as she spoke of this woman. "She had very poor eyesight, yet she would sit with a magnifying glass and tediously translate all of a baby's documents and records from Portuguese to English."

"Is she still around?" asked Daisy. "I'd like to meet this person."

"Yes, she still gets involved with these little lives."

"So, what else do I need, Isabella?"

"Your fingerprints will have to be sent to the FBI to check if you have a criminal record."

"You made up that part, right, Isabella? My fingerprints?"

"The INS takes this requirement very seriously and once you have all of this verified by them, we can start to work on Clay's papers. He will need his birth certificate, which, luckily I have. Then you will need an irrevocable release signed by one of his sole surviving biological parents. Again, fortunately, I have the signature of the young woman who carried him. Of course, all of this has to be translated into English before it is sent off to the States for approval by INS. I know it sounds like an awful lot."

Daisy stared at Isabella. "I've never heard of such a complicated process."

Isabella smiled for the first time that day. "I know. But it will get done. You'll see."

Daisy and Luis had a quiet dinner in a small restaurant near Leblon Beach. Daisy hardly ate. Instead, she pushed the food around on her plate and sipped wine. Finally, she put her fork down.

"Luis, how long will it take to finish the film? I want to fly home as soon as possible and begin the home study. What do you think?"

"Well, we still need to go to Fortaleza and then Charlie and I can rent a helicopter and spend a couple of days getting some film in the Amazon region. That should complete our work."

"And what about me? You go on that helicopter, I go."

"No, we will rent a small chopper, get in, get out. You can wait for us. No argument."

Daisy shook her head. "Oh, we'll talk more about that. Trust me. But, if possible, I would like to see Clay safely back at A Candeia before we fly to the northeast."

Luis reached for her hand across the table and squeezed it. "We'll begin work on this tomorrow and before you know it, we'll be bringing Clay back to Rio. That is a promise, Daisy."

TWENTY-ONE

Daisy spent most of the next three days calling people in Washington D.C. who could help her expedite Clay's adoption. She talked with Miki often and he assured her he would do everything in his power to make contact with social workers who could do home studies and hurry the process.

Daisy called Luci Mendes, Beto's wife, and told her about Clay. Before two sentences were out, Luci broke in with, "Do not worry, Daisy, we know many important officials who have the kind of power you are going to need. We will begin contacting them and I feel strongly we can gain support for you. Trust us."

I do, thought Daisy, as she put the phone down. It was Wednesday. She and Isabella and Luis were planning to drive back to the funabem that Friday. Isabella had all of Clay's papers and had found Gustavo, her attorney friend, to be most cooperative. He had even offered to go with them but Isabella had declined. "You have done enough," she said. "I do not want you to put your livelihood on the line."

"Let's just pray it works," he had told Isabella.

Despite the persistent butterfly feelings in her stomach, Daisy felt optimistic for the first time.

The phone rang and Daisy was surprised to find a friendly-sounding female voice on the other end ask, "So you want to adopt a baby?"

"Uh, yes, I do," Daisy answered "May I ask who is calling?"

"My name is Kitty Howard and I am a social worker. I do home studies for people in the D.C. area. I took a history course once at Georgetown and my professor called me today and told me your story. Dr. Tsuru spoke very highly of you."

Daisy smiled. Miki had done what he promised.

"You will have to return to the states, but if there are no glitches, I may be able to speed up the home study portion of this adoption," Kitty said. "We have to do a very thorough job of checking out applicants and there are no short cuts, I'm afraid. However, because you have already found a child, this will speed up the process. Do you have any idea when you can get back to D.C.?"

"Well, I was supposed to make a brief trip to the Brazilian northeast to finish the filming for Dr Tsuru within the week but the baby I'm trying to adopt has been taken from A Candeia by the Brazilian Federal Police. He's now in a state run orphanage. He's getting less than humane care and won't survive long in that horrible place. I have to get him out as soon as possible. I want to start this adoption process as soon as possible. The sooner Clay is mine, the safer he will be. I'm thinking I would like to get the home study done before I complete the filming now. Maybe even get the court work started. What do you think? Can we do any of the work by telephone, Kitty? You know, questions, basic things?"

"Yes," she answered, "but that's a pretty expensive way to conduct interviews."

"I know, but right now time is so important. Whatever can be done by phone I must do it."

Kitty heard the urgency in Daisy's voice. "All right. Let's set up a time for tonight. At least the cost of the call will be cheaper in the evening and we will begin with the questions. Daisy, I promise to do all I can to help. I'll also go to the INS office this afternoon and pick up your forms and express mail them to you overnight. If you can quickly fill out those papers and get the fingerprints done and returned to INS, I'll follow up and walk any papers through that I can."

"I honestly don't know how to thank you," Daisy said. "You don't even know me and you're going to so much trouble."

Kitty was silent for a few moments. "You don't have to thank me, Daisy. I understand your fears about the baby. My husband and I lived in Korea for five years and our one-year old son died there. The red tape we had to fight just to bring his body home was unbelievable...and cruel. Had it not been for an American social worker located in Korea who took pity on us, I'm not sure what we would or could have done. Just know that I understand and will do all I can to help you get your baby safely out of Brazil."

On Friday Daisy, Carrie, Luis, and Isabella headed back to the funabem to see Roberto and hopefully, bring Clay and Gracie home. Isabella had a grey folder full of legal papers, signed, stamped and notarized, all bearing Gustavo's signature.

They reached the funabem and Isabella went straight to the office of the administrator. Luis, Carrie, and Daisy waited outside in the waiting room. The decision now rested on Isabella's persuasiveness and the contents of the grey folder that she carried close to her. It seemed forever before the door opened and a smiling Isabella appeared.

"It worked! We can get Clay and Gracie out today. It was Gustavo's signature that did the trick. Nobody argues with his authority and I shall be eternally grateful to him. So, they will bring the babies out before too long. Now, I'll ask to see Roberto."

The hefty woman behind the desk told Isabella she would have to make a phone call to Roberto's ward before she could give permission to send her back. She dialed the extension and turned her chair toward the wall behind her. She spoke in low tones, mostly in one syllable words. Then she placed the phone back on the hook and turned to face the three.

"Uh, you will be able to take Roberto home with you today, as well," she said. "Drive around to the side entrance where boxes of food and other supplies are delivered. He will be brought to you there."

Isabella's eyes filled with tears and she hugged Daisy and Luis excitedly.

"I cannot believe it. I only asked for the infants and they never give you more than you ask for, but I will not question what I do not understand. I will simply pick him up and hold him close to me all the way back to Rio. I told Roberto I would get him out of here. I never dreamed it would be this soon. What a wonderful surprise."

A door opened and a uniformed woman came into the waiting room carrying Clay and Gracie wrapped in their blankets from A Candeia. Daisy stood and watched Isabella take the tiny bundles from the attendant. She yearned to hold Clay close but Isabella had warned Daisy that nothing must give away her real relationship to Clay. "It will all be over for us if they even suspect the real story behind Clay. Just be silent and show no signs of emotion," she had warned.

"Okay," said the woman behind the desk, "you may pick up the other child now. It's the side entrance just past…"

"We will find it," interrupted Isabella, anxious to get to her Roberto.

They piled in the car and drove to the side of the building. Two large men in jumpsuits were standing on the platform.

"Stay inside the car," Luis said and he cut the ignition. He got out and addressed the taller of the two men.

"We're supposed to pick up a little boy here. His name is Roberto and he…"

"Yes, we know about it," the guard said. He turned and went inside the building. He returned a few minutes later with a dark green burlap bag which he threw haphazardly in Luis's direction. Daisy watched as Luis barely caught the bundle before it hit the ground. She noticed Luis' expression suddenly change as the weight of the bundle almost threw him off balance.

"Are these his things?" he asked.

"You have him. He's inside that bag. They said he died sometime yesterday."

On the drive back to Rio, Isabella held Roberto close to her, as she had imagined she would just hours before. She had unzipped the rough, foul-smelling bag and now she held his lifeless little body as she rocked back and forth. Tears coursed down her cheeks as she caressed the soft brown curls and ran her fingers lovingly over his face.

During the entire drive Isabella never stopped talking to him. Over and over, she told him, as she rocked him back and forth, "You do have a family, little one. I will bury you beside my own two babies I lost years ago. You do have a family and you are loved."

In the front seat, Daisy watched Clay as he hungrily nursed on a bottle of rich formula. As happy as she was to have Clay back in her arms, she couldn't keep the tears back as she listened to Isabella talk to Roberto. Carrie, too, was sobbing. With Gracie in one arm, she had draped her other over Isabella as she rocked the tiny body.

As soon as they arrived back at A Candeia, Isabella ordered a tiny wooden coffin to be built. It was brought to the house on the hill early the next morning and that afternoon, Luis, Daisy, Isabella, Charlie, Carrie and a few staff women, gathered at the family gravesite on a small hill behind the garden. The little coffin was covered in flowers and Isabella led the group in singing, *Jesus Loves the Little Children.*

Daisy watched Isabella as she stood, back straight, head high and she knew that this strong woman was using all the faith and strength she could muster. She cleared her throat and began.

"Today we lay to rest a member of my family," she said in an unwavering voice. "Not born of my flesh but of my heart, he is a son, nevertheless. A child who belongs to all of us. From this day forward, he will be remembered as Roberto Paes. His headstone will bear our family name.

Roberto Paes was no mistake, for God does not make mistakes. We stand here now, in the quietness of this place, with the Christ statue above us, arms outstretched, to honor this beautiful boy. He will not be denied a loving memorial to his existence. Our hearts are broken, remembering this trusting child but we are thankful he lived among us, even if for a short while. Goodbye, Roberto Paes. You are loved and you will never be forgotten. For as long as children's laughter can be heard, we will see your face, your dancing brown eyes, and feel your sweet, innocent trust warming our hearts and spirits. You are every child in Brazil now and for generations to come, you, my son, shall never die."

TWENTY-TWO

After the little service, Charlie, Luis, Carrie, and Daisy again found themselves around the dining room table with Isabella. Daisy held Clay who had fallen asleep in her arms after devouring another bottle of formula. Daisy exchanged a look between her and Charlie and Luis. It wasn't lost on Isabella.

"Is there something you need to tell me?"

"I've decided to get the home study done before we complete the rest of the film." She turned to face Isabella. "Maybe as soon as I get back, we can even get the paperwork done in front of the judge as well."

Isabella sighed. "I know you're afraid for Clay but it isn't necessary for you to change your plans so drastically. No, I think you all should head to the northeast as you had planned," urged Isabella. "I need to stay busy and besides, I am not alone. I have the women here and Carrie. Taking care of Clayzinho and working on his adoption papers will help me very much. I can do nothing more for little Roberto now. Please, I beg you, go, and finish your film."

Daisy shook her head. "I hate the idea of you being alone after all that has happened. Besides," she looked at Carrie, "aren't you scheduled to go home within the week?"

"Yes, Isabella believes if all goes well and my immigration papers come soon, Gracie and I could be on our way by the end of this week," said Carrie.

Daisy turned to Luis and Charlie. "I'll feel better if you guys can hang around to protect Isabella and the babies while I'm gone. Then when I come back, I'll do what I can to get the paperwork in order. Hopefully, things will go smoothly and we can wrap the film up after that in time to take Clay back to the States with us."

Daisy rose and patted Clay's back to urge a burp. When he complied, she smiled and kissed the top of his head. "My mind's made up, Isabella. It's what's best after all that has happened. If I can get reservations, I could leave in a couple of days. I'll call Kitty and get some more work done on the home study process. She's taping our phone conversations and then typing from the tapes. I think we're progressing. Oh, and I received the forms from INS this morning."

"Don't get too optimistic, Daisy," Isabella looked at her across the table, not smiling. "You've not begun your work with the Brazilians yet. It won't be smooth going here and don't expect anything but opposition all the way. You saw what happened to Roberto – they don't put much value on tiny lives. What I'm trying to say is don't count on much, if any, support from the authorities in Rio. They don't care if Clay lives, dies, goes to America, or wastes away in the funabem."

Isabella's hands were resting on the table, but her fingers were curled into her palms, making a tight fist. Her knuckles were white.

"Daisy, my friend," Isabella continued, "pardon me for painting such a bleak picture. It is just that I don't want you to be hurt and you are very likely to be. You must, of course, continue with your home study, go to Washington and do all that is legally required. However, at the same time, you must be aware that you may never get permission to take Clay out of this country. Never."

"Never? That's a strong word. But if that's what I'm facing, so be it. Mama always said that anything worth having was worth fighting for." *And I'm talking about the big Brazilian, too.*

Daisy's words were prophetic. She was able to get reservations for Washington, leaving within two days' time. She telephoned Kitty right after that and told her she would be in Washington soon and would like to get the home study completed. She then called Miki.

"I'll be flying back to D.C. the day after tomorrow to finish my home study and, hopefully, walk some papers through immigration. I was hoping we could get together, Miki, while I'm in town. I can update you on the film. I'm also going to need all the advice and support I can get to take Clay out of Brazil. Isabella tells me that even with all my paperwork in order I will probably still have a difficult time getting the Federal Police to issue Clay a passport and the American Embassy to sign off on his visa. She says they drag their feet in the courts and at the translators. I'm sure you know what I am talking about. Do you know some people who can help?"

"I know one man who will prove invaluable to you. Our friend, Beto, knows many people in the court system, especially the minors' court. Call Beto, if you haven't already, before you leave for the states and see if he has some encouraging words for you."

She immediately telephoned Beto and told him about Clay. He promised to meet with a judge he knew as well as a couple of officials in the passport division at the Federal Police.

"Call Luci and me just as soon as you return to Rio and we will bring you up to date on the progress we've made. How long do you expect to be in the states?"

"I hope to be back in Rio in less than ten days. Kitty, my social worker, says she won't need but a week. I surely hope she is right. I'm not sure about immigration, though. Also, I'd like to get some baby furniture and a few other things while I'm there."

"Daisy, why don't you wait on that part," Beto said softly. "I don't want to frighten you but so many things could go wrong here."

"Are you saying that I may not be able to go through with all this, Beto?"

"No, I am not saying that but I am planting the remote possibility so that you do not get your hopes too high. As I promised, I will do everything I can to help you but there is a limit to what a private citizen can do within the inner workings of government affairs in Brazil."

"Is there anything I can do to speed up Clay's paperwork before I leave for the states?"

"Yes, I do know that you can apply for his passport. Other than that I believe everything else depends on your meeting all the qualifications from immigration and the U.S. Government's standards for adoption. We'll be waiting to hear from you very soon, Daisy."

Daisy's time in Washington passed quickly. She liked Kitty immediately and was grateful for all the extra time and effort her new friend was putting in to get the study information compiled. Kitty gave Daisy helpful hints to help expedite the interactions with the INS. It turned out there was nothing Miki could do to speed things up but Daisy was grateful for his support.

And, despite what Beto had said to her just before leaving Rio, Daisy purchased a complete nursery for Clay. The night before she left, she sat cross-legged on the floor in the middle of the room that she had turned into Clay's room, and folded baby outfits. P.D. jumped around, sniffing everything, glad to have his friend back.

Daisy held a tiny shirt aloft and then offered it to P.D. "Do you think you can share me with a little baby, P.D.?" She smiled when he growled at the tiny garment. "Is that your answer?"

Then just as quickly her smile faded. She suddenly had the urge to hear her mother's voice.

"Mama, it's good to hear you," she said as soon as her mother answered the phone. "You sound wonderful. I just wanted to tell you that I have one more trip to make to Brazil and then I'll be back in the states for good. And do I ever have a surprise for you!" Daisy said as she rocked in the new rocking chair next to Clay's crib. "I think you're going to like this surprise very much. In fact, I know you will."

"Does it concern that Brazilian cameraman you had your eye on?"

"Luis? No, not exactly." Daisy smiled. "The surprise I spoke of is that I'm adopting a beautiful baby boy I found in an orphanage in

Rio. The baby's name is Clay and you'll love him, too, Mama."

"A baby! You're kidding. I never would have guessed that in a million years. Are you sure you want to do this? A baby is so much work..." Sybil stopped in mid-sentence. "Are you getting married? To Luis?"

"No, Mama, I'm not getting married. At least, not as far as I know. Yes, Luis is still in the picture but I have no idea where that is going to go. No, baby Clay is going to be just mine."

"Daisy, do you want to come home for a few days? Maybe it would do you good and I'd just love to see you. We have so much to talk about."

"Thank you, but no. I need to get back to Rio as soon as I can. There is so much paperwork to get done and only I can do it. I promise, though, as soon as I get the baby out of Brazil and I have Clay checked out by a pediatrician here in D.C., we'll fly straight to Fort Worth. After all, a boy needs to be hugged by his grandmother. Just say some extra prayers for Clay and me, please, and that I'll be able to make it through all this. I love you, Mama." Daisy said a quick goodbye and put the phone down.

When Daisy returned to Rio, she went straight to the condo at Copacabana Beach. She walked through the first floor and then climbed the stairs to her bedroom. She dropped her suitcase on her bed and then noticed a small envelope on her pillow with 'Daisy' scribbled in Charlie's unmistakable handwriting.

> *Daisy,*
> *So glad you're back, little sis. I'm spending some time at A Candeia. I think they should have a man around right now. We don't want Isabella to have to face the Federal Police again and certainly not by herself. So, I'm the Protector.*
> *Call me there as soon as you get in and Luis or I will come and get you.*
> *C.*

Daisy knew that Isabella had received several phone calls lately that bordered on threats and both Luis and Charlie were worried about the safety of the babies as well as Isabella and her staff. Moving in was certainly a noble gesture for Charlie to make but Daisy wondered if Deni, Isabella's attractive young niece, who had moved in to help care for the babies, didn't have something to do with Charlie's eagerness to stay at A Candeia. Well, whatever the reason, Daisy thought, I'm glad he is with Isabella and Clay.

When Charlie arrived later that day, he found all of Daisy's things packed and ready to go. Daisy was glad to see him but her disappointment was obvious.

"I know. You wanted Luis here. He got a small job that he thought he would grab while we waited to get back to work on our film. He said to tell you he'll see you tonight." Charlie pointed to Daisy's packed bags. "What's going on? You just got here."

"There's no point in me staying here and you staying there. I'll move in at A Candeia, too. We can get more accomplished that way. You and Luis can both work on completing the editing of the film as we have it so far while I work on Clay's paperwork. Then we'll take a few days to film the Amazon portion and we can add that to the film at home, if we need to. The sooner we get back to the States, the better."

"What about Luis?"

"What about him?"

"I thought you two were getting close. Is there..."

"Is there what? Something going on between us? If there is, only Luis knows it and besides, I have Clay to worry about now."

"Whatever you say, sis."

The following afternoon, Daisy was sitting in A Candeia's kitchen going over yet again the many steps that would make it possible to get Clay out of Brazil.

"Why is it going to be so difficult since you already have the power of attorney from the biological mother?" asked Daisy. "It's not like we're starting from the beginning."

"Until the wheels of the plane carrying you and Clay lift off the ground in Rio, it won't be over," said Isabella.

The next two days were filled from morning until night while she and Isabella walked all over Rio going from one federal building to another. And always Daisy carried a large, gray folder under her right arm. Isabella had printed in large red letters on the front: CLAY GARDNER. IMPORTANT PAPERS. With each passing day the gray folder grew fatter with forms, pages of rules about adoption and every single scrap of paper that had anything to do with Clay.

In the late evenings, when they returned to the house on the hill, Daisy would carefully place the folder on one of the two desks in Isabella's study. Then, after dinner and playtime with Clay, Daisy would visit with Charlie and Luis and they would update her on their day. Their documentary was at a standstill while Daisy tried to expedite Clay's passage to the States. Daisy felt bad about wasting valuable time but knew Clay's departure from Brazil was more important. Miki had himself told her to do whatever had to be done to get Clay home.

On the third night, Daisy and Isabella were in the large front room, sipping coffee.

"Tomorrow we go before one of the toughest judges in Brazil," Isabella said. "Her name is Luciana de Silva and she is in charge of the minor's court for Fuegas, the village where Clay was born. It's sixty-five miles one way so we will have an early start. You better be prepared to take some rough verbal treatment."

Sleep did not come quickly, that night, however. Daisy tossed and turned, dreamed and woke, only to start the process all over again. The sun finally crept over the mountains, and Daisy dragged herself out of bed, anxious to start, and end, this day.

Driving the many-times rebuilt dune buggy that Isabella used as a real car was quite an experience. Daisy looked down and saw the highway pass beneath her feet. This particular morning traffic seemed unusually heavy and drivers yelled obscenities out their windows. Daisy held on tightly to her precious folder and prayed there really was safety in the dune buggy's homemade seat belts.

Before long, Isabella pulled into a small parking lot next to a two-story, beige stucco building. The sign on the front door read: Fuegas Central.

On their walk into the building and up the creaky wooden stairs to the second floor court room, Isabella kept up a running set of directives to Daisy about things she should and should not say

Twenty-Three

Isabella and Daisy took seats in the front row of the small courtroom. Daisy looked around and saw only four other people in the room, all sitting in the back.

"Isabella, is this a good or a bad sign that this courtroom is almost empty? What do you think it means?"

"I don't think it means anything. Just focus on what we hope to accomplish today."

Court time was scheduled for ten o'clock. Daisy looked at her watch. It was almost eleven.

"Will they send someone in to tell us if she's not coming?"

"She will be here," said Isabella. "I've been in this courtroom many times. Be patient, Daisy. This is just the beginning."

A handsome young man appeared in the doorway with folders and papers tucked under his right arm. Daisy noticed he wore a badge with the name 'Eduardo' printed on it. He looked around and then walked to the judge's bench and stacked the folders and papers on the right side. He left and returned with a large glass of water, no ice, which he placed next to the folders. He then stood, arms by his side and looked straight ahead.

"Does that mean the judge is on her way?"

"Maybe. That young man is the judge's assistant and he is waiting just like us."

Daisy looked at Eduardo and smiled. To her surprise, he smiled back. Then he looked in the direction of the door and Judge Luciana de Silva made her appearance. Daisy had expected an old woman, stark, imperious-looking. But Luciana de Silva was beautiful. Her short dark brown hair was streaked with blonde highlights. She wore a perfectly tailored, black herringbone suit with just the right accessories – earrings, rings and bracelets. Without a look at her clerk, she walked directly to her place and sat down. Judge de Silva was definitely all business.

The young clerk approached the judge and leaned over her shoulder. It was clear he was discussing the folders he had just placed moments before on her desk. Daisy could see Clay's file because of the red capital letters Isabella had printed on it.

Judge de Silva shuffled through the folders, first placing Clay's file in the middle of the stack and then, after a moment's hesitation, she pulled it out and placed it on top.

Daisy squeezed Isabella's arm. "This is a good sign, right?"

Isabella whispered to Daisy, "This is like watching a tennis match. You have to keep your eyes on the judge and watch everything closely."

The judge pulled a folder from the middle of the stack, handed it to her clerk, and folded her arms.

Eduardo opened the folder and read from it. Two people from the back of the courtroom came forward and Judge de Silva talked softly to them. She signed several documents and other papers and handed them to the two and they left the room.

"Well, that didn't take long. We're making good time," Daisy said.

"We are not making any time at all," said Isabella. "She just pulled another folder from the stack, this time from the bottom."

Judge de Silva looked through the folder and called a woman to her bench. She talked animatedly with the woman, using her hands to help her get her message across. Daisy couldn't tell if she was angry or if the person who stood before her was irritating her in some way. Finally, the judge signed one paper and dismissed the woman who walked to the door and out of sight.

Luciana de Silva picked up a gavel that Daisy had not seen until now and struck it twice on a wooden block. She stood up, spoke something to her assistant, and quickly left the courtroom.

Before Isabella had time to say anything to her, Daisy was out of her seat and headed toward the judge's bench. Eduardo was busily gathering up the remaining papers and documents when he saw Daisy standing before him.

"Do you speak English?" she asked.

"Yes, I do. The judge is gone for the day but she left word for you to return to her courtroom tomorrow at the same time."

"But, it was a long journey today and..."

"I am sorry. That is all I can do." He smiled at her and added, "Come back in the morning."

"Why, when my folder was on top? Why didn't she call on me? Why did she keep pulling folders from the middle of the stack? I just need her signature on one document."

"I cannot answer your questions. I don't know. She just said to come back. Maybe tomorrow she will call you up. I'm only her assistant."

By this time Isabella was at Daisy's side.

"Let's go, Daisy," she said, tugging on Daisy's arm. "This is all that will happen here today. We will return in the morning and see how things go. Do not talk to anyone here but the judge. Let's go." Isabella squeezed Daisy's arm a little harder.

Daisy mumbled an "I'm sorry" to the clerk and allowed Isabella to lead her out the door.

The next morning Daisy and Isabella were back in the courtroom, again sitting in the front row. Judge de Silva was late for the second day and when she did arrive she sat down at her bench and looked directly at Daisy. She didn't smile or show any acknowledgment. She simply stared. Daisy couldn't discern the meaning of her look, if it had any. Judge de Silva looked down at the folders in front of her and began shuffling through them. She picked up one, opened it, and read aloud "Emilio Marinho." A man, with a woman following close behind, came and stood before the judge.

Daisy watched the judge speak to the man before her. A few minutes later, the judge smiled and the two people left the courtroom.

The clerk motioned for a young woman to approach the bench. Her folder had been pulled from the middle of the stack that was slowly getting smaller. After the woman talked with the judge a few minutes, she, too, left the courtroom. There were only three folders left before the judge. Daisy could see her folder with the red ink on top of the stack. Her heart beat faster. At last, she would be called to the bench. The judge pulled out the bottom folder, read a name aloud but no one came forward. She handed the folder to the Eduardo and said something in Portuguese. Then, she rose and quickly left the room.

Daisy bolted to the table where the clerk was busy writing in each of the remaining folders.

"Won't you please help me?" she asked.

He looked up and smiled. "Yes? What can I do for you?"

Isabella was on her feet and came and stood beside Daisy. She placed her hand on Daisy's arm but Daisy continued.

"Can you tell me how to get through to this woman? I spend my days traveling all the way out here and she never picks up my folder. Then, we're told to come back the next day. I came back but nothing happened. Please, can't you do anything? I have a tiny son I want to adopt and take to the United States as soon as I can. Can you help?" Daisy asked once more.

Eduardo had quietly listened to all Daisy had said, but he leaned in close to her, said, "I'm sorry," took all the folders, and left.

Isabella and Daisy walked out into the sunlight and headed for the dune buggy. After climbing into the driver's seat, Isabella sat and stared straight ahead, her mouth set in a firm line. She sighed and turned to Daisy, clearly irritated.

"Daisy, you have just put the entire proceedings in a precarious position by talking to that young man so frankly. I predict that he will turn on you and not do one thing to help. Behind his charming smile and sparkling eyes is just a man who is enjoying flirting with an attractive woman. He will not help you. Why should he?" She turned on the ignition and pulled out into the traffic.

The same boring trip to Fuegas continued for five more days and as always, nothing was accomplished in the courtroom. Daisy's folder was never touched and they were told at the end of each session that those left in the courtroom should come back the following morning. Daisy had done her best to keep silent as Isabella had warned but came close several times to addressing the judge. Her assistant continued to smile and seemed compassionate but Daisy felt Isabella was right. Why should he want to take a risk and try to help her?

On Friday they were told to return on Monday and they quickly left the courtroom. Eduardo came down the steps behind them and approached Daisy.

"Excuse. I know you don't understand and I am sorry. I have watched you come every day and patiently wait only to be sent home. I have decided to put in a word for you and your son. I promise you I will do what I can."

As he walked away he turned and gave Daisy a wink and a thumbs up sign.

"We'll see," said Isabella. "I hope your trust in him won't turn on you."

TWENTY-FOUR

Monday morning, Daisy and Isabella were back in the dune buggy bouncing along, headed, once again, to Fuegas. The weekend had been good for Daisy and she felt renewed, refreshed, and believed in her heart that this would be the day she had been waiting for. The judge would pull her file, talk with her, sign the much-needed papers, and soon she and Isabella would be on their way back to Rio, ready to continue the struggle to finally take Clay out of Brazil.

They were lucky this day to find a parking spot right in front of the building that had become much too familiar. As the two sat in the dune buggy it began to sprinkle and soon the droplets turned into giant pellets of rain.

"Let's get into the courthouse, Daisy," said Isabella, already out of the vehicle and running up the steps. Daisy caught up with her and they both entered the small foyer.

"Don't worry, these showers won't last long," said Isabella, "but if the sun doesn't come out soon we will be riding back in a wet car."

The courtroom was not so full this day and again, Daisy's hopes soared. When Judge de Silva and Eduardo, whose arms were full of folders and papers, entered the room Daisy noticed the judge was actually smiling. Daisy took it as a good sign.

Eduardo called for Joam Gilberto and he came and stood before the judge. They talked for a moment, the judge smiling all the while, and then Judge de Silva signed a paper and the man left. In anticipation, Daisy moved to the edge of her seat for there was only one other person left in the room.

"Vitor Fonseca," Eduardo called out, looking past Daisy. A man in a dark suit came to the front of the room. There seemed to be some kind of disagreement between the judge and this man and at one point he slammed the desk with his hand and raised his voice. Judge de Silva took all the papers from in front of her, shoved them into his folder, and handed it to Eduardo. She pointed toward the door and glared at the man who lost no time in leaving the courtroom. Then the judge stood in preparation to leave.

Before Isabella could stop her, Daisy headed toward the judge.

"Stop. This time you wait on me! I am not invisible. I only want a small favor from you – your signature on one line on one piece of paper. It is your responsibility as a judge to do your job. As far as I'm concerned that job right now is me."

Isabella was now at Daisy's side, tugging on her arm. Daisy would not be silenced.

"Ever since I came into this courtroom, you have ignored me completely. Never once did you say, or have your assistant say to me, that you wouldn't get to my case for a day or two or a week. You have required us to be here every single day and we have complied. Why are you ignoring me and my son? By not signing those papers in my folder you are keeping me from going through with a legal adoption and then taking him to the United States. But, you know all of this. I beg you," Daisy continued, her voice now shaky, "won't you sign these papers and let me go home with my baby?"

Isabella started to say something but Judge de Silva raised her hand, silencing her.

"I order you, as judge of this state, to get out of my courtroom." She was still standing and looking directly at Daisy. "Come back tomorrow." With that, she and Eduardo left the room.

Isabella and Daisy walked back to the buggy in silence. Daisy knew she had probably ruined all chances to ever get her paperwork signed. There was nothing left to say.

The little dune buggy made its way up the dusty street with Daisy and Isabella bouncing through all the potholes in the road.

Daisy and Isabella found Luis, Beto, and Luci waiting for them when they arrived at A Candeia. All three were sitting in the garden. Luis and Beto were sipping beer from bottles. Luci was holding Clay who was wrapped in a blanket to ward off the evening chill.

Luis put his beer on a small table next to the bench he was sitting on and hurried over to Daisy. He hugged her. "I can tell by the look on your face, it didn't go well today."

"No, it didn't but they are not going to break me."

As soon as Luis released her, Daisy hurried over to where Beto and Luci sat.

"How wonderful to see you both." Daisy said. She kissed each in turn. "What a nice surprise." She gently took Clay from Luci and pulled back the edge of the blanket. Two big black eyes looked back at her.

"How's my handsome boy?"

Luci leaned over and stroked Clay's cheek. "He's such a good baby. We have been looking at the leaves on the trees and watching them move in the wind. Not a sound from him except an occasional baby gurgle."

"How are things going in Fuegas?" Beto asked. "Any cooperation yet from the judge?

"Anything but," said Daisy. "It seems she has singled me out and is purposely ignoring me. If this keeps up, I'll never get the papers signed."

Beto nodded. "I've been talking to some of my patients who are attorneys and work in the judicial system. We have tried to think of a way to expedite this but it is not easy to usurp a judge's authority and sometimes any meddling on the part of officials outside of Fuegas could result in throwing your case out of court, entirely. We are all walking a very fine line. Too much help, too little help." He looked at Luci. A look passed between them and she nodded. "But I have a feeling your time is coming."

"Why do you say that?'

"No special reason, just a feeling." Beto said.

Later that night, after Luci and Beto had left, Daisy and Luis sat together on the bench beneath one of the palm trees. It was the same bench where, just weeks before, Luis had played with Roberto the first day they had seen him. It seemed so long ago now.

Daisy rested her head on Luis' shoulder while he caressed her fingers. It was times like this that Daisy wondered what Luis felt about her. Some days he seemed so far away, his emotions locked away. And then there were times like this when his heart seemed to be right out in the open. She felt like shaking him and screaming "What do you see for us? Do you love me?" but she knew it would only drive him away. He needed to express himself in his own way, in his own time. She was sure the death of his wife and child was still heavy on his heart.

"Querida, what are you thinking?" Luis asked.

Daisy smiled. If only he knew. Instead, she removed her hand from his and pushed her hair out her eyes. "That I want it to be weeks from now and I want Clay to be safe in his nursery in Washington." *With you by my side.*

"I wish that, too. Come, it's getting chilly. You should go in and I should be on my way home."

TWENTY-FIVE

The following morning, Daisy and Isabella once again arrived in Fuegas, praying this would be the day for success. Daisy was unusually quiet on the drive and had been thinking that she would try a different tact with Judge de Silva. She would just sit and look pleasant and not make any waves but her heart sank when they entered the courtroom and she saw it was filled to capacity.

By noon, the judge and her assistant had gone through several folders when Daisy saw the judge pick up her folder. The judge called her name and Daisy stood where she was beginning to think she would never stand – in front of Judge De Silva herself. Daisy waited for the Judge to speak.

"It seems we are acquainted with the same people," she said cryptically. "I have seen you in this court for many days and perhaps this is the time to see if we can accommodate each other. What is your wish of me?"

"I need your signature on the papers inside my folder. I cannot go any further, as you know, until you sign off on my son's original birth certificate registered here in Fuegas. Once I get your signature I can start the legal work to get his passport and his American visa. You are the most important step in the whole process and I will be forever grateful for your signature today."

"Why do you want to adopt a Brazilian baby? Why don't you adopt an American infant? It would all be much easier for everyone if you would take my suggestion and do this," Judge de Silva said.

"When I came to Brazil to work I had no thoughts of babies, adoption or anything but making a documentary film for a U.S. university. As part of our work, we went to a small orphanage and shot some footage there. I saw this tiny infant and was told that he had no waiting parents and when I looked at him, so helpless, so beautiful, I just fell in love with him." Daisy fought to keep back the tears. She wanted to be strong in front of this imposing woman. "I couldn't find one single reason why I should leave this baby in Rio when I was capable of taking him to the States and being his mother."

Daisy leaned closer to the judge. "Now I'm standing in front of you, pleading with you to sign the paper that will start him on his way home. There is much more to do, I know, but you hold the key in your hands."

Daisy noticed that the judge had a gold necklace around her neck and hanging from a chain were two little gold heads, both silhouettes of small boys. When the judge moved her head, light glistened off the golden heads and Daisy thought of Clay.

Judge de Silva replaced Daisy's folder back in the stack of others on the desk. Daisy's heart sank and her head pounded. This woman was totally in charge of whether she could adopt Clay or not. Clay's life was literally in her hands. One quick signature would grant this baby freedom. No signature would place him at the mercy of the Brazilian courts and from what Daisy had witnessed, there wasn't much mercy there.

Daisy reached into her purse and pulled out the small black and white passport photo of Clay that had been taken at A Candeia the week before. She cupped the tiny portrait in her right hand. This was it. Now was the moment to take a stand, to say her piece, to make one last attempt to win the all important signature.

"Judge de Silva, I have noticed that you wear a necklace with two little boys' faces in gold. Are those your sons?" Daisy asked.

The judge's face was transformed and her stark, unsmiling expression changed in an instant to a wide smile as she answered, "Yes, these are my two sons. One is now an attorney in Sao Paulo and the other has just finished medical school and is working at a hospital in Rio." Her left index finger lightly touched the gold silhouettes as she talked.

"I know you are so proud of them," said Daisy. Then Daisy held up the tiny photo of Clay, asleep. She held the picture close to the judge's face and was aware that tears were forming in her eyes. "This is my little boy and I am all he has in this world. I cannot give up so that is why I am fighting so hard to take him home with me. I want him to have the same opportunities that your two sons had, the chance to be anything he may want to be. I want him to know love and family and all about dreams coming true. I want for him all that you wanted for your children. Someday, I hope to wear a gold necklace with Clay's picture on it just like the one you have. I assure you I will wear it with as much pride as you. Won't you please help me?" Tears ran down Daisy's cheeks.

Judge de Silva took the small picture of Clay from Daisy, looked at it, handed it back and said, "You do not give up easily. I like that. I will sign your document today and you can get on with trying to get him out of the country. It will be difficult but I believe you will have success. You are strong and determination is on your side. And, you will need both to raise this boy. That is another kind of job," and she smiled.

Daisy thanked her and took the papers she had signed. Before she left, Judge de Silva reached over and touched Daisy's hand.

"I sincerely wish you well. Va com Deus."

Once outside the courtroom, Daisy grabbed Isabella and spun her around. "We did it! I never thought I would ever hear those words from that woman or get this signature. We're home free!"

"Not yet, but closer," said Isabella, herself relieved they had made their last trip to Fuegas.

It rained on the way back to Rio and with no top on the dune buggy, they were soaked by the time they got into the city. The rain had stopped but the streets were wet and Isabella had told Daisy to hold on. "These cobblestones are very slippery and the tires on this vehicle have no tread. We don't want to slide into someone else. We should be back at Cosme Velho in twenty minutes or so and then we'll make plans about the next steps."

Isabella sharply turned the little car into the narrow lane that led straight up to the Corcovado house. She made several attempts to get some traction on the wet cobblestones that paved the way but the little buggy kept sliding backwards down the steep hill.

"Daisy," Isabella said, "get out of the car and come get behind the wheel. I have an idea. I'm afraid we are going to keep sliding until we lose control of the car and it will slide backwards into the busy traffic. We wouldn't stand much of a chance up against those bigger cars and trucks."

Isabella got out and Daisy sat behind the wheel. She had no idea what Isabella's plan was and she was even more confused when she saw Isabella crawl up on the hood of the car and lay flat, holding onto the sides of the windshield. Daisy wanted to laugh out loud. This was the funniest sight she had ever seen. Here was dignified Isabella wearing a dress, dripping wet, looking like a deer someone had tied to the hood of a car, her face smushed flat against the windshield and her large eyes looking straight at Daisy.

"Now," she yelled, "when I say 'Go', you hit the gas pedal and try and get us up this steep incline before we start slipping back. I think my added weight to this little car will help. Ready?"

Daisy wasn't ready but what could she say with Isabella lying on the hood of the car, face to face with her, only a thin piece of windshield between them? She took a deep breath and yelled out, "Ready. Hold on, Isabella." Daisy pushed the accelerator hard to the floor and with a few slips and slides, the little car found traction and began to edge its way up the steep, slippery hill.

"Daisy, don't stop this car. Keep it going. Keep going. That's it."

Within a few minutes they jostled to the top of the narrow road and Daisy pulled over to level ground with Isabella still holding on to the windshield. Through it, Daisy could see that Isabella's knuckles were white and she wondered if her own face might be the same color. Only after she turned off the ignition and let go of her grip on the steering wheel did Daisy begin to shake at the realization if what had just happened.

"Good job, Daisy," said Isabella as she slid off the wet hood. "Excellent driving. I couldn't have done better myself." Daisy knew that one day she would tell Clay this story of floor boarding a dune buggy straight up a rain-slick mountain in Rio with a real-life hood ornament.

TWENTY-SIX

Early in the morning, three days later, Daisy, Charlie, and Luis were at the airport, standing in line to board a small plane, the only non-stop flight to Fortaleza that day.

"I got the last three seats on the plane," Luis said, "so I guess we're supposed to go today. Frankly, I think it will do us all good to get out of Rio for awhile. We can all use the distraction. Aren't you looking forward to some new scenery and time away from A Candeia, Daisy?"

"In a way, yes, but I hate leaving Clay right now. Maybe I'm paranoid, but I'm afraid he won't be there when we return."

"Nothing is going to happen to that baby, Daisy. Isabella will take excellent care of him. Do you understand what I'm saying? She will take him and literally hide from the authorities if she has to. Whatever the cost, Clay is under no better protection."

They boarded the plane, Charlie headed toward the rear while Daisy and Luis found two empty seats directly behind the bulkhead.

The plane was not in the air a half hour before Daisy's eyes became very heavy. She scooted close to Luis, and put her head on his shoulder. Soon, she was sound asleep.

She awoke when the little plane bumped as it made contact with the tarmac. It had been a long flight and Daisy was still drowsy with sleep. A short time later, they picked up a rental jeep at the airport, loaded their equipment and suitcases in the back, and headed for Colima. They stopped at a tiny market on the outskirts of Fortaleza on their way out of town and bought several kinds of cheese, three tins of beef, and some thick bread. Charlie iced down some soft drinks and fruit juices and put them in a small cooler he'd bought.

They had an eighty-five mile drive to their destination but the roads were only paved part of the way so the trip seemed much longer.

"We'll stop about twenty miles outside of Colima and pick up Geraldo who will act as our guide while we are in the area," said Luis. "He's lived in and around the northeast most of his life and he'll come in handy. Besides, I want someone I can trust to watch out for you while Charlie and I whiz around above the jungles shooting film. Geraldo will be good company as well as providing good research material for you, too."

They stopped at a small hut with one gas pump just after dark and Luis called out to a figure standing in the doorway of the hut. "Geraldo. It's me, Luis. Come. Meet my friends and let's continue our journey."

Introductions over, Geraldo piled in the back and sat with Charlie on the hard bench seat for the twenty mile trip to their lodgings for the night. Before long they saw faint lights in the distance and Luis announced, "We're here. This is our home for the next few hours."

He drove the jeep under a tall tree and turned off the engine. They all crawled out and stretched. Then, Geraldo led the three to a clump of crude huts and small buildings that he called a village. The village was only a wide place in the road but Daisy thought it funny that there was a very large sign by the side of the road reading – COLIMA. Luis had told Daisy this would be a good place to spend the night before getting into some rough terrain and gutted roads and scorching temperatures the next day. He and Charlie would meet the helicopter the following afternoon and fly into the deep interior of the Amazon region itself.

Miki had said he wanted some footage of the real interior of the Amazon area, not village life near the civilized part of Brazil but a look at the Brazil that was still a mystery to the world. He had explained to them that while they did not have to spend but a few hours in the untamed jungle, no "almost-like-it" shots would do. So Luis had asked Geraldo to find a helicopter that would fly them into the Amazon the next afternoon. Daisy would stay behind in the little settlement of Pincu with Geraldo and wait for Luis and Charlie. A small chopper that usually held only the pilot and one passenger was the only type generally used for this close, precise jungle work. To squeeze Charlie in would make quarters tight and strain the weight limits but the smiling Texan insisted that Luis not make this trip alone. They would drop off Daisy in Pincu and continue the short drive to the spot where the helicopter made its headquarters.

Geraldo walked them to their sleeping quarters. Daisy stopped short in the doorway of her room, taken aback by the stark interior. Luis touched her arm and whispered, "At least we've come this far and in the morning we'll have some good, strong coffee, hot bread and some fruit and then be on our way."

Daisy's eyes still looked despondent. Luis added, "I know that you would love to see a Holiday Inn behind those bushes but this little place is not so bad. It's small but clean and that is all that really matters, right?"

"You're right. I've survived worse."

Charlie had been watching Luis talk to Daisy. He couldn't refrain from adding, "Luis, my friend, you're making a noble attempt but you're talking to a real lover of hotels. You know, if it doesn't have a carpet and central air, we keep driving?" He and Luis laughed but Daisy saw little humor in this exchange.

"I'm no sissy and you know it. This will be fine."

"There's only one problem, Daisy," Luis continued. "There is only one empty room in this little place but it has two beds, a wash basin, towels, and clean sheets. If you have no objection, I will share the room with you tonight. Besides, I know nothing of this little settlement or the people who live here, so I would feel safer being near enough to help if you needed me."

"Sure," Daisy said, trying to sound confident. "I'd probably lie awake waiting for something to happen. Fine. No problem. But, what about Charlie? Where does he sleep?"

"He and Geraldo will stay in one of the huts with Geraldo's cousin and her family."

"That's very convenient for Charlie. He always is forced to stay where there are women. Poor baby. Okay, let's do this. We need to get our sleep."

Geraldo and Charlie walked off into the darkness, leaving them alone. Daisy still hesitated.

Sensing her discomfort, Luis, said, "I'll go to the jeep and bring in our equipment. That kerosene lamp on the table isn't much but it does hide many things that would probably frighten you, like lizards, alligators......"

"Very funny, Luis. Go. I'll be fine."

"Okay," said Luis, standing in the doorway. "You go ahead and wash up and get in bed. This has been a pretty full day for you and I think you deserve some privacy, even a small measure. I'll give you ten minutes. Call if you need anything."

Daisy threw her duffle bag on the little bed and heard it thud. So much for a soft mattress. She removed her clothes and had to admit that the cool water from the basin felt good on her body that was gritty from the dusty jeep ride and sweaty from the heat. She dried off with half the towel, leaving the other half for Luis, slipped on a short cotton gown and got into the bed next to the wall, leaving the little bed next to the window for Luis. Within minutes, she heard faint singing and then a knock on the door.

"Daisy, may I come in?" Luis asked.

"Door's open, and I'm tucked in for the night."

Luis came in and shut the door behind him.

"Oh, and I saved you half the clean dry towel and..."

"Thank you, but Geraldo's cousin let me use an extra basin in their room. So, I have had my shower!"

Luis blew out the lamp and for a moment the room was filled with darkness. As Daisy's eyes became accustomed to the blackness, she could make out Luis's silhouette against the open window. She lay still and watched him take off his shirt, sit on the bed, and remove his sandals. He stood and unbuttoned his pants and they slid to the floor. Next, he took off his underwear and stood for a brief moment in the near light.

Daisy thought that he had the most beautiful body in the world even if she could only see the outline. Luis folded his clothes and placed them on a chair before getting into bed. She watched him pull the sheet up to his waist and heard him poking and jamming his fist into a pillow.

"What are you doing?" she asked.

"This thing they call a pillow feels like it has lumps of sand in it."

"Do you want to trade? I really don't sleep on a pillow anyway." She tossed her pillow over to his bed.

Luis went through the motions of fluffing up Daisy's pillow, sighed, and said, "Not much better but it will do. Thanks. Have a good sleep. Geraldo said he would awaken us at five-thirty. Goodnight."

"Goodnight, Luis."

Daisy lay in the small bed and listened to Luis' soft breathing and knew he was asleep. She turned on her side but sleep wouldn't come. Instead she kept imagining Luis' smooth naked skin under the sheets, mere inches from her. She tossed over on to her other side, willing the thoughts to go away.

They wouldn't.

Instead, an idea formed and stayed. Soon, the idea turned into a chant, a cheer, urging her on, until it became a thunder in her head.

She turned on to her back, but the little cheerleader began in earnest now.

Go! Go! Go! All the way!

Daisy sat up in bed. She took a deep breath and stood up in the small bed. Then she stepped carefully across to Luis's bed, one foot on the left side of his body, the other foot on the right side. Luis stirred and Daisy heard him say, "What is it? Who...? What's going on?" Then he opened his eyes and saw Daisy astride him, looking down.

"Daisy, are you okay?" he asked, still looking at her standing over him.

"Yes, I'm fine."

He watched as her gown come up over her head. Daisy tossed it out the window. She dropped slowly to her knees and began to pull the sheet down from around Luis's body. He didn't move. When the sheet dropped to the floor, he felt the warmth and softness of her body on his. He could lie still no longer.

"Sorry to be so pushy, Senhor Campos, but I just cannot wait any longer. Either you love me or you don't, but tonight I need you. I've needed you so long, Luis..."

"Shhhhh, shhhhh," and Luis began to kiss her neck, her eyes, her ears, then finally her mouth and she felt she would cry. He tasted so good. His mouth was hot and soft and she never wanted to move. *We don't need air. I will be his breath and he will be mine. Oh, Luis, please never stop kissing me.*

The little cheerleader was yelling.

He moved his mouth but only to cover her breasts with his kisses. She was supporting herself over him with her arms. He kissed one breast and then the other. His arms wrapped around her as he continued kissing her. His hands moved slowly up and down her body, creating new life. Daisy could be still no more.

Luis whispered, "Oh, how I have wanted you. For so long I have wanted you." He was kissing her navel, his tongue making circles, wild and hot all the way down. She was moving faster now and she knew he could feel her wetness.

She was on her back now, Luis atop her body that would not be still. "Why did you wait, Luis? Why?"

"Because I didn't want to care. I didn't ever want to care again. Oh, but I do, my love. Oh, but I do."

Her legs were around him and she felt him go easily inside her and she knew this was the first time a man had ever truly made love to her. Nothing else existed in that moment. She felt herself climbing higher and higher until she couldn't think anymore. Didn't want to think ever again.

They moved in rhythm together, faster, and then Luis would slow down to an almost stop. Daisy knew she would die if he didn't continue. He began to move again, this time faster, harder, and with one push they held on to each other for fear of falling off the face of the earth. Daisy felt waves of throbbing deep inside her. All she could do was hold on and pray this man would never take himself from inside her soul.

At last they lay quietly, Luis touching her softly all over and whispering, "Amante, my love, I will never stop loving you. You have given me back my life. I will love you forever."

Daisy touched Luis. First, his soft, curly hair that was wet at the nape of his neck, his furry chest, and then, that wondrous part of Luis between his legs that was coming alive once more. She continued to touch him and soon he was inside her again.

Somewhere in Daisy's distant consciousness little cheerleaders were shouting. Go! Go! Go! All the way!

And they did.

Twenty-seven

As the quartet bounced along toward Pincu the next morning, Daisy was unaware of the gutted, corduroy roads, the boulders that lay strewn along the way, or the strong wind that blew stinging dust in her eyes. Nothing could ever be the same again. Not life itself. Not after last night.

Luis and Daisy had fallen asleep sometime just before Geraldo came to their hut to awaken them. Even though both were bone tired, sleep had been the last thing on their minds. Now, as the sun climbed in the sky and the air heated and the dust rose, Daisy wished they had been a little more practical.

But only a little.

She and Luis sat in the front seat of the Jeep and Charlie and Geraldo took the back, each holding on to the uprights as Luis maneuvered the old car back and forth in an effort to avoid the worst of the ruts. But Daisy hardly noticed. She couldn't keep her eyes off Luis as they bounced along. He looked the same this morning but everything else was different. Ever so often he would look in her direction and smile. Daisy couldn't get the silly grin off her face.

"Hey, Daisy," Charlie yelled over the car's engine. "How'd you sleep last night? I thought about you on those little, hard cots. Get any shut eye?"

"I was so tired, I hardly noticed."

"Really? You seem a little tired to me."

Daisy twisted in her seat to face him. "Yes, really. Actually, I feel very refreshed this morning. It's a wonder what just a few hours will do for you." She saw the beginning of a smile on Luis's face and thought she heard the faint, faraway sound of "Go, all the way..."

Just before noon they arrived in Pincu and Geraldo guided them to the small cafe where he and Daisy would wait for Luis and Charlie to return from the Amazon.

"We'll eat a bite here," said Luis. "Geraldo says they have the only palatable food for miles. You two can take a tour of the area, which won't take long. Charlie and I should be back before dark but if we are a little late, don't worry. According to Geraldo the rains are pretty unpredictable up where we're going. So that could slow us down a bit. It is about a thirty minute ride to the helicopter. Charlie and I will take the jeep and leave it there. We'll be fine."

"Luis, maybe we should all drive to the area and film together. It worries me that the little helicopter is so small."

"Daisy, my love, please don't worry. I know this pilot and he is an excellent one so just enjoy an afternoon of doing nothing and before you know it, Charlie and I will be back to bother you once again."

"I'll be counting the hours." She turned and faced Charlie, "Watch out for this Brazilian, won't you?"

"Sure, but who's going to look out for me? A Texan out of his element down here in Brazil? How about me?"

"Charlie, you've never been out of your element in your entire life and you know it. You both take care of each other for me, okay?"

Charlie lifted his right thumb in affirmation. "Deal, lady. Now, let's get out of this jeep and get some food. This is going to be a long day."

Luis gently put his hand on Daisy's arm and steered her to a table in a corner of the small café.

"I want to be alone with you for a few minutes. This is not too private but at least we can talk. There is so much I want to say and this isn't the place I imagined I would be saying these things." Luis held one of Daisy's hands in both of his. "Eu te amo, Daisy. I have loved you for a long time. I want you to know that I totally support you in adopting Clayzinho. I don't know how good a father I'll be but I would like very much to try. The baby and I have much in common and when everything is settled, I'd like to be his father. And, Daisy, before that, very soon in fact, I would like you to be my wife."

Daisy squeezed Luis' hands. Tears welled in her eyes and she found it hard to speak. "Luis, I want that, too. Yes, yes, a thousand times yes." She stroked his cheek. "I love you so much. I wish I could marry you today."

Luis pushed a stray lock of Daisy's hair behind her ear. "I wish that, too, but we have the rest of our lives to be together. Let's just get this film done and get back to our baby."

Daisy put Luis' hand to her lips and gently kissed it. "Our baby. That sounds so good." Then her eyes clouded over. "Luis, let me come with you, please. Is there no way I can persuade you to drive in to the jungle?"

Luis smiled. "It is not a matter of persuading me, my love. It is simply that this is the only way to get into this area. I promise you we will be back here by nightfall. Why, you and Geraldo will hardly know we have gone until you'll see our jeep in a cloud of dust bouncing back into town. Please, do not worry. This pilot has years of experience and I trust him very much. We have made many trips together all over this country and I wouldn't fly with anyone else. Enjoy the day and think about last night and know that I can't wait until we can make love again. You are a part of me now, Daisy. I will never leave you."

Daisy leaned over, softly touched Luis' face with her index finger. "My heart is so full, Luis. Why has it taken this long for us to open up to each other? I think I've known since the first day I saw you near Ipanema that I loved you. Please be careful today."

Luis took her hands and they stood up.

"I guarantee you now that we will have a flawless trip today. I will return in time for us to start back to Fortaleza and then on to Rio tomorrow. And then…I'm going to marry you, Daisy, and we are going to stop the world long enough to have an unforgettable honeymoon. If you thought the French or the Italians were the experts in the romance business, then you are going to discover that it is the Brazilians who know the ways of love."

He held her close to him and whispered, "It is this Brazilian who intends to love you forever. My love, I do not know how to tell you how I feel but wait until Rio and I will show you. Can you wait?"

"No, I cannot and you know it so why are you teasing me?" and she kissed the front and back of both his hands and then pressed them against her breasts. "Oh, my darling, I think of last night and want you right now. Here in this little café in the middle of nowhere. I want you to make love to me again and...."

"Again and again," interrupted Luis as he held her closer. "We must be off, Charlie and I, but I will be back soon."

He led her to the door of the café and pointed.

"You just keep watching that road and time will fly and that crazy Texan and I will be coming down the road with beautiful film of the Amazon. Then, we will talk some more about 'again and again'."

They ate a quick meal and then it was time for Charlie and Luis to leave. In front of Charlie and Geraldo and the four or five people in the café, Luis kissed Daisy long and passionately. "I'll be back soon."

Charlie piled into the jeep after hugging Daisy, and Luis climbed into the driver's seat. Daisy, standing next to the vehicle, put her arms around Luis's neck and gave him one more kiss. He saw tears welling up in her eyes, started the engine, and said to her, "See that sun up in the sky? I'll be holding you again before that sun sets behind those hills. Remember that. Before the sun sets."

And they were gone, dust almost blocking the view of the little jeep as it made its way down the road to the helicopter.

Daisy was getting nervous. The sun was heading rapidly toward the hills where Luis had pointed earlier in the day just before he left. She paced outside the café. Geraldo had joined her as she walked back and forth, straining to see if the jeep was coming up the road. When she heard the familiar sound of the jeep's engine, relief swept over her. She squeezed Geraldo's hand as they literally danced little circles in the dusty street. At last Daisy could make out the jeep and started running towards it when she stopped in her tracks.

There was only one person in the jeep. She couldn't quite make out all the details in all the dust but she recognized the hat Charlie had been wearing that morning.

Luis must be asleep in the back seat.

Charlie pulled the jeep up in front of the café and turned off the engine. He climbed out quickly and walked to Daisy. The look on his face told her everything she needed to know. He didn't have to say a word. She knew something bad had happened.

"Where is Luis, Charlie? Why isn't he with you? What has happened?" Daisy screamed through her tears.

Charlie grabbed Daisy's shoulders and shook her. "Stop. Listen to me, Daisy. I didn't fly in with Luis. The chopper was too small so Luis and the pilot took off without me. We got word about two hours ago that they went down in the dense jungle."

"Went down? What does that mean? Are you telling me they crashed? Charlie?"

Charlie opened his mouth. Then stopped. He took a deep breath and started again. "They crashed, Daisy. Lots of black smoke was seen coming from the crash site. I hired a chopper pilot to fly me to Luis's last known location. Daisy, we were in the air minutes after we heard about the crash and soon I, too, saw the smoke and the wreckage for myself. There's no chance of anyone surviving that. Luis is gone. I'm so sorry."

Charlie held Daisy while she sobbed into his shoulder. He guided her back into the café, to the same corner table where she and Luis had planned the rest of their life just hours before. After a few minutes, Daisy's tears slowed. She dug her fingers into Charlie's arm. "Tell me everything. Don't leave out a thing."

For the first time in a long while, Charlie wished he had a cold beer. Instead, he took a drink of the water the café owner had brought.

Over the next few minutes, he relayed what had transpired that day.

It had been a thirty minute drive to the chopper and when Charlie and Luis rounded a curve in the road they saw the pilot standing by the rear of the aircraft. He looked up and yelled, "Right on time. The weather is great. We shouldn't have any trouble."

Luis parked the jeep near a small shed that held maintenance equipment and he and Charlie unloaded their camera gear. As they began to load the chopper it soon became apparent they could only carry one passenger in addition to the pilot. Charlie had volunteered that they leave some equipment behind. The pilot looked inside carefully, rearranging a few pieces of the baggage but when he crawled out he said, "I'm afraid we have a problem. About half this stuff can go but for sure only one man can go up with me. We'd be risking far too much to try and carry the additional weight of another person."

Charlie had tried to push Luis aside. "Then I'll go." But Luis wouldn't hear of it.

"Good try, my friend and soon-to-be brother-in-law, but if anybody is going up in the chopper today, it is me. I've flown with Alejandro many times and we know what the other is thinking. Also, his English is about as good as your Portuguese, Charlie. I've talked to Miki and I feel I know exactly what he wants from this area. Besides, I've flown over this region many times and I am fairly familiar with the territory. We'll be back before long and there is a small bar about a half mile from the field. It probably doesn't have the greatest atmosphere but you only drink soft drinks anyway. Besides, knowing you, you'll spot a pretty girl and can spend the afternoon charming her. You can hear the motor and come back out and pick me up."

Luis had climbed in beside Alejandro and closed the small door. Within seconds, the tiny helicopter was airborne and Charlie stood waving at his friend. Luis was right. Charlie found a beautiful girl in the cantina up the road from the airfield and between his poor Portuguese and her small knowledge of English, the two managed to spend a comfortable time together.

Around five o'clock Charlie found himself looking at his watch every few minutes and listening for the sound of the chopper. He lost interest in his female friend, excused himself, and headed back to the airfield. When he arrived a man was inside the hangar talking on a radio.

"Everything okay? When is the last time you had voice contact with Luis and Alejandro? Shouldn't they be heading back by now?"

The man at the radio removed his headset.

"Lamento. I am sorry but my English is only fair, Senhor, but I will tell you what I can. I have been in constant contact with several radio spotters along their route. The last I heard was that they had been seen getting down pretty close to a native village. Don't worry, Alejandro is a fine pilot."

It was nearly six o'clock and Charlie had a knot in the middle of his stomach. The radio began to make loud squawking sounds and the man put the headphones back against his ears. Charlie couldn't understand what he was saying but knew from the frantic tone that the news was not good, that Luis and Alejandro would not be flying over the trees in the next few minutes. The old man put down his headset and looked into Charlie's face.

"I am sorry, Senhor. There has been an accident. Your friends are not returning."

"My God, man, what are you saying? What has happened?"

"The chopper went down in the jungle. He said another radio man on the ground saw the little helicopter swoop down and then saw black smoke coming up from the forest. I am sorry. Lamento. Lamento. They are gone. No aircraft can survive that crash. That is a desolate region with no hope of help."

"As I told you," Charlie continued, "I went up to look for the chopper. When we saw the debris at the crash site and the heavy smoke I knew it was bad but I had to search for Luis. I had to know. You had to know. As soon as I landed I got in the jeep and came straight here to you."

Daisy grabbed Charlie's arm. "But you said they crashed near a village. Maybe they got help."

Charlie shook his head. "Only if they survived. It was a small aircraft, Daisy. It just didn't happen."

"But we can send out a search party. We..."

Charlie shook his head.

"Charlie, we can't give up. It's Luis. We can't just leave him out there."

He hugged her close. "Daisy, you have to accept it. Luis isn't coming back."

Daisy looked toward the low hills. The sun had set long ago. Quietly she whispered, "But, Luis, you promised." Then sobs wracked her body.

Twenty-eight

The sound of the chopper engines was deafening in Luis's ears. Combined with the smothering small space inside, Luis was working on the beginning of a major headache. The heat was overwhelming and with perspiration running from his forehead into his eyes, he was finding it harder and harder to lean against the small window and film the seemingly unending rainforest below.

Luis and Alejandro had been airborne for a little over an hour. Soon they would begin the return journey back to the airfield. The camera was heavy on his shoulder and Luis was happy to see that the sun was beginning its slow descent toward the horizon, unseen, somewhere beyond the dense foliage.

"Luis," said Alejandro, half turning to face his friend and passenger, "I'm flying on for four or five more kilometers and then we will need to turn and head back."

"Good. I'm losing the good light anyway." Luis placed his camera back in its case.

Alejandro took the little helicopter down lower into the jungle. Luis turned and asked, "We're pretty close to the top of those trees, aren't we?"

"I see some smoke rising up through the trees. It could be a native village so you might want to get your camera out again. These little villages are scattered throughout the rainforest and are very difficult to spot from the air. That smoke up ahead just might give you some rare pictures. I'll get as close as I can without putting us in any danger," explained Alejandro.

Luis was looking through the lens of the camera when he heard the noise.

"Merda!" Alejandro yelled. "We've been shot at. Get down as low as you can, Luis. I'm going to pull up and get us out of here, fast! Keep your head down. Now!"

More shots rang out and Luis heard his friend call out, "I'm hit! Grab the controls!"

Luis saw Alejandro fall hard against the door, blood turning his tan shirt a bright red. Gunfire did a chilling tap dance on the left side of the chopper. No matter how hard he tried, Luis could not force the controls to move in any direction. The chopper was dropping like a rock, headed straight for the forest below.

Luis was cold. Pain shot arrows through his whole body. He opened his eyes and turned his head but focusing was an impossibility. He couldn't stay awake and the harder he tried, the quicker he disappeared into the darkness and silence of a world where he had never been before.

Twenty-nine

Charlie and Daisy drove back to Colima that night. The following day, they drove on to Fortaleza and then flew back to Rio. Daisy said very little during the entire trip back. Her mind was in the jungle, alternating between hovering over a streak of black smoke, and remembering Luis and their last night together.

Once back at the beach house, Daisy retreated to her room. She spent her waking hours staring at the hills from her bedroom window. Charlie did his best to encourage her to eat, to engage her in talk of the project, to make plans for baby Clay once they got back to the States. But after several failed attempts, he finally gave up.

On the second day, Charlie suggested they go to A Candeia.

"Don't you miss Clay?" he asked.

Daisy stared at him. "I'm not sure it's a good idea if I see him anymore. I don't think I have anything to offer him. He deserves a mother who can love him. That's not me. I feel so dead inside."

"Well, then, let's go see Isabella and tell her that. She deserves to know. If you've decided not to go through with the adoption, she should hear it from you. And not over the phone either. You owe her that much."

Daisy sighed. "You're right."

An hour later, Daisy was back in the familiar living room, staring up at the Christ statue while Charlie went in search of Isabella.

When Isabella walked in, it was apparent that Charlie had filled her in. Her eyes were narrowed in anger.

"What's this I hear? You've given up on your baby?"

"He's not my baby. He never was. He's yours and he deserves better than me right now. He needs a full-time mother. Not some woman who trots around the world and gets people killed."

"I see. You seem to have this all figured out."

"I do."

"All right. I do have a couple in mind. I recently heard from a man and his wife in Tennessee who can fly down next week. All of their paperwork is in order and we can probably place Clay very quickly. He won't even know the difference." Isabella turned to go. At that moment, Margarita walked in holding Clay.

"Here he is, all warm from his nap. I told him his mother was here to see him," she sang out, unaware of the conversation that had just occurred.

Isabella motioned to Margarita. "I am sorry, Daisy has changed her mind. Take Clay back to the nursery."

Margarita turned to go. Clay cried and Daisy jumped out of her seat, all composure gone.

She snatched Clay from Margarita's arms. "Don't cry. I'm here. I'm here." Tears coursed down Daisy's cheeks. She kissed Clay's face and held him close.

"Isabella, please don't give him away," Daisy said. "Please. You won't, will you?

"Yes, I would give Clay to new parents. He needs a home and love," Isabella said as she stood next to Daisy. She reached over and gently stroked Daisy's hair. "But I have already promised him to a lovely young woman from Washington, D.C. Although she is very upset at a great loss in her life right now, I believe she still wants this baby as her son. Doesn't she?"

Daisy just nodded and held Clay close.

"Daisy, I know your grief is not going away for a long time. In fact, it may never leave you. But you must go on with life – your life and this baby's. He has no choice and neither do you. You have made a commitment to him and he is counting on you. Do not let him down, or yourself. I asked you before if you still wanted Clay. I will ask it no more."

Daisy sat back at the window and looked up at the Christ statue, Clay now quiet in her arms. "Yes, I do want Clay. I have lost one of my Brazilian loves but I do not intend to lose another. If it means I'll have to fight the whole country of Brazil to get Clay out of here, then I guess I had better get busy. I know Luis would not give up without a fight. He left me with wonderful memories and so much love – enough for me and for Clay."

Daisy looked down at the black-haired little baby and whispered, "Clay Luis Gardner, there have been some major changes in our lives but nothing the two of us can't handle. You just hang in there a little while longer and before you know it, you and I will be headed for home."

Isabella walked away, stood in the door, watched Daisy hold the tiny dark-haired baby, and smiled.

THIRTY

Charlie helped Daisy move some of her things back into one of the little rooms at A Candeia that afternoon. She wanted to be as close to Clay as she could until they both left for home.

"You take care of Clay. I'll take care of the film. Fair enough?"

"Charlie, sweet person, I am thankful for you. Yes, it is fair enough."

That afternoon, Beto and Luci visited again. Daisy had just laid a sleeping Clay in his bassinette in the nursery. She found Beto, Luci, and Isabella sitting at the kitchen table. There were small cakes and glasses of fruit juice set out in front of them. Daisy sat across from Luci and sighed. Luci placed her hand over Daisy's.

"You look so tired."

"I am but it's more emotional than physical. Even though the judge has signed off on Clay's paperwork, there is still much to be done. I just can't seem to find the energy to do it though."

"Daisy, you need some rest. You're exhausted," said Luci.

"I can't afford to rest. There will be plenty of time for that when Clay is safe with me in Washington."

"But you'll be no use to anyone if you wear yourself out."

"I won't. But I think I will go lie down for a while, if you'll excuse me. Isabella, will you send Charlie to my room when he comes in? I need to talk to him."

Daisy was sitting up in bed, reading when Charlie popped his head into her room.

"Hey, sis." Charlie leaned against the door frame. "Isabella said you were looking for me."

Daisy gave Charlie a big smile. She patted the side of her bed and he sat next to her. He smiled broadly and she realized that he really had many expressions just like her father - his father. It was a familiar, good face. She was surprised she had never noticed it before.

"What? You're staring at me," he said.

"I was just noticing how much you look like Dad."

Charlie put his head down. "Is that going to be a problem?"

"Are you kidding? I think it's great." She playfully poked him in the stomach. "Just watch out for that Gardner gut when you get older, though. But let's talk about something else. With everything that has been going on lately, we haven't talked much about the film and we need to get it finished. I gave Miki a deadline and I would like to keep it or come very close. We still have no film of the Amazon region and Brazil's story wouldn't be complete if that were not a large part of it. I'm not sure what to do about that. I had mentioned to Luis before..." Daisy's voice caught and she took a deep breath. "I had talked to Luis about using some stock footage but he wouldn't hear of it. Maybe now we should."

"Well, I've been thinking about that, too, and I think I have a solution. I would like to go back to the Northeast and finish the job Luis began and..."

"No, absolutely out of the question. I will not lose another person I love. Don't even think about it!"

"Hear me out, Daisy. Listen to me. I want to fly into Fortaleza and take a small team with me and go into the jungle by jeep and when we can't go any further that way, then we hike the rest of the journey. I've already talked with some photographers who have great experience in the Amazon region and they are based in

Fortaleza. They have lined up three guys who know every inch of that place up there so I won't be alone on any part of this trip. I feel good about it. It will take a little longer than we had planned and we won't be able to get quite the footage that we would have by helicopter but I think this is a good compromise. Unless, you want me to rent a helicopter again?"

"No. I won't risk any more lives on this project. Let's go with your original plan, Charlie."

"That's what I thought you'd say. Then, this is the only way. We have to finish the job we started. Luis would want us to. And that way, you can continue with all this legal work while I head north."

Daisy looked out her window, then turned to face Charlie.

"You're right. But you have to promise me you'll turn back at the first sign of trouble. I love you, Charlie. I don't want anything to happen to you."

She placed her hand over Charlie's and squeezed. "Thank you for being here for me. The remainder of the film is in good hands and I promise not to worry about it if you promise to be careful."

They hugged and Charlie said softly in Daisy's ear, "Thanks for trusting me with all of this. The documentary will be fantastic. I promise."

Soon after Charlie left, Daisy heard Beto and Luci leave as well. An idea formed in her mind and Daisy got up in search of Isabella. Daisy knew she had to see Vovo Maria and tell her what had happened to her beloved Luis. She walked to the study and found Isabella working on her many folders. She asked Isabella if she would go with her to Vovo's to translate. Also, most importantly, she wanted to take Clay for she hoped this would soften the terrible message she had to deliver.

"Isabella, I have a pretty good idea where Vovo Maria lives. Her house is in the extreme south part of Zona Norte and the day Luis and I went there he pointed out an observatory on the back side of Tijuca Forest. The house is down that same street and I would recognize it with no problem. I'll always remember the bright yellow house with the almost iridescent blue shutters."

Daisy, Isabella, and the baby took a cab from A Candeia and soon Daisy saw the familiar house with all the steps. She prayed she was strong enough for what lay ahead.

Josephina came to the door and welcomed them in, then took them to the back of the house where Daisy had first met Vovo Maria.

Recognizing Daisy, Vovo smiled broadly and said, "Boa tarde, pero onde Luis?"

"She wished us good day and asked where Luis is," said Isabella who was now kneeling by Vovo's wheelchair.

Holding Clay, Daisy stood by Vovo and as she talked to her, Isabella smoothly and with no hesitations translated her words.

"Vovo Maria, I am so sad to have to bring you this news of your Luis…" and Daisy told the story as Charlie had related it to her. Vovo Maria's eyes never left Daisy's and her shoulders dropped and silent sobs showed her pain.

Then, Daisy held Clay up to Vovo and with no sound Luis's grandmother reached her arms out to hold him. She stroked his hair, touched his face, and kissed both of his tiny hands.

"Vovo Maria, I want you to know that Luis and I were planning to be married and together we were going to adopt this baby boy. His full name is Clay Luis and his last name would have been Campos. Luis had such a strong bond with this baby. They both were born in favelas. Luis was anxious to be his father and care for him. Can you see, Vovo, that Clay has eyes just like Luis's? Just like yours. As I look at you now I can feel Luis looking out at me. You and Luis were so much alike. I had to come here today and tell you the news but I also wanted you to meet your grandson, Clay Luis. You will always be his Brazilian Vovo and we will come and visit and stay close. Luis would have liked that. I will like that. We will have our own little family here in Rio." Daisy stood and kissed Vovo on her forehead.

Vovo motioned for Josephina and whispered in her ear. Within seconds Josephina returned with something wrapped in tissue paper and handed it to Vovo. Vovo handed the small packet to Daisy and as Isabella translated, Daisy listened. Her eyes filled to the brim as Isabella spoke Vovo's words to her.

"She says, 'This little bundle holds a lock of Luis's hair. I used to cut it for him when he was a little boy and one time I decided to keep a piece of my darling baby. One lock of his dark hair. See how it curls, even now, after all these years.'"

She unfolded the paper and held the piece of hair, tied with a little blue ribbon, next to Clay's head. Isabella smiled and repeated Vovo's words, "She says, 'See, it is the same color. That is a very good sign.'" Vovo put the lock back in the paper and handed it to Daisy.

After the goodbyes, they were almost at the door when Vovo spoke again.

"Muito obrigada. Meu amor sempre." and she waved until the front door closed behind them.

Isabella was having a difficult time getting her words out but at last said, "She said, 'Thank you so much. My love always.'"

For the first time in days, Daisy felt a small measure of peace.

THIRTY-ONE

A stabbing hot pain in his leg awakened Luis. He had no control over his eyes. He worked hard to see his hand clearly. His head was throbbing and he felt nauseous.

Suddenly, he was aware of a voice calling to him in the distance. He tried to concentrate on the words being yelled and struggled to sit up. The voice yelled again, closer now.

"Wake up! Hey, do you hear me!"

Luis opened his eyes. A tall bearded man stood before him, a rifle slung over his shoulder. "You speak English?" Luis asked. His throat felt scratched and raw and he could barely get the words out.

"Good," the man said, looking down at him. "Glad I don't have to speak that God-forsaken language with you. Here," he bent and offered Luis a wooden bowl filled with a pungent brown liquid. "Drink this. It's some kind of soup these Indians around here stir up. It's supposed to be medicinal. It'll keep you alive long enough to tell me what I want to know."

Luis sipped the liquid and was surprised to find it warm, almost good.

"Okay, that's enough." The man grabbed the cup from Luis's mouth and flung it aside. "We need to talk. Now!"

He sat down on a mat next to Luis and lit a cigarette. By the dim light of the match's flame Luis saw that he was in a small thatched hut with a dirt floor.

"Where am I?" he asked.

"Somewhere in the Amazon rainforest," the man answered with a sneer. "Is that close enough for you?"

"How did I get here?" Luis asked.

"Well, your little bumble bee had some engine trouble," he patted his rifle, "and just fell out of the sky. Your friend didn't make it. I pulled you out of the wreckage and brought you here. Now," he leaned in closer to Luis, "I need to know what you were taking pictures of. I found your camera in the pile of junk that's left of your chopper. You taking pictures of my little set-up here? And, who paid you to take these pictures?"

"I was filming for a documentary on Brazil. A history professor hired us to make this film."

The man kicked Luis' leg, sending shards of pain through his body. "Don't lie to me. You're alive as long as you tell me what I need to know."

"I'm not lying. I thought I was filming a native village."

The man was quiet for a few moments and then spoke in hushed tones to Luis. "I've worked a long time setting up my little empire here in the Amazon and nobody is gonna mess it up for me."

"What are you talking about?" asked Luis.

"You don't need to know. But I could use a little help and since you speak English, you'll do. As long as you make yourself useful, I'll let you live."

Luis sat up a little straighter. "What do you want?"

"Don't get any ideas. I'm going to kill you when the time comes. You already know too much and I don't buy your story about any documentary. You messed up real bad this time, fella. But in the meantime, I may have use for you." The man stood and reached for the overturned bowl. "Here, drink what's left of this. You're going to need it."

Luis took the bowl and downed the now cold liquid.

"I have to go into Fortaleza in the morning and meet a plane," continued the man. "I won't be gone a day and the two tough-looking natives outside this hut will watch you for me so don't try anything. They have orders to kill you if you do."

Early the next morning Luis heard loud talking outside the hut. He twisted to look through the narrow cracks in the bamboo and palm fronds that made up the sides of the crude hut. He could see the man loading up boxes and plastic bags on a sled-like contraption. Then he heard him yell at the two natives in Portuguese, "Do not leave this spot or when I come back I'll track you down and hang you both from one of these trees."

Luis watched as the man picked up ropes that were attached to the sled and slowly headed off into the jungle, pulling his treasure.

Minutes later, Luis saw the two natives pick up their spears. They talked animatedly, pointed to the thick jungle, and took off.

Luis knew it was now or never. He stood and tested his leg. Almost unbearable pain forced him to limp. He tried a few steps and knew he'd have to ignore the pain as best he could. He rummaged through the junk piled on the dirt floor and grabbed what was left of his jacket. He also found a canteen of what he hoped was safe water. He slung the canteen over his shoulder, and stumbled out of the hut into the small clearing.

Once outside the little dwelling, Luis realized he had no idea about direction. He stood in front of the little lean-to, wondering which way to choose. His leg ached and throbbed, and he knew it was going to be slow going in his condition. But to stay was certain death. He looked up through the jungle's thick foliage, looking for any signs of the sun. Making a quick decision, he limped off into what he hoped was the direction of Colima, then Fortaleza – and Daisy.

THIRTY-TWO

The next day, Daisy and Isabella made their way to the main office of the Brazilian Federal Police in downtown Rio. They walked down the hill and jumped on an open-sided bus to ride to police headquarters. Here they would show Daisy's passport and apply for Clay's. We're getting closer, Clay.

They entered the large building and walked straight to a window whose sign read, Passaporte. Fortunately, there was no one in line so Daisy was able to show Clay's tiny passport photo and request a passport for him. The uniformed man behind the desk filled out some papers, took Clay's photo from her and then told Daisy, "Now, I must see your passport."

Daisy removed it from the zipped compartment in her large leather purse and placed it on the counter, both her hands gripping the top of the document. The man said, "I must take this and present it to my superior. I shall return it. Wait here ," and he disappeared from sight.

An empty feeling gripped Daisy's stomach and Isabella said softly, "This has to be done. Better say a prayer, though."

The man who had taken Daisy's passport was nowhere in sight and according to the large clock on the wall, she had been waiting for over half an hour. Another man walked up behind the counter and Daisy asked him about her passport. His answer was short and to the point, "It takes time."

The man Daisy had given her passport to returned but went to another person in line.

"Excuse me," said Daisy. "If we are finished here, I need you to return my passport."

"What do you mean? I do not have your passport nor have I seen it," he answered. "Perhaps you have misplaced it."

"I put my passport on the counter, as you asked, and you took it and went behind that partition. You said you had to show it to your superior. Now you tell me you have not seen my passport. I can assure you, sir, that I have not misplaced that important document. I gave it to you and you did not bring it back and..."

Isabella stepped up to the counter and pulled Daisy away. "That is enough. If you make an enemy here it will stop the remainder of the legal process. The Federal Police run this country and even though this man is lying, don't make waves. It will only get you in trouble with the police and you will need them until your plane leaves the runway for America. They are involved in every single step from now on."

"But, what can I do, Isabella?" Daisy whispered. "They have my passport and I can do nothing without it. What can we do?" Fear gripped Daisy's heart. The man behind the counter walked around the partition once more and returned with two other men. One uniformed man with a black moustache asked, "What seems to be the problem?"

Daisy repeated her story.

"I am afraid you are very mistaken. I am his superior and I have not seen your passport. The Federal Police are honorable people, and we are trying to help you, but you must be honest with us. No one here, and there are witnesses, has seen your passport. Why don't you leave, retrieve your passport, and come back. Then, when all things are in order, we will help you fill out the papers you need. We only want to be of assistance, senhora."

Isabella tugged on Daisy's arm and pulled her toward the back of the room, out of earshot of the Police.

"Daisy, don't let them fool you. They know who I am and have probably been following us to Fuegas and back each day. Because of what happened at the funabem, they would like nothing better than to arrest me for obstructing justice when we took the babies and Roberto back to Rio. That's why I can't speak up."

"But I just can't leave here without my passport, Isabella," said Daisy, her voice shaking.

"Well, you don't have any choice right now. We have to play this their way for now. Tell the man we will be back in the morning and see if he makes any positive comments," said Isabella.

Daisy turned to the first officer who was back now behind the counter. "I will return in the morning," she said.

He looked at her and smiled. "Excelente, and don't forget to bring your passport with you."

Daisy and Isabella walked out into the noisy Brazilian traffic and stood on the sidewalk, waiting for the next bus. Soon, one creaked by, belching smoke. They paid their fare and sat toward the back so as not to be overheard.

"What's really going on?" Daisy asked. "Why did they so obviously lie about my passport today? What will happen now?"

"Daisy, the Federal Police, like Judge de Silva, are all trying to stop you from getting this baby out of the country. Everyone is doing all they can to discourage you so you will give up. I'm sure word has spread about what happened at the funabem. And," Isabella added, "never forget for one minute, they can bring everything to a halt. There will be nothing on the books that you even applied, officials will say they never saw you and they will block you even if you happen to make any ground at all."

They rode in silence for a block or two before Isabella spoke again.

"From my heart, I do not think our task is impossible. I respect your diligence and fighting spirit on Clay's behalf. I just haven't figured out exactly what key will open the doors, if only for a little while. From past experience, I know that in every system of government there are little chinks in the armor of those in authority. I believe we will find a weak link or two that will allow us to get the necessary things done. It will be slow moving but as long as we are moving at all, that, my dear, is progress. Progresso."

The bus stopped on Cosme Velho and the two tired women began their hike up the steep hill to the house.

THIRTY-THREE

Isabella and Daisy were back at the Federal Police building the next morning. Once again, Daisy addressed the man who had taken her passport the day before.

"Bom dia," said Daisy, trying to sound as cheery as possible.

He smiled at her as though they had never argued.

"I see you have come back. May I have your passport, please?" he asked.

Daisy sighed. "As I may have mentioned yesterday," she said articulating every word precisely, "I presented my passport to you, and you took it into the back to show to someone. I have not seen it since."

Continuing to smile, the man whose name tag read Emilio, said, "I am sorry if you have lost your passport, but I will say again that I never saw it. I'm afraid I can be of no further service to you without that document."

"Do you mind going behind that partition and looking around? I promise you that I saw you take my passport, leave this front counter and return saying you never saw it. You held it in your hands. I saw you. Will you at least look for it, please?"

"Just a moment," and Emilio left the front counter.

Emilio returned just moments later and said, "I have looked everywhere and your passport is not here and no one else has seen it either. I suggest you go to the American Embassy and apply for another one."

Isabella touched Daisy's arm and motioned with her eyes that they should leave the building.

Once outside, Isabella said, "We need to talk. Let's find a small street café, have some coffee, and see if we can come up with any solutions."

They found a small café a block away and sat at a small round table under a bright red awning. Isabella ordered two cups of the dark liquid for both of them. Daisy added lots of cream, but as she expected, Isabella drank hers black and hot.

"Isabella, the trips to Fuegas took so long and now this. What do you think is going to happen? I'm stuck without my passport. Do you think they will return it to me? I have absolutely no idea what to do next, do you?"

"I think it's time we talk to my attorney, Alberto, and see if he has any thoughts. He is well-versed in Brazilian law. Let's finish up here and go back to the house. I'll try to get in touch with him this afternoon."

While Daisy bathed and fed Clay, Isabella was at her desk trying to get through to Alberto. His secretary finally told her he was at the minor's court and would telephone her when he returned to his office.

With Clay asleep, Daisy and Isabella decided to have an early dinner. Isabella sliced some homemade bread, and added cheese and ham. She then heated up a waffle iron and placed each sandwich on the bottom part and pulled the top down over the sandwich. Soon, the sweet aroma of ham and cheese filled the small kitchen.

"That smells wonderful," Daisy said as she took a seat at the small table in the kitchen.

"It was a favorite food when my children were growing up. I'll just add a bowl of fresh fruit and this will be our meal. The sandwich is pretty filling and we both are going to need our energy."

Halfway through their meal, the phone rang and Isabella picked up the extension.

"Isabella here. Oh, Alberto, thank you for returning my call. Daisy and I are in a bit of a legal jam with the federal police and I wanted to know if there is anything you can do." Isabella went on to relate to him what had happened with Daisy's passport.

After a few minutes of conversation, some in Portuguese, Isabella hung up. "Alberto said he does not like to get involved in the affairs of the federal police. He is an attorney for the city of Rio and the federal police have jurisdiction over the entire country of Brazil so they look down on anyone other than their own legal teams. They run the country and would probably pay no heed to anything Alberto tried to say. Even though he is an attorney, he carries absolutely no weight with the police. He just said he thinks he would hurt far more than help. He also pointed out that there is no evidence that the police have your passport. It's your word against the police and that does not hold any power at all."

Daisy looked down at the table top, fear gripping her. "I guess that's it then."

"He did say he would come here in the morning so you could ask him questions yourself," Isabella continued. "He thinks he might still have a lot of information that could be helpful. You must continue to have faith, Daisy. Somehow everything will work out. I honestly believe this."

After breakfast the next morning, the large bell outside the kitchen clanged, signaling that someone had arrived. Daisy opened the door to a very tall, curly-haired, handsome older man who extended his hand and said, "I am Alberto Morais. You must be Daisy. Let's sit and talk and see if we can find any solution to your current problem. I assume Isabella told you I am not optimistic though."

They sat in the living room. Someone had placed a tray of tea and sweet breads in front of the sofa. Daisy could smell the hot tea, brewing in the pot alongside two cups.

With warm tea cups in their hands, Alberto spoke first.

"Daisy, with daily images of violence on television and

newspapers some feel there seems to be no other existence for Brazil. I believe, at the funabem, you got a small look at what I'm talking about, but things are much worse than you know. Without going into detail, let me just say that violence against children in this country is extreme. Of course, the street children are a problem because there are so many of them. In just six months last year alone, over two hundred children were murdered."

Daisy gasped. "Oh my God, I had no idea."

"The problem is overwhelming. Approximately ten million children make their living on the streets in Brazil. You can imagine what that has done to the tourism business here. There are little thieves everywhere tourists go. I have seen some with two or three authentic Rolex watches in their pockets. If some get murdered..." He shrugged and let Daisy come to her own conclusions.

Daisy was quiet for a moment and then said, "If Clay is not adopted and taken out of Brazil, could he wind up like these children?"

"Without a doubt," Alberto answered quickly. "Daisy, I'm telling you all this because I want you to know just what kind of people you are up against and I want you to promise that you will keep fighting. Perhaps you will be one of the lucky few who somehow can get this baby out of the country. But, I also want you to know just what an insurmountable government brick wall you are facing. I wish I could assist you but even though I am an attorney the law doesn't work for me or people I represent."

Isabella walked into the room and sat down on the sofa. She had heard most of what Alberto had said.

"Daisy, I know all of this is so discouraging," she said helping herself to some of the tea. "Most people outside Brazil have no idea just how bad it is. Even Alberto, a servant of the law, can do nothing to help you. His best help, I think, is to be honest with you and present the best, most realistic picture of Rio. It helps to know the face of the enemy and to know as much about them as you can. He has given you some good information today."

"Well, I certainly have the picture now," answered Daisy. "It's still hard for me to understand why they fight so hard to keep one infant from leaving the country. It seems to me that it would just be one less street child." She faced Alberto. "Are you telling me that it is impossible to get Clay out?"

"No, I am not saying that," said Alberto, "but it is tricky business. Daisy, listen to me carefully now," and he moved in closer to her as though he was telling a secret. "Do you know who your very strongest ally is?"

"You?" she answered.

"No, as I have said, I cannot help at all."

"My government in the States?"

"No."

"Well, I don't have a clue then."

Alberto looked at Isabella and smiled. "Your best ally is Isabella."

Daisy looked from Alberto to Isabella and started to speak but Alberto interrupted her. "I know Isabella has made some enemies because she is doing all she can to get babies out of Brazil and she has not always been quiet with her feelings about the military government that watches her every move. But there is a certain respect for her and they know, I think, that she is a strong-willed woman who doesn't ever give up and they are aware that she will do whatever it takes to get Clay and others like him out of Brazil. They know she has connections all over this city and she will pull every string to get 'her' babies to freedom."

The following afternoon, Daisy and Isabella returned to the Federal Police office and once again inquired about Daisy's passport. Emilio motioned for her to come to the far end of the front counter. In hushed tones, he said, "I have found your passport and I have put the necessary stamp in it. Here," and he reached into his inside jacket pocket and slid it across the counter, "put this quickly into your purse and leave."

"I want to thank you for…"

Isabella, who had been watching the transaction gripped Daisy's arm, and said, "Do as he said. Walk straight out that door and do not look back."

On the street Daisy asked, "But, I don't understand. Why now?

What happened to change his mind?"

"Those are questions we will never know the answers to, Daisy. A look. A word from someone we don't even know. All that matters is that you are now in possession of your passport, the most precious thing you have. I, personally, didn't know if you would ever see it again. Now we can get to the remainder of the work. Let's head to the American Embassy and apply for Clay's visa. Want to walk or take a cab?" Isabella asked.

Daisy was smiling broadly and she answered, "I feel like I could fly but let's walk. I'm so relieved. We're a step closer, aren't we, Isabella?"

"Yes we are, my friend. Yes we are," and Isabella took Daisy's arm as they walked briskly down the busy streets of Rio headed for Avenida Wilson and the American Embassy.

THIRTY-FOUR

That evening, Daisy and Isabella sat in their now familiar places at the desks in the living room. They had been talking animatedly about one of the babies and her parents who were on their way down to adopt her.

"Despite all the hoops we have to go through, I am both amazed and grateful that I am still able to get babies out and on their way to a new life," Isabella said. She reached for Clay's well-worn folder and leafed through it. After a few moments she looked up and was actually smiling at Daisy.

"I've checked everything and I can see light for the first time. We'll get Clay's visa tomorrow, we have the papers from Fuegas, your stamped passport and the visa application from the Federal Police. Now, I must find and decide on just the right translator to turn all these papers from Portuguese to English and then, the final step. Once translated, and with a copy of all the papers for you to keep with you forever, we then send the other package with all Clay's legal work to Immigration and Naturalization Services in Washington, D.C. It usually takes forty-eight hours for them to check everything and return them to us. When that's done and with a statement from INS saying everything is in order, I believe, Daisy, that we can book a flight home for you and Clayzinho."

The following morning Isabella was on the phone for hours trying to locate a translator. She wanted to get Clay's file to INS and back before any more problems arose.

Daisy came and sat at the desk across from Isabella and watched her work.

"Well, no surprise, Daisy," Isabella said after she had spoken to the fifth potential translator. "We seem to have come upon another little roadblock. There are only certain government-approved translators whose work will be accepted on official documents. So, we have to use one on the government list."

"And?" Daisy had a feeling she wasn't going to like the answer.

"And, all five translators on the list have refused. When I gave them either your name or Clay's, they cut me off and made flimsy excuses."

"Why?"

"I believe word has spread that you are not to get Clay out of Brazil. They know about the funabem and your film work here and are being very obstinate. Whatever the Federal Police tell the translators, that is what they will do. They get a kickback from the work they do for them. Daisy, I don't mean to frighten you, but these translators can stop everything."

"But, Isabella, the judge signed the papers, the Federal Police even helped."

"Yes, I know, but we cannot send any of this to the INS without the papers being in the original Portuguese and also copies in English. All of these papers have to be on file in Rio as well as in the U.S and you have to carry a complete copy of everything with you back to the States or they won't let you enter your country at the airport in D.C." Isabella opened a tattered book on her desk.

"I have two more names I can possibly use. One is marked retired but I will call anyway. Her name is Julieta Brita. I have worked with her in the past and she is excellent but I haven't seen her in years."

Daisy got up and brought Clay to the desk and quietly played with him while Isabella made her call. The conversation seemed long but soon Isabella placed the phone back on the hook.

"We have to go to her home. She said she would do the work but I have to see her myself. We have to be so careful. Wrap Clay up and let's take him for a ride. This young man hasn't seen much of his city. It is not far from here."

The dune buggy pulled up in front of a stone house with bunches of colorful flowers surrounding the small house. As they walked up the cobblestone steps, the front door opened, and a white-haired woman greeted them. She smiled broadly when she recognized Isabella. The two women spoke rapidly in Portuguese for a few minutes and then Isabella turned and introduced Daisy and Clay.

The old woman reached out and touched Clay's little hands. They walked into the small house and Julieta motioned for them to sit at a table near a large window. Julieta smiled down at Clay and then looked up at Daisy.

"I will be happy to help you if I can. My eyesight is almost gone but I get by with my best friend." She picked up an oversized magnifying glass lying over a newspaper on the table. "It takes me time but I am accurate."

"Does the government still recognize your work?" Isabella asked. "I noticed your name is still on an old list of translators. We just must be sure they will accept you."

"Yes, I am still recognized as a government translator and just finished some work for the Federal Police. I am qualified and ready to assist you."

Julieta looked down at Clay, lying quietly in Daisy's arms, and said, "I am doing this because it means one more Brazilian child will have a chance to live. I will work around the clock and have this completed for INS to inspect in twenty-four hours. Trust me. I think God guided you to me. This will be a labor of love. This beautiful child will remain in my memory always and I am glad to do the work. I usually charge large sums because the government can afford it. For you, and do not disagree with me, I am translating this as a gift from my heart."

Daisy couldn't believe her ears. They were on their way!

Back in the car, Daisy asked, "Could Julieta get into any trouble by doing this for me?"

"I don't think so because she doesn't do much of this anymore and they don't check her carefully now. They know she is almost blind, too, so I think she will be safe. If she doesn't charge, there will be no record of payment anywhere. But, she will initial each page that she translates so there is that identifying mark. We will just pray no one will notice."

Clay started to fuss on the way home. Daisy put him over her left shoulder and patted his back. "I think this little guy has put on several pounds since we rescued him from the funabem. I can't wait to get him home to meet his Grandmother in Texas."

Isabella reached over and patted Daisy's knee. "That day will make me happy, too."

The call from Julieta came the following afternoon. The papers were ready to be picked up. Isabella and Daisy left immediately and then hurried to the Post Office to mail the precious package. They both held the parcel and placed a kiss on it. Then they handed it to the supervisor who promised to take it to the plane personally.

As the two drove away from the Post Office, Daisy said, "Isabella, I feel so empty. All our work, our tears, our frustrations, Clay's life, it's all been wrapped up in that little package and is out of our hands,"

"And will soon be in the hands of the immigration people who will check it and then send it back. We then get Clay's visa and you will be on your way home."

For the next two days all Daisy could do was watch the clock on the wall in the kitchen. Isabella would occasionally walk through, look in her direction and say, "Soon, Daisy. Soon."

Isabella made several calls to the Federal Express office but the answer was always the same. Nothing had arrived from D.C. for Daisy Gardner. And, as always, they promised to call the minute anything came in.

On the morning of the third day, Isabella brought Daisy a cup of tea as she was sitting by the window looking up at her beloved Christ statue.

"I have a suggestion to make," said Isabella, her voice sounding weary. "We have waited long enough. I am going to telephone INS in D.C. and put a tracker on this package. Perhaps it is on its way right now, but we need to know."

Daisy followed Isabella to her desk and sipped her tea while watching her dial the number of INS in Washington. Isabella talked to someone quite awhile and then was transferred to another person.

"Yes, let me give you the return address once more," and she repeated the street and numbers. "Yes, I will hold."

Silence for several agonizing minutes and then Isabella said, "Yes, I am speaking for Daisy Gardner. I am Isabella Paes, her friend. I see. Are you sure? What can be done? Please call me as soon as you can." Isabella hung up the phone.

"What? Didn't they receive the package?" Daisy asked.

"Yes, they received the package by air on the same day we sent it. But they have no record of where it went after it was initially checked in. It seems that at the moment your package is missing."

"But every single legal paper we need is in that..."

"Yes, I know, Daisy."

THIRTY-FIVE

"Daisy, all we can do is wait, as nerve-wracking as that is," Isabella said. "I do know the package will arrive at Federal Express and they will notify us. Now, the good part, and we must concentrate on this, is that as soon as the package is found and gone over by INS officials, they will send off a certified letter to the American Embassy saying everything is approved. They won't accept phone calls so we wait for that communication, too. But, that will be the last order of business and then you can go to the Embassy and pick up Clay's visa and be on your flight home."

Daisy said nothing. She turned and looked out the window at the Christ statue. Visions of Luis came unbidden. A tear trickled down her check and she didn't even bother to wipe it away.

Isabella stood behind her and patted her back, not unlike the way Daisy patted Clay.

"Why don't you get things packed because when the papers get back here things will move faster than you can imagine. You may hear about the approval in the morning and have to be on a flight the same evening."

While Daisy folded things into her suitcase, she mentally ran through people she might know in D.C. who could help her. She knew Miki didn't know anything about this situation and would be in over his head when it came to INS issues. Then she thought of the perfect person – U.S. Senator Howell Heflin.

She had worked with him the year before on a documentary he had narrated about his home state of Alabama. They had become friends during the project and he had told her that if she needed any help with anything to let him know. Now was surely that time.

Daisy ran into the kitchen and found Isabella chopping vegetables. She grabbed the knife from her hand and spun her around. "Isabella, I know someone who can help."

"Who?"

"Senator Howell Heflin in D.C. Let's call him. Now."

Isabella followed Daisy into the living room and between the two of them they eventually got through to Senator Heflin's secretary in Washington.

She remembered Daisy. Daisy gave her a short version of her problem and was immediately transferred to the Senator. She recognized his deep, very Southern voice.

"Hello, Daisy. I hear you need a little Southern miracle worked down there in Brazil. What can I do for you?"

Daisy told him about the missing legal papers. "I have no idea what to do. This is the end of the fourth day and I am stuck here in Rio until they find those papers and send them back, with INS's official stamp, along with a letter to the American Embassy. As you know, I can't get Clay's visa without these things. If they are lost permanently, it is a disaster because I could never get this far in the process again. Sir, I am so very close and it's been amazing that I'm almost to the finish line. But Senator Heflin, I'm very frightened."

Just as she had expected he would, he said in his slow, calming voice, "Well, now, let's don't worry until we know we have something to worry about. I'll get right on this and I promise you I'll find the right person who can tell me the status of your papers. Do you know if the Embassy there will accept a phone call regarding the visa?"

"No, the Embassy has a policy that they will not accept any phone calls at all. The communiqué has to be sent by mail. What do we do?" asked Daisy.

"Leave all this in my hands. I'll get back to you as soon as I know something. I'm glad you called me, Daisy. I will do everything in my power to help. Remember, don't worry."

Daisy hung up the phone and relayed Senator Heflin's message to Isabella.

"I think this is the only chance we have," said Isabella. "Can you trust this man to look into this right away or do you think he'll get around to it in a day or so?"

"Above all, I trust this man. I think he is probably on his way from the Capitol to INS right this moment. He does what he promises and I'll hear from him one way or the other."

The phone rang and both Daisy and Isabella jumped. It was Charlie.

"Are you back in Rio? I'm so relieved. Tell me you finished?"

"Yes, we are! We got some great stuff, Daisy. You're going to love it but, no, I'm not on my way back. I'm still in Fortaleza."

"Why, Charlie? I could really use you here. I'm waiting now on word about the immigration papers. As soon as we get them cleared, I have to leave with Clay. It could be as soon as tonight. Is there any way you can get here?"

"That's wonderful news about Clay but there's no way I can make it there in time. Besides, I need to take care of something here. Trust me, I can't leave right at the moment. Look, don't you let anything stop you from getting Clay out of the country. I'll see you at the christening in Washington. I promise. Nothing will keep me from being my nephew's Godfather."

As soon as Daisy and Isabella sat down for lunch the phone rang again. They looked at each other. Isabella told Daisy to answer it. "All the calls now, I think, will be for you."

"Hello, may I speak to Daisy Gardner?" the voice on the other end of the phone asked.

"This is she. Who is calling, please?"

"I am Luna Vincenes from the American Embassy. Ambassador Donald Morrow, has asked me to call you with a message."

Daisy wanted to scream into the phone, "Hurry up. Just

say it," but she waited as she heard Luna shuffling papers in the background.

"I am sorry I am so slow but I have to read this part to you: Immigration in Washington D.C. has approved your papers concerning a Clay Luis Gardner. All the legal work is in order. The American Embassy can now issue him a visa and he is released to leave the country."

Tears ran down Daisy's face. She gave the thumbs up sign to Isabella who raised both fists in the air in victory. "Oh, before you hang up," Daisy said to Luna, "is there a signature or name on the bottom of that paper?"

"Yes, and this is very unusual, but this message was received and accepted telephonically, something that has never happened before. In answer to your question about the signature, the Embassy operator wrote down the name of the person making the call. It is a Howell Heflin, United States Senator."

As soon as Daisy got off the phone, Isabella looked through her thick address book for the number of Varig Airlines. Daisy slipped out of the room and went to the nursery. Clay was in his basket, sleeping. She gently picked him up and held him close. She walked into the living room and stood in front of the window she knew so well. She whispered softly in his ear, "Clayzinho, we got our miracle and we are going home tonight. You know nothing about what has gone on but one day I will tell you everything. And, just as I am right now, you will be amazed."

Daisy looked up at the Christ statue and prayed. *Every day you have stood on the mountain outside this window. I will miss your powerful presence. On days when fog and clouds covered your face, I still knew you were there. Today, there is no fog and I am thankful, for I will remember this moment always, holding my baby in my arms and being so grateful for your nearness. You have been a monumental strength for me and I don't believe it was any accident that Isabella's home just happened to be on the side of Corcovado Mountain.*

Daisy turned to look at Isabella and her wide smile told her all she needed to know.

"I hope it won't take long to get your things together, Daisy. You and Clay have reservations on the seven-thirty flight tonight, direct to Washington. I will get busy making some bottles of formula for Clay, getting his diapers ready. I don't know what I am going to do without you, Daisy. I love you like one of my daughters and we've been through so much together. I will miss you and Clayzinho very much but we will keep in touch always. I have to tell you things like this now because when we arrive at the airport everything is going to move very fast and there will not be any time for talk or goodbyes. I'll tell you more about this in the car on the way."

In that moment, the realization that Isabella wouldn't be around every day to help her find solutions to problems, to encourage her, to be strong when she was weak – it was frightening to Daisy to realize that Isabella would not be flying out with her and Clay. She knew, deep in her heart, that she could never have accomplished all that she had if not for Isabella. But she was a mother now and she would do all she needed to for Clay. She and Clay were going home! *Oh, if only Luis were going with us*, she thought.

Daisy had her bag packed, Clay's diaper bag was ready, and before long she carried her things out to the kitchen and placed them by the back door. Daisy thought about calling Miki and asking him to meet them at the airport in D.C. but decided to just get a cab and head for her apartment instead. There was no telling how long she would be detained in immigration. She would call Miki later.

Charlie called again just as they were getting ready to walk out the door. Daisy told him she was hurrying to get to the airport before the Federal Police received word that a visa had been issued to Clay. "Isabella says they may try and stop me so send up a prayer for us. Love you, Charlie, and I wish you were leaving with us."

"It's okay, sis. Try not to worry. You just get that little guy home. I'll be seeing you in a couple of weeks and then we'll have lots to celebrate, believe me."

Fifteen minutes later, the cab Isabella had ordered honked out front. "No dune buggy for this special trip," she had said.

Once at the airport, Isabella took Daisy's tickets and checked in at the Varig counter for her. She had told Daisy in the cab that the best thing for her was to be as inconspicuous as possible.

"When you get to your gate and while they check your tickets for the last time, be sure to have Clay covered with the blanket. We don't want to call any attention to you at all. I've told you before, until the wheels of the plane lift off the runway, you and Clay are not safe. Don't speak to any of the airport personnel. Simply show both passports, get your boarding pass, and quickly board the plane. Do not look back. You know I am here wishing you well. Look straight ahead and keep walking."

Then, Isabella hugged Daisy and reached over, pulled the blanket back and kissed Clay on his forehead.

Just as Isabella had said, things moved swiftly when they got to the airport and soon she was boarding the plane. She didn't look back, but she wanted to.

Isabella had bought two seats for Daisy, one for her and one for Clay and it gave Daisy more than enough room to stretch out and try to relax. She leaned over and looked out the window but couldn't see Isabella. She did, however, see Federal Police walking up and down the tarmac carrying machine guns and she prayed the plane would not linger on the ground. Isabella had been right.

Soon, Daisy felt the engines revving up and she hugged Clay close to her as the plane raced down the runway and lifted off. She whispered quietly to the little boy sleeping in her arms, "We're going home, Clay. It won't be long now."

Thirty-six

One year later, Washington, D.C.

Luis sat on the edge of the sofa, his arms outstretched.
"Come to me, Clayzinho. Papa is waiting," he called to the
dark-haired toddler standing next to a leather ottoman that
was almost as tall as the little boy. Big, black eyes stared back at him
and Luis felt as though he was looking in a mirror.

With a tiny red truck in one chubby hand, Clay began his
unsteady journey to Luis, smiling, falling, getting up, trying again,
and finally, safely in the arms of the man he called, "Pa-Pa."

P.D. was close by, eyeing the baby, but keeping safely away from
little grabbing fingers. Daisy stood in the doorway, watching the
scene play out before her, loving the laughter, and feeling thankful.
She walked over and sat down next to Luis, her hand on his knee.

She reached over and touched Clay's hair. "The two of you
amaze me."

"How do you mean?" asked Luis.

"This baby adores you. You have a bond with him stronger than
blood. I am so blessed."

Clay rubbed his eyes, ready for his morning nap. Daisy took him
from Luis' arms and held him close. The baby put his head down on
her lap and she continued to run her fingers through his soft hair.

Soon he was sleeping, breathing deeply.

"I love that sound, Luis. It's a sound I never thought I would hear from my own son. It makes me feel so warm and safe...and loved."

Luis put his arm around her. "Daisy, my love, I know exactly what you mean. That is how I feel every time I look at you and Clay. I catch myself just staring at you, not believing that I am here, that we are a family, and that we are together for always. "Sometimes when I watch Clay playing on the carpet and he pulls himself up to walk, he's not too steady on his feet. I look at him and it reminds me of last year when I was trying to make my way out of the Amazon, one leg injured, no sense of direction. To walk was very painful but I had no choice. Like Clay, I would fall, but knew I had to get up and continue moving."

"I thank God you were able to reach that mission house in Fortaleza," said Daisy, looking intently at Luis.

"Everything is a matter of timing, Daisy," Luis continued. "You getting permission to leave Rio with Clay, me making it to Fortaleza, Charlie being smart enough to figure out where to look for me when he heard about the crazy photographer who had been lost in the Amazon...it all was a coming together of many events, Daisy, and that timing brought the three of us to this moment."

Daisy reached over and kissed Luis full on the lips.

"You promised you would come back. Somewhere inside me I always believed you would keep that promise."

The phone on the table behind the sofa broke the soft moment and Luis reached for it.

"Hello, my world-traveler brother-in-law," he laughed into the phone. "Where on earth are you?" Luis turned and winked at Daisy. Clay had stirred but did not awaken. "Okay, maybe. Seriously? I don't know."

Daisy stared at Luis who seemed to be enjoying the conversation with Charlie, albeit one-sided. She raised her eyebrows to Luis. He put up a finger, indicating he would explain in a minute.

"I don't know what my wife would say about that," said Luis. He watched Daisy as she carried Clay to his room to finish his nap. "Let me call you back in a couple of hours. Give me your number. Oh, out of curiosity, what hat are you wearing right now? I know, a baseball cap, but what does it say?" Luis laughed. "I can see it now.

Talk to you soon."

Daisy returned and sat next to Luis, putting her head on his shoulder.

"Now, what was all that about? Charlie's not the type to call up and chat about nothing, certainly not about what hat he's wearing. What's up?"

"You know him too well, I think," said Luis. "You are correct about his call. Right now, he is in Tokyo, sitting in a sushi bar with a cute Japanese girl whom I could hear giggling in the background. He has just finished his filming there."

"So, why did he call?" probed Daisy. "And what do you have to ask me about?" She knew something had Luis' interest. She could see his dark eyes sparkling with excitement.

"Okay, Charlie was asked this morning by Global Peace Partners to do a documentary for them in Tibet. They asked him to bring what he needed and he needs another cameraman."

"And that cameraman would be...you! Right?"

"Well, he just asked if I could join him on this one. You know, we work so well together and..."

"And you really want to go on this assignment," said Daisy. "So, is there any reason why you can't go?"

"Well, I don't like to leave you and Clay behind. I will miss you so."

"And I will miss you, my darling, but the three of us can make other trips when our son is a little older. We'll be fine. When do you have to meet Charlie in Tokyo?"

"In four days."

"That much time, huh?" Daisy hugged Luis hard. "We have lots of shopping to do for this trip...cold weather stuff."

"By the way," she added. "What hat was Charlie wearing this time? I heard you laugh."

"A baseball cap. His first item for the new trip. It read, 'Tibet. You bet.' They may not let him in the country."

They stood. Luis held Daisy close and if she wasn't mistaken, she thought she heard him softly humming *The Girl From Ipanema*, the same melody he had hummed to her in Rio when she knew she was falling in love with him.

And here she was, falling in love once more.

Joyce Norman, was born in Ft. Worth, Texas and is a graduate of Texas Wesleyan University and the University of Alabama. She taught high school and college before becoming a journalist. She is the author of three other books including *Personal Assignment* and *Come and See*. This is her first novel.

Joy Collins has wanted to be a writer since she was a child. Educated as a nurse, she has written a health newsletter for Baby Boomers, as well as many medical articles for journals and web sites. But making up stories has always been her passion. Her debut novel *Second Chance* centers on the many pitfalls of living in a stepfamily. *Coming Together* is her second novel and she is now at work on her third.

Joy shares her Arizona home with her husband and several fur-kids. For more information, visit her at www.joycollins.com.

Printed in the United States
222306BV00003B/3/P